Frankau, Pamela, 1908–
    Road through the woods.
Doubleday [1961] $3.95

ROAD THROUGH THE WOODS

By Pamela Frankau

Road Through

the Woods

BY PAMELA FRANKAU

Doubleday & Company, Inc., Garden City, New York

1961

LIBRARY OF CONGRESS CATALOG CARD NUMBER 60–13523

COPYRIGHT © 1960 BY PAMELA FRANKAU

ALL RIGHTS RESERVED

PRINTED IN THE UNITED STATES OF AMERICA

FIRST EDITION IN THE UNITED STATES OF AMERICA

AUTHOR'S NOTE

Though the village of Drumnair owes its geographical position and some of its looks to Adare, County Limerick, it is basically an imagined place, peopled by imaginary characters. The Book of Drumnair is likewise imaginary. No trace of it can be seen in Trinity College Library, Dublin, where I found much help and courtesy, here gratefully acknowledged

P F.

Thursday   May 28th

CHAPTER ONE

"Would this be yours?"

The boy turned. He looked at the shiny sealskin wallet held out to him in the woman's hand. He saw that it was stamped in the corner with gold initials, D.C.B. "No," he said. "Not mine."

"You're quite sure, now?" She was panting a little; she must have run. "I found it on the counter. Just where you were putting the stamp on your postcard."

He shook his head, smiling at her. "No. Really. But thank you for coming after me."

She said she hoped the owner would come back for it; a valuable thing to lose; perhaps that couple in the big car? There had been a lot of people in and out all the morning. Then she hurried off, leaving the boy standing at the corner. Dreamily, he looked this way and that; he saw a wide sunny street. Stretching away to his right there was a double line of eighteenth-century façades in red brick; a statue on a high pedestal; to his left, the shop-windows began. He went towards the shops.

He felt light-hearted, a little vague and lost, but in the careless, accepting mood of a dream. At the back of his head there was the notion that he ought to be thinking hard about something; but he couldn't remember what the thing was. He found the dream-walking sensation comfortable. Over his head, strung across the street, bright pennons were fluttering. He liked them. He wondered why the town had put out all these flags. He went on loitering, looking in the shop-windows. At the next traffic-light he halted again; here the side street to his left beguiled him with the sight of a bridge running across a wide river. He reached a small ornamental fountain in a paved yard; on the other side there was a stone memorial with bronze figures. And now the bridge; 'Sarsfield Bridge' he read aloud from a stone plaque. An imposing bridge, with traffic sweeping over it.

The boy hesitated. He wanted to lean out over the coping and stare down into the water; always a favourite thing to do. But the coping was too high; the pillars supporting it were the shape of urns, set close together on a foot-high stone ledge. After a moment, he unshipped the rucksack from his shoulders. Freed of its weight, he managed to get a toe-hold between the bases of the pillars, and stretch his arms across the coping. Here he hung happily, looking up-river. The river made a tantalizing curve just where a castle began to appear at the water's edge. The horizon was made of roof-tops piling up, one square red tower higher than the rest, a church-tower highest of all.

The boy stared down at the water. As before, he found it beautiful and hypnotic, the smooth brown water that dappled on and on. He could hear a woman's voice singing; a woman who looked like a tinker, in a dirty, dragging red dress. (Wait a minute. . was he seeing her or remembering her? The loud, sweet voice seemed a part of the air; part of the fabric made by blue sky, white cloud and the drum-towers of the castle; it mixed with the silk-ribbed water; it sang through his head.)

The boy blinked. This was like the moment of awaking in a new room, not knowing just where you were, nor why. With a kind of bright mist in your head, and nothing else.

The singing voice had stopped. He let go of the coping and jumped down. He thought "What am I doing here? Where am I going? Silly. . but this is *awfully* silly." Inside his head the bright mist stayed; there was nothing; nothing but the moment of Now.

Perplexed, he began to shake his head as though his ears were blocked and he hoped to clear them. He did it again and again. A plump young girl, walking past, stared, giggled. She embarrassed the boy and he moved quickly off the bridge. He began to hurry, back by the way that he had come. (Was it the way that he had come? He thought it was; traffic-lights, and then shop-windows; yes.) He thought that if he kept walking, the mist in his head would clear. He wasn't frightened; merely puzzled. "Snap out of it now, can't you?" he said as he went,—"Wake up. Come on. Think. What's this town? Begins with an L, doesn't it? But how did you get here? You don't know. Well, all right— where do you live? What's your name? Oh, *honestly.* ."

He was aware of himself, aware of his own familiar company, knowing that there was an "I" and knowing nothing more. A tobacconist's window advertised 'Sweet Afton' with a green label. He knew that 'Sweet Afton' meant Irish cigarettes. Well, that was something. 'Ireland' rang a bell behind the mist. But as he groped, the word 'Ireland' seemed to belong to the future, not the present. He knew that he was going there; but how had he got there? This again was like a dream, wherein, though one found oneself in a vivid foreign land, one could not remember the journey.

In the next shop-window there was an angled strip of looking-glass that gave him his reflection. This was what he had expected; the details were quite uninteresting, just his own familiar face; dark curly hair, light grey eyes and wide mouth; his own familiar body: medium height, broad shoulders. But his clothes puzzled him. A light sweater, an open-necked shirt, corduroy shorts. He wore thick socks and heavy, crepe-soled shoes Clothes for walking. Had he been walking? When had he put on these clothes, and where?

Fishing in the pockets he found a handful of Irish coins; he knew the harp and the fish; the hound, the horse and the rabbit; pretty coins; there was a medal mixed up with them, a St. Christopher; he couldn't remember that. There was a map sticking out of the other pocket; he unfolded it; a section of a large-scale map. He read the words "County Limerick."

"Well, now we know where we are," he said to himself. The half-laughing, half-serious mood of the dream persisted; he couldn't worry. From the map, a folded piece of paper fell to the pavement; he read some notes of bus-times. Limerick—Listowel; Listowel—Tralee. These said nothing to him.

"Hullo, there!"

The voice was loud and friendly. He was facing a large fair man with a little moustache; he had not, to his knowledge, seen the face before. The eyes were small and blue, the pouting lower lip unattractively wet. The man wore grey flannels; he had a camera slung over his shoulder and he was carrying yellow boxes of new film.

"Hullo," said the boy.

"Are you the one for Shannon, or the one for Tralee?"

Obedient to the piece of paper in his hand, the boy said "Tralee."

"Well, I got my phone-call. My pals are meeting me in Listowel; so I can give you a lift that far. Hop in." He opened the door of the dusty Hillman parked beside the pavement. "Hey, what's happened to your luggage?"

"I haven't any."

"I mean your rucksack."

"Oh, that. ." he hesitated. He had made the large fair man suspicious, he thought. "Perhaps I sent it on ahead."

"What d'you mean perhaps? Anyway that's pretty silly, isn't it? I mean one doesn't send a *rucksack* on ahead."

"No. Well. ." He had no solution to this.

The man looked at his watch. "Going to be late," he said peevishly. "Have you left it at the hotel?"

"I really can't think."

"Are you having a game with me?"

"No, sir."

"Didn't skip without paying the bill and leave the rucksack as hostage, eh?"

"No," he said, "I don't do things like that." (Odd, to be so certain of one's behaviour and not to know one's name.)

"Pawned it? Running out of cash?"

"Could be."

"You're a queer customer," said the man with the moustache. The wet lips pursed; the blue eyes looked wary; the voice barked, "I don't want any trouble, you know. And I don't like funny business."

"Nothing very funny about losing one's luggage, is there?" said the boy.

"You just lost it?"

"Obviously."

"Well why not say so? In that case, you'd better stick around and look for it."

"No, thank you. I'd rather get on to Tralee " There must

be a clue in Tralee, if he was headed that way. As it seemed he was.

"I told you. I'm only going as far as Listowel."

"Good enough," said the boy, climbing into the car.

"Queer customer, you are," the man repeated. "Still, none of my business. Maybe your pal took your rucksack."

So he had a pal. He wondered about this while the driver navigated the town traffic, punctuating his progress with groans and grumbles. The fluttering pennons, the crowds, a group carrying a banner, seemed to annoy him. "Honestly," he said—"You'd think the Queen was coming, wouldn't you? Lucky to get out before the procession starts up. Look at those kids." They were between the red-brick façades now, passing a church. Outside the church he saw a cluster of little girls in white dresses and veils, shepherded by a nun. " 'Look like child-brides, don't they?" the man said.

"I've seen them before. In France—I've been in France."

"Well, so've I, more than once, no need to sound so cocky about it."

"It was just a discovery," said the boy,—"What are the flags for?"

"It's a religious thing. Corpus Christi."

("Now those words are quite familiar, and quite important. Or they were once. . I must try to keep my trap shut; I don't want him to know I'm having this thing.")

"Bloody backward country. Another hundred years and it won't be here at all. Know the population-statistics?" While he talked, the boy was watching his hands on the wheel, his impatient way with the gear-shift. He wanted to take the wheel himself. ("I can drive a lot better than he can. That's another thing I know.")

They were out of the town, into a scattered suburban

road; then into true countryside that kept the boy contentedly watchful. The low hills, the greenness, the hedges of
scarlet fuchsia were familiar. He stared, still hunting clues.
He was interrupted:—

"Well—we'd better introduce ourselves. My name's Allard. . Bruce Allard. What's yours?"

"My name. ." (Albert? Arthur? — Bob? Bill? Bertie?
Charles? Christian? Carus. . ? Carus, now. C.A.R.U.S. It
was a name, at least, that pierced the fog in his head,—
that tried to mean something.) He said "My name's Carus"

"Carus? Carus—what? Or what—Carus? Surname, is it?"

"I don't know." His watchful attention had been diverted
by a sudden runnel of cows pouring through a gate and making a solid, leisurely barrier across the road. At their heels
came a man with a stick and a small black-and-white collie
dog with a smiling face Neither man nor dog showed any
inclination to hustle the cows.

"You don't *know*? What on earth do you mean?" Allard
had slowed the car to a crawl and was staring at him with
an outraged expression. The boy began to laugh.

"It's quite true, sir." Really, he thought, trying to keep
up the deception was too difficult. He plunged further in;
"Mind you, I'm not a hundred per cent sure I *am* Carus.
But at least it's a name I remember." There was a certain
satisfaction in saying to the goggling face, "To tell you the
truth it's the only thing I do remember. Except Sweet
Afton and Corpus Christi. Everything else is a blank."

They were at a halt, because of the cows. Allard now
looked babyish with perplexity.

"You're pulling my leg, aren't you?"

"No, I'm not."

1 5

"Are you seriously trying to tell me you've lost your memory?"

"I suppose that's what's happened. 'Does happen, doesn't it? I've read about it in the papers, I think. People found wandering. That's what I was doing when you found me. wasn't I?"

"But,—Good Lord—" Allard seemed quite unable to take it in. . "It's impossible. You weren't like this last night."

"Could you tell me about last night?"

A rearguard cow lurched close to the bonnet. Allard sounded his horn wildly. Some of the cows hooted back and emptied their bowels. The dog, losing interest, jumped into the hedge and disappeared; the man cut a slow, ineffectual swathe in the air with his stick. Allard took so long to negotiate the herd that the boy began to despair of getting an answer. He repeated "Could you tell me? It might help."

Allard braked suddenly and pulled the car to the side of the road. He now looked very cross indeed: "One question first, my lad," he said. "If your mind's a blank, how d'you know you've got to get to Tralee? And if you didn't recognize me, why did you let me give you a lift? And what's your business in Tralee, anyway?"

"That's three questions," said the boy. "And I can only answer one. I knew about Tralee because of this bit of paper—" He handed it over. . "Why won't you tell me about last night?"

Allard gave a groan, lit a cigarette, observed to nobody in particular:—"This would have to happen to me, wouldn't it? Okay. You and your chum came into the bar at the Royal George; about nine o'clock. You told me you'd been hitch-hiking all over the country; and we had a couple of minutes natter with our beer. The other boy was bigger than you;

fair-haired chap He said you were splitting up this morning. One of you had to go to Shannon Airport, and the other was on his way South, to Tralee. I was waiting for a phone-call. 'Said I might be good for a lift as far as Listowel. You both cleared out when you'd had your beer. Dead on your feet, you said. And you both had rucksacks. That's about all. I gathered you were staying in the hotel."

"Very odd," said the boy, "isn't it?"

Allard's sceptical expression endured. "You really mean you don't remember any of that?"

"Not one thing."

"Not your friend, even?"

"No."

"You *must* have a clue on you somewhere. Turn out your pockets No papers? Letters? Nothing. . 'That all the money you've got? Looks as if you'd been robbed. Sure somebody didn't slug you?" He felt the back of the boy's head with busy, maddening fingers. "Tender? No? H'm. This sort of thing ever happened to you before? Don't *giggle*."

"Excuse me, but—if it had—how could I know?"

Allard threw away the cigarette. He whistled between his teeth. "Best thing I can think of is to run you back to the Royal George. You probably registered. May find your name and home-address. 'Get in touch with your family. All I can think of."

"No" said the boy. "You're late. We needn't do that. We can stop at the next place and telephone the Royal George."

Another suspicious look:—"What's the idea?"

"Just thinking about you—and your being late. We're six miles out of Limerick already."

"Okay," said Allard, after a moment. "Take a look at that

map of yours, see where we're getting to? Rathkeale, is it?"

The boy ran his finger along the road-line on the map. "No. Drumnair comes first." A curious tingle of pleasure came with the sound of the name. "Drumnair" he repeated. "Five more miles."

Allard, having started up the car, left him in peace for a while He was glad. If it was true that he had been hitch-hiking all over the country, this would account for the comfortable familiarity of the things he saw. That broken sign-post, snapped off and useless; that tinker's encampment in a bay of grass by the road; naked children, a dog, a brown woman knitting on the steps of the van; over towards the mountains, the glimpse of a craggy ruin, desolately tranquil; now a green field spattered with gold buttercups; a reedy pond. The cloud inside his head seemed to make the visual landscape sharper, more important. He was enjoying the glimpse of a heron, a hooded statue among the reeds and the yellow iris, when Allard's voice brought him back.

"Must say, you're taking it very calmly. If I'd lost my memory I'd think I was going crackers. 'Tell you what I was doing, then—trying to see how it felt. Couldn't do it. Couldn't make my mind a blank; all I was doing was hold-ing my breath. And *remembering* all the time; little things. . little pictures that just bobbed up for no reason. My garden at home,—'chap I knew in the war who hated the Irish—, dirty poem someone gave me at a business-dinner. Don't know why."

"Well, but—one's memories are always *there*, aren't they?" said the boy. He looked at the map again; a picture pierced the fog; a carved archway, leading into roofless ruins, sun-light striking through on to green grass and gravestones; the shape of a high Celtic cross and all the little figures sculptured on the shaft. He blinked and it was gone.

"It'll come back," he thought. "It will all come back."

A tiny village opened up, closed again behind them; just a scatter of poor houses, whitewashed, roofed with mangy thatch. At the gate of a yard, three yelling geese, their long necks stretched, their heads in the air, protesting blindly with their tongues out, made him laugh.

"You aren't worried at all?"

"No, sir, thank you very much."

"I would be, if I were you," Allard persisted.

The boy was conscious of a faint compassion, a smiling pity somewhere inside him; as if a child had spoken.

"It doesn't feel bad," he said indifferently. He watched the road. Something was happening now. To his right, past Allard's shoulder, he could see a broken tower beside a sycamore grove, a thin flutter of jackdaws flying round the tower. "Hey," he said to himself, "I know that tower." He looked to his left, yes, that was what he had known he would see; the wall of the demesne; a long stone wall, with the trees growing thick and high. The wall went on. Now, to the right, a little river. The road crossed it. The river ran through the demesne; he knew that too.

"Drumnair" he said "We're here."

In a blink, there came the wide village street, with all the flags strung and fluttering from roof to roof. An enormous joy seized him, as if the flags were flying for him, because he had come home. He knew it all. At the head of the street there was the Nellon Inn; a white building, long and low, with its bright blazon above the door, and the cars lined up outside. The two pretty, prosperous cottages facing the inn had been painted yellow; the thatch was new on each curving roof; the gardens were full of roses and yellow lupins; red valerian grew along the walls.

He heard music coming up the street; down by the church he could see the crowds forming. His heart thudded; this was easy; this was magic; this, for some reason, was where he had longed to be.

"Pretty village, ain't it?" Allard was saying—"Plushy pub, too. Looks as if the damn procession's starting up. We'd better telephone from here." He swung the car into line with the other cars facing the Nellon Inn.

The boy said quickly—"No, no. It's all right now." He was shaking with excitement. He burst open the door of the car and jumped out. When Allard scrambled after him, catching him by the shoulder, he felt a vast impatience.

"Look—you needn't telephone—or anything. I know where I am."

Still the hand gripped his shoulder: "You mean, it's come back?"

"I know this place as well as—" he was about to say "as my own name" and stopped with a shout of laughter. "Goodbye, Mr. Allard. You've been very kind to me."

He wrenched himself free and ran. He heard Allard shouting after him, but he didn't look back; he raced on towards the music and the crowd. His eyes picked up familiar things; the gates of the parish school; the grey stone presbytery; the huge sycamore leaning out over the churchyard wall. The crowd engulfed him; the crowd was everywhere; it was milling around the gate; it was inside the gate, packed solidly under the vivid, lurching banners. He had to get in there, too. But it wasn't easy. He was squeezed, shoved, flung backward and forward, shouted at by two boys carrying staves that swished against the sycamore. He dived at the wall and clung to it, looking in, dodging his head this way and that, because there were people standing on the wall. Everybody was singing; the hymn thundered out above his head:

"Faith of our fathers, Holy Faith,
We will be true to thee, till death."

The boy knew it. He tried to sing too, but the crowd wedged him so tightly that he had no breath. With a desperate scramble, he squeezed himself up onto the wall. Here he lurched and swayed between friendly elbows; someone trod heavily on his foot. He caught at a low branch of the sycamore, swung, and dropped down among the watchers on the grass inside the wall. "Mind me hat," said an indignant face, close to his own. He pushed his way through, until he got to the edge of the grass.

Here, he could see what was happening. At the gate two policemen were operating patiently, somehow keeping the broad path to the church door free and empty, somehow dividing the procession as it formed, from the turbulent onlookers. The snaking colours of the banners moved forward, crimson and green, yellow and blue; lines of little girls in white, lines of little boys with white armlets following the nuns. It was a humble, blazing pageant that rang enchanted echoes through the mist. (Where? When?) Now a hush, a gilt cross carried high, strong voices pouring upward.

"Pange lingua, gloriosi,
Corporis mysterium."

He was down on his knees in the grass with the rest of them.

This was automatic. He wasn't aware of imitating his packed neighbours, nor of having done it before; it was just a thing that happened to his knees and his body The murmuring prayers all around him throbbed like the buzz of a hive. He bent his head and covered his face with his hands. Peeping between his fingers, he saw a golden glitter of vestments going by; a golden canopy; he heard the clink of censer-chains swinging. It was old in memory. It was a glimpse through a door that swung shut again before he had time to know what was inside. The mist closed over the dazzling sliver of truth. It was gone.

He did not know how long the kneeling lasted; ecstasy was out of him; his knees hurt, the warm bodies pressed too close; he smelt human smells and heard human noises. The enchantment was broken. Then at last they were all scrambling up to their feet, heaving him up with them. He stood islanded in a rough, swirling chorus of talk and laughter. He came back to himself.

And found nobody there.

This was the first realization that although in a familiar place, he was still without identity. The name Carus alone endured.

Hearty human disorder reigned about him; men shaking hands, mothers embracing the little white girls and the white-banded boys; priests and nuns and the lay crowd mixing merrily. The boy sat down at the foot of the sycamore-tree and picked the grass-blades out of the criss-cross patterns on his bare, painful knees.

Then he looked at his watch; one-fifteen. It occurred to him now to take off the watch and look on the back of it for a possible inscription. This was something that Allard hadn't thought of. He found the initials D.C.B., and below them, the words 'From I.' which looked pretty silly. " 'From me', surely," he said to himself. Did the 'C' stand for Carus? The 'D' foxed him completely. (Dick? David? Douglas?) And the 'B' meant nothing at all. He put the watch back on his wrist.

He was hungry. Since the money counted by Allard and himself added up to six shillings, he could buy something to eat. He would, he thought, like to go into the church first. Something important about that church. But the hearty drifters, the businesslike groups rolling up the banners, a young priest talking to a tall, fat girl in a red dress, scared him off. As he rose, the girl with the priest leaned back her head and laughed; he saw her face, a handsome, exuberant, damn-your-eyes face; he liked it.

He thought "She's my friend." But he knew he had never seen her before.

Coming out of the gate he was pulled up on his heels. Across the street, below the line of thatched cottages and the gap where you could see a field of the demesne stretch away behind the wall, he could recognize Mrs. O'Toole's grocery shop and Mulligan's garage. ("But it isn't remembering," he said, "It's knowing, and that's quite different.") Outside Mulligan's garage there stood a dusty grey Hillman that looked like the one driven by Allard. Was Allard hanging about, waiting for him? Surely not. Still, he disliked the idea; he turned left, up the street again towards the Nellon Inn. It wouldn't seem to be a place where one could eat for six shillings, but there was something important about it, as for the church. Seeing the two yellow cottages again, he thought that the first cottage belonged to a very old lady with a marmalade cat. She made a picture in his mind, standing at her door; the cat rubbed against her skirts; the door was open; and there was a red lamp burning under a little statue in the hall. But not now. The door was shut.

And here, beyond the last cottage, there was a sweeping inlet of empty road, with the grey, curved wall of the demesne surrounding the inlet. The wall, and the gate. Two stone gateposts; two stone urns. But a solid wooden door built between. (Once, surely, you could see right through.) This entry faced the Nellon Inn. The boy stood looking across the road at it for a while.

Then, turning back from it, staring at the painted sign, he got another hint. Not from the sign itself. But the name was Hogan, surely; the Nellon Inn was owned by Mr. and Mrs. Hogan. "Well, if I know them, perhaps they'll know me. They'll have to, won't they? Isn't that a point in metaphysics? 'If I meet you and you don't meet me, it's the end of cognition'. . When was I studying metaphysics, I wonder? Maybe I'm a well-educated chap, though I can't say I feel like one."

He went in, to look for Mr. and Mrs. Hogan.

The lobby was grander than it used to be; not unpleasantly grand, but giving off an air of up-to-date comfort; on tiptoe for tourists, he thought; rich tourists. The walls, which he had expected to be of dark wood panelling, were painted white. There was a red carpet. There were glass panels engraved with the words 'Bar' and 'Dining Room.' The small, neat reception desk on the left was new. Nobody in it. He stood here, looking straight ahead, through the open door of the bar; a back room whose windows framed the garden beyond; a long shallow room. The sun filled it; the sun lit up the colours of the garden. As he strolled in, a noisy group came chattering out and headed for the dining-room. He was alone here, except for a waiter madly collecting empty glasses. Nobody behind the bar. Knowing the lay-out, the boy took a peep into the small dark alcove on the other side of the counter. It was cut off, a private corner.

Here he was presented with an apparent museum-piece, or collection of museum-pieces, all as still as waxworks and, oddly, suggesting them. An elaborate old man was seated at a table spread for his lunch. He had white, bobbed hair and a yellow-pink, eagle face. His napkin was tucked under his chin. He read from a book precariously propped against a toast-rack. A bottle of wine stood at his elbow and he was surrounded by his paraphernalia. A second chair, pulled up to the table, accommodated two large parcels, a sort of cowboy hat and a blackthorn stick with a silver knob. A cream-coloured greyhound, tied by its leash to the table-leg, was sound asleep.

The old man read on in the gloom, while the boy stared, collecting the details as though he were studying the composition of a picture.

"Excuse me—" he began.

The white head roused itself; enormous blue eyes opened widely and the smile was most sweet. "Pippin!" cried the old man. "My dear Pippin! After all this time. . Where did you spring from?" It was the voice of a singer or an actor, the boy thought, a voice full of faded melody. "Oh, I am *extremely* glad to see you. ." it fluted on; the old man tossed his arms in the air and the boy made a saving clutch at the wine-bottle.

"Am I Pippin?" he asked. "Is that my name?"

"Ah. . ." There was a drop in the temperature, a pause while the large dim eyes wavered in their search. "I'm rather blind, you know. And it's dark in here. I thought for a minute you were Pippin Black. You have a most remarkable look of him. But of course not, of course not. It's too long ago. Everything delightful *is*, have you noticed? No, not at your age. It will be; just you wait. Do you know me?"

"I'm not sure."

"Not *sure?*" said the old man with some petulance. "Then that proves it; you don't. If you did, you'd be sure enough."

"Luke?" said the boy; the name had flashed up, like the name of Carus.

"Oh-ho. So you do. I'm not certain I allow young people —on what may or may not be first acquaintance—to use my Christian name. You may call me Mr. Courtney."

"Thank you, sir."

"Sit down. Have a glass of wine. Tell me who you are if you aren't Pippin."

One swallow of wine made the mist inside his head thicken and dazzle. . It was easy to say, "Well, as a matter of fact I don't quite know *who* I am."

"Splendid! Naturally you don't; you're much too young to know; how very intelligent of you to be aware of this fact. . No pepper mill. . Disgusting." He clapped his hands and began to shout "George! George!"

"The barman isn't there," said the boy.

"Well, he will be. . George! George! . . Quiet, Dana, my lovely," he added as the greyhound woke up. " 'Only oasis of tranquillity in the whole of Drumnair, this, you know. The Corpus Christi fandango sends them all into delirium. Ah. . there you are, George. What the devil were you up to? Taking Mattins or Vespers or something?"

The barman, sweating at the temples, said reproachfully,

"I was fetching the pepper mill from the dining-room, Mr. Luke, just as you asked me to do."

"And why should that take you three hours?"

The barman shrugged his shoulders and winked at the boy.

"Now you're here, take a look at this young gentleman. Does he remind you of anybody? No? You're a numskull. Or perhaps Pippin Black was before your time. Yes, he must have been."

"I'm afraid he was," said the barman.

"This fellow" said Mr. Courtney, raising a talon of a forefinger with a green ring on it and pointing—"is Pippin's living, breathing image."

"Is he indeed?"

"He is indeed."

They both stared benignly. The boy, with the wine warming his stomach and making him hungrier every moment, asked "Who is Pippin?"

The old man blinked. "Now, that's more difficult. Who is Pippin? I've no idea. I haven't seen him for years, you see, and therefore he is very much changed; or he may be dead. People do change," he fluted on, "and they do die. And of course they can die without being dead; which is what one means by changing. Do you follow me?"

"Not quite."

"You should, a clever young man like you. . By the time you're *my* age, God help you, you'll have been a whole various crew of people who would never recognize one another if they met again. Is that clear?"

The barman was out of the conversation now; a fresh stream of drinkers had poured into the long room. Mr. Courtney sent a peevish glance towards the noise and repeated—"Is that clear?"

"Yes," said the boy untruthfully. "It's clear, but it doesn't tell me who Pippin is."

"If you asked me who he *was*—" said Mr. Courtney severely, "I'd say he was a young man with a great deal of quicksilver; a fortunate young man; a person who might have risen to great heights. . doing what? Who can tell? In those days he was just a merry little pirate, sailing the seas. I liked to see him about. Another foreigner, of course. But then we've always had foreigners at the Manor. *She's* a foreigner. My poor son Tom was indigenous. . and look what it did for him. *I* lived away from my own country for years. Twice," he added. "Pippin, now. . I don't believe he'd have settled. Well, he didn't, did he?" Here he began to chuckle. Then he looked at the boy. "I'm sorry. You don't know, of course. But take it from me, Pippin was a grand little fellow. I like young people to be merry. I like—" He peered at the cold chicken. "I don't really like a cold lunch. But when the servants—all two of them—are Massing and processing and carrying banners about . . . well, there it is. You aren't listening."

The boy longed to say "I can eat the chicken, if you can't." While he was hesitating upon this boldness, the thought of the Hogans returned. "I'm sorry; I *was* listening. But there's something I'd like to know. I'm sure you can help me—"

—"I can't help anybody. I'm as near bankrupt as it's convenient to be. *She* is, too. We all are. I can't possibly help you." He pushed away his plate. "Unless, that is, you would take an unpaid job as a chauffeur-gardener in exchange for a really pretty little cottage and some of your meals . . . When you laugh in that asinine but rather charming way, you really might *be* Pippin. . I was serious."

"So'm I—" the boy began. Mr. Courtney interrupted him.

"You are? I don't know that I believe you. You seem frivolous to me. . as you should be at your time of life. 'Time
of life'" he added thoughtfully "is more usually applied to
the old, is it not? I wonder why."

"I wanted to ask—"

—"My advice? You have a problem? I can guess. Some
young woman. Doubtless unworthy."

"It isn't anything to do with a young woman."

"Then it ought to be," said Mr. Courtney.

"Oh lord—" said the boy. "All I want to know is does
this hotel—"

—"Inn. It prefers to be called an Inn."

"Well, damn,—inn. Does it belong to Mr. and Mrs.
Hogan?"

"It did once" said the old man. "But they sold it years
ago. Before you were born, I shouldn't wonder. . Is that
all you wanted to ask me? Taken an interminable time to
do it, haven't you? Who told you about the Hogans?"

The boy said "Can't remember." Now he felt lost again;
the wine had confused him. Mr. Courtney was absorbed in
prising open the lid of a flat, gaily-painted tin. He took a
knife to it. Then he began to make his selection from an
assortment of cigarettes and small cigars, some of which were
broken. Meanwhile the barman, at cruel speed, removed
the half-eaten lunch.

"Do you smoke?" asked Mr. Courtney. "It's interesting,
I think. . You won't? I thought all young people smoked
their heads off in the intervals of rocking and rolling and
stabbing policemen. You're English, of course."

"I think so."

"I like that very much. Nationality is a matter for individual choice. And, judging by your clothes, you're one of

2 9

these healthy outdoors lads, who tramp about on their holi-
days, making up their minds. . I used to. . But not here,
of course; in Spain; in the Alps. Why aren't you doing
something of the sort, I ask myself, instead of favouring
the pretty-pretty, picture-postcard village of Drumnair?
What is there to see, after all, except the demesne itself, and
a few ruins—the abbey—the Friary?"

The Friary . . .

"Why are you looking pop-eyed, Pippin? I'm determined
to call you Pippin."

"You said 'the Friary.'" He felt a gust of excitement
blowing through the fog.

"I did say the Friary. I can tell you one supremely interesting thing about it: Don't you believe a word the guide-
book says, now, will you?"

The boy was on his feet. "Forgive me," he said "I'd like
to go there."

The eagle-face became petulant again. "Now? Really?
Well, it's in the demesne, you know. . you'll have to get an
estate-pass. They issue them at the reception desk. If you're
not staying here they won't. Tell them they must; tell them
I said so. But I can't imagine why you're in such a hurry.
There's nothing much to see. Far better stay here and let
me tell you the true legend. Besides, it's going to rain. ."

"How do you know?" the boy asked.

"Because it always is. In that scout-uniform of yours,
you'll get wet. Off you go; I see you straining upon the start.
Nobody has any consideration for me at all. . but not at all."
He added "I shan't be here when you get back. I have some
Americans pending."

"I'm terribly sorry. I know it seems rude. But—"

He saw that Mr. Courtney had resumed his waxwork

appearance; the white head was bent over the book. He tried "I hope I'll see you again," and this time received a mumble: "Better not let *her* see you."

"Who? Why? I mean why not?"

"Looking as you do," said Mr. Courtney, "it might be a mistake. Don't hover. I'm reading."

The girl at the reception desk gave him the pass, a paper ticket He crossed the street. The sunlight was still strong and the shadows sharp He came to the gate in the curve of wall. The solid wooden door, set between the high stone posts, puzzled him again. He read the notice:—NO ADMITTANCE EXCEPT ON BUSINESS, OR TO PERSONS HAVING AN ESTATE PASS. He lifted the latch and went in.

Shutting the heavy doors behind him, he found himself in a quiet green world that he knew. He was walking beside the river that ran in under the wall of the demesne; a swan, on her nest in the rushes, looked painted and still. The avenue divided; looping to the right, it vanished among high rhododendrons. That was the way to the Manor. No sign of the Manor from here; it was hidden by the crowding trees. He walked on to the left, came to a low bridge and crossed the river; the Friary was close now, grey walls on a low green glacis. A framework at once delicate and stubborn, the original shape still enduring, the purpose still to be found. The boy stared at it. The only comment in his mind was "Yes, . of course; this couldn't change."

At the foot of the grey walls, the big brown hares were playing. Until he began to walk up the glacis, they were unconcerned with him; doing what they always did; scudding, rocketing, leaping; then, suddenly, as though invisible strings twitched them away, they were gone.

His feet swished through the long grass; he walked under

the first archway into the chapel. Roofless beneath the blue sky, the humble and stately skeleton endured. The high East window, the columns, the low altar-stone; all quiet, all over, all going on. Nothing changed. The jackdaws were still fussing in the ivy on the West wall. This low arch led to the cloister. Here the light dimmed; peering through the fragile pillars, he looked for the tomb. Huge weeds had sprouted avidly, making a tree-tangle in the square plot, thistle, burdock and darnel growing high, making a screen for the slab where the worn figure lay, in its muffle of carved robes. "Nobody comes here any more," he said to himself, but this didn't make him sad. The place, he knew, needed nobody.

He traced the old way, around the cloister to the last arch that let him out into a hall of height and grandeur, the refectory room. No roof; just the sky and the grey skeleton and the green grass. The boy stood still in the sunlight. His eyes found the line around the walls above his head; the line of bigger stones, the sockets, the jutting stabs of broken masonry that showed where the floor of the upper room used to be. His eyes came to the corner steps; a squat craggy flight, curling up to the level of that lost floor. The steps ended at a deep embrasure, shaggy now with weed, with ivy and valerian. Something about the shape of this big, crumbling gap began to puzzle him.

Slowly he mounted the steps. He held on to the lip of the embrasure with his hands. Then, trusting the thickness of the broken wall, he went up. He stood on a broad sill; he could almost span the gap with his arms. The jackdaws flew off, yelling. He stared all around him, feeling like a watchman on a tower; gazing at the sward and the avenue, the hushed, endless trees. While he watched, the shadows dulled in the grass. White webs of cloud were crossing the sun; dark, hurrying rags came up and after. "Luke was right; it's going to rain" said the boy.

Here he felt the sill begin to sway under his left foot, and shifted his weight quickly. The movement dislodged a whole layer of stones; they toppled off; they clattered down, tumbling into the grass. The boy squeezed himself into the right-hand corner of the embrasure; he clutched handfuls of ivy; he squatted perilously, waiting for the whole sill to break off and throw him down. But no more happened. Now, where his left foot had rested, he could see a dark, gaping hole, as though he had uncovered a shaft going down through the wall. Still grasping the tough tangle of ivy-stems, he pulled himself up to a standing position again. He felt a little awed, a little guilty; yet the moment was ecstatic, as though he stood on the edge of all adventure; he knew that he must crawl to the open shaft and look in.

"What are you doing up there?"

He had not heard the car. He saw it now, in the avenue at the edge of the glacis, standing still. The shout and the barking of dogs were nearer; a woman was striding furiously up to the wall; the dogs were plumy-tailed red setters.

"Come down at once! It's forbidden! It's dangerous. Didn't you see the notice? Can't you read?"

He stayed where he was; he didn't answer for a moment. He saw that her head was tied up in a coloured turban, that her face looked white and pink and powdery like a mask. She came on, to the foot of the wall. "Come *down*, d'you hear?"

He took a show-off risk and jumped; he landed neatly; the dogs charged upon him, began to greet him, pushing up their heads under his hands. He fondled them, still staring at the woman. She stared back; her long blue-green eyes, set far apart, looked at him with positive hate. She put up her hand to her forehead, let it fall. She muttered "It—isn't—possible."

He knew her now, though she seemed to have grown much older. "Hullo, Geraldine" he said. It was her turn to make no reply. She had taken a spectacle-case from the pocket of her raincoat; she put on horn-rimmed glasses. The peacock-hued scarf wrapped her head all round, tying below the chin; the raincoat collar was turned up high; all this enclosed the almond-shaped mask, tortured with thin wrinkles; blinded now by the greenish glasses. He was sorry for her, without knowing why.

She snapped "Why are you here?"

"I don't quite know." He was baffled again. Nothing came with this woman but herself; it was odd to find her wholly familiar, yet to have no recollection. He felt her hatred lunging at him. Now she was looking down at his hands. She said "Same hands, even—" as though talking to herself, and added angrily "It's ridiculous."

"Why are you cross?" the boy asked.

"You're Carus' son—you must be."

"I may be."

"*May* be? What sort of talk is that? Daniel. You're Daniel."

(Dick? David?) Yes, he thought, I could be Daniel. Carus' son Daniel. He said "Mr. Luke Courtney thought I was Pippin Black."

She repeated "*Pippin!*" with a snort of a laugh. "Pippin. . Damn silly nickname. It always was. Can't imagine you call your father Pippin. . Is he with you?"

"I'm alone."

"But *why?*"

He held out the estate-pass.

"All right, all right; it doesn't entitle you to climb on the Friary—*nor* to come to the house, d'you understand? I don't know what sort of a joke this is, but I won't have you at the house."

While he stared at her bewilderedly, she said "I can only assume Carus has told you everything. Very charming."

"Nobody's told me anything."

"You know my name."

He countered with "Well, you seem to know mine."

"I happen to be cursed, among other useless gifts, with an elephant's memory," she told him.

He was interested. "*Useless?* D'you mean that? A memory's no use?"

She was taking off her glasses. He saw the blue-green eyes again. Why should a line of poetry flash in through the mist? It said "*La Belle Dame Sans Merci hath thee in thrall.*"

CHAPTER TWO

In the car, below the Friary, Monsignor Francis Merrion sat waiting for his old friend Geraldine Courtney. At first he amused himself by studying his own face. Not a habit of his; but in her hurried exit, Geraldine had knocked the driving-mirror crooked, and it tilted down to frame his reflection. "You still," she had said to him a little earlier, "look like an elegant owl." He saw no elegance; he saw the owl, the round intellectual face, pallid today; the clerical collar and the purple silk triangle below. There was a deep cleft running vertically between his eyebrows; Geraldine had noticed that: "You've got the pleat in your forehead, too. Are you in pain?" She remembered everything. She was right; his enemy sawed through all his bones, making a pain-shape of his skeleton; skull, vertebrae and lumbar regions. A little sad to remember this feast of Corpus Christi, his first in Ireland for several years, as a day of pain. He offered it up with a grunt.

His own fault, in any case. He had taken on too much with this journey. Quite enough work ahead of him tomorrow, when the Retreat began.

"How one capitulation does lead to another, does it not?" said Francis to Francis. First he had succumbed to the appeal of his old friend Mother Paula from the convent at Castleisland. He had not meant to do this. But having written to say that he would take the five-day Retreat, he had seen doors opening to other cherished places, to other old friends. So there had been two nights in Dublin, one night under the Bishop's roof in Limerick, and now a night in Drumnair—of all places.

Of all places, he thought again. . Thus far, it seemed little changed. Geraldine a little paler, a little more shrill and tense. The trees and the pasture surrounding him now, the great stretches of the demesne, held their old beauty; their old magic. Something mournful and malevolent here too; as always. And, as always, a crisis. Only a small one, perhaps, this young tourist scrambling about in the Friary, but enough to anger Geraldine. When he saw that she was still talking to the boy up there beside the ruin, he climbed out, to stretch his tired back and legs.

They were only a hundred yards away; she was haranguing the boy and the boy stood still. He had his hands in his pockets; his attitude was jaunty and composed, the tilt of his dark head most reminiscent. "How very strange," said Francis. (In a blink, he travelled back thirty years; he saw another young man standing on that same spot, with the sunlight fading off the grass; Geraldine talking, Carus Black standing comfortably speechless, hoarding up his thoughts inside his head.)

It was over in a moment. He saw Geraldine point towards the gate, the boy turn away, round the Friary wall. Francis was still watching the deject figure when Geraldine came storming back with the dogs. She said briskly, "Half-witted. Kicked a great piece off the wall. I'm seriously thinking of stopping the estate-passes. At least, checking somehow on the people who get in. I must talk to Luke." She set the driving-mirror straight and started up the car. He saw that her hands shook on the rim of the wheel.

3 7

"Did he," Francis asked musingly, "remind you of any-one?"

"That boy? No. Why?"

"Nothing. ." It was wiser not to say the name of Carus. Looking at her profile he saw that she was in one of her vizor-down moods.

"I would very much like you to have a word with Antonia," she said. "If you're not too tired, that is."

"Of course," said Francis.

"Better alone, I think; better without me. If you'll go into the drawing-room, I'll send her to you."

They drove up through the rhododendrons, through the tree-tunnel, and came to the house. *"Oh monstrous house."* Francis cocked an eye to the phrase; it came from Carus, surely. 'Monstrous' had been one of his words. Geraldine circled the terrace, bringing the car close to the steps for the comfort of his descent.

'Oh, monstrous house.' The main wing was a high-shouldered, early Victorian horror, built of brown stone, with some fake Tudor ornament wriggling here and there, some fake Tudor chimneys. It had long, melancholy ground-floor windows and a grim portico. To the right, the old wing slanted placidly away, with its little tower jutting out against the trees. The lavish, untidy garden spread around and about until the woods began.

As he limped up the steps, Francis heard the noise of the rain come suddenly; a dance of wind shook all the leaves; there was a twirling and pattering behind him, a movement of witches. Then the front door flew open and Antonia rushed out. She had grown up; she had grown larger, very much larger. Big and buoyant, wearing a trench-coat and what looked like a ski-ing cap, she was pulled up on her heels. Her expression was that of a child caught at mischief.

Beside his shoulder, he heard Geraldine asking coolly "And where do you think you're going?"

"To see Luke." Since old Luke Courtney had, with pains-taking malice, sealed up all the doors originally connecting the two wings, it was, Francis remembered, necessary to approach him by way of the terrace.

"To see Luke? When I specifically asked you—"

—"I know. I'm sorry."

"So I should hope." Geraldine's voice now became so-cially affable: "You remember Antonia, don't you, Francis? You remember the Monsignor, of course. . He would like to talk to you." She had seized Francis' luggage: "No, nobody need help me. I want you both to go into the draw-ing-room. You can have tea there quietly, together; I shan't disturb you."

Francis shook hands with Antonia. The eyes with the bloom of a grape, the rich skin and the dazzling teeth, added up to beauty. More than beauty, he thought; there was a demon in the face, an oddly adult prisoner trapped between the laugh and the scowl.

But there was no disguising the fact that she was an elephant of a girl, a big fat girl. He knew the pain suffered by big fat girls. In London, not long ago, he had taken tea with some ladies of pious vivacity, waited on by the daughter of the house, also a big fat girl. He could hear the ladies hustling out their comfortable words:—"Puppy-fat"; "She'll fine down"; "She's tall *with* it—and that makes such a difference." Antonia was "tall *with* it." Still, poor Antonia. . Was Geraldine, as she offered this, her adopted child, to the cloister, considering that the nun's habit would, among

39

other advantages, cover all? An amiably frivolous thought. He smiled into the face of the rebel. . "We could talk a little later," he said "If you have a rendezvous."

"I haven't, strictly speaking," said Antonia. In the hall, she pulled off the cap and the trench-coat with a gesture of resignation. The hall was unchanged; he saw its country-house clichés; moth-eaten stags' heads; a case of stuffed birds; the stairs that mounted to a broad landing; above the landing the ugly stained-glass window crammed with family crests and quarterings. On the table in the centre of the stone floor there lay bunches of pinks, freshly plucked, waiting to be arranged in the big silver bowl. Familiar, too.

"Tea won't be long," Geraldine said abruptly. She opened the drawing-room door. As on any rainy day, the long room looked drowned, cold, colourless. Bright sunshine, he recalled, made for tarnish and shabbiness everywhere. The long windows showed the room no mercy. Once the curtains were drawn, it would become its old self again in the lamplight. At the moment, Francis gazed into an aqueous gloom of oil-paintings, tapestries, dull rose damask, peeling gilt and bruised parquet. According to Geraldine, people said "Such a lovely room" because it was too pathetic in its tired grandeur to be ignored; it made a demand. "They have to say something—the way one does for a friend's new, awful hat. ."

He saw that the colours had faded still more from the biggest tapestry; where a hunter chased a stag through pale tree-trunks and a team of curling, prancing dogs followed the hunter. He stood picking up the lost detail while Antonia went ahead of him. Below the gilt and marble chimney-piece from Versailles there stood an embroidered fire-screen. The girl put the screen aside; this revealed a modern electric fire in a long steel shell. She switched it on. The red bar began to glow. "Always cold in this room. . even in May," said Antonia.

"Inclement weather" Francis agreed.

"What's happened to Geraldine?"

"She intends us to be alone" said Francis, choosing the wing-chair by the fire.

Antonia looked at him with a twinkle. "I didn't mean that, Monsignor. I meant. . well, she looks so queer. As if she's just seen a ghost."

"Well, perhaps she has. I think I did, too."

"Honestly? Which? Monk-sort? Walled-up-nun sort? Weeping-child sort?"

"I wouldn't," said Francis, "Call this ghost one of the locals."

"Surely not a *new* one? Nothing new happens here."

"It wasn't really a ghost."

She looked disappointed. He wondered what he was supposed to say to her. He had known her last as a twelve-year-old tomboy. He tried, "I understand you're being made to suffer my Retreat tomorrow."

She nodded. "I'm glad it's you," she said.

"Thank you." He frowned over the chilly words spoken by Geraldine on the way from Limerick. The word "difficulties" stood out. He said—"Is it true you're having difficulties these days?"

"I've been having pleurisy. So's not to go back to school. I did it on purpose."

"Ah."

"It was quite easy. I had a cold, so I didn't change my shirt when I came in from riding. Then I had a bath, leaving

41

all the windows wide open." She added, "I have confessed it, so not to worry."

"I won't. And after the Retreat," he said "You'll be going back?"

It was a convent-school in England. It was Geraldine's belief that Antonia would begin life as a postulant next October. Looking at Antonia now, he thought her about as likely a postulant as a black panther-cub in the Zoo would be. She was saying, "I don't want to go back. Or stay here, either, the Lord He knows. I suppose I've just gone bloody-minded. Isn't it queer one can't talk to Geraldine?"

Francis thought about it. "N-no,—not really. Seeing that she herself talks to nobody."

"Was she always like this? I can't remember it when I was a tot. I remember being sorry for her."

"Not frightened of her?"

Antonia said "Goodness, no. But you've known her forever. Was she always—?"

—"No. She wasn't. Or less so. She has shut herself up gradually."

"Looks like *I'm* the one that's going to be shut up," said Antonia with a giggle.

"You're worried?"

She cocked her head on one side; she stuck her thumbs ungracefully into the belt of her skirt: "I don't worry about having no vocation, Monsignor. Seems to me they know that already at the convent. And if they don't yet, they will; they'll find out faster than light. What gets me down is that it's spoiling all the fun *now*; spoiling God, even. And that," she said "I won't have. See?"

"I think I see." It was a more reasonable attitude than he had been led to expect. But at this instant he could see her only as one more of Geraldine's failures. He went back to the beginning; to the first rapturous letter. Geraldine had enclosed snapshots of the plump, dark baby, brought from England after its parents were killed by a flying-bomb She had written "Wonderful to have something so small and gay to look after and live for." Her son, Godfrey, was already an adult, already a problem. She had written, "I have rechristened her Antonia. Please pray for her, won't you?"

Poor Geraldine.

Antonia said "I'm afraid I shan't make at all a good Retreat."

"Why do you say that?"

"I can't get close to God any more."

"I know the feeling. I've had it myself. It doesn't last."

"*Promise?*" She looked as beseeching as a spaniel. "I promise," he said.

"Monsignor. . . . 'can't say this without sounding horrible. . but it's all become so—so impregnated with Geraldine. *She's* in the way. Every time I aim at the Lord there's only Geraldine. Like getting the wrong number on the telephone. I go on and on saying 'Speak, Lord, for thy servant heareth' and nothing happens. Except Geraldine's voice saying 'No.'" Here she startled him by giving an anguished bellow: "*Ow*—and it used all to be so lovely. It was my favourite thing. And it's gone. It's not *fair*."

"Now you cheer up," said Francis. "Remember it hasn't gone. Love of God can't go, unless you want it to."

"Well but of course I don't *want* it to."

"All right, then." He smiled at her: "You run along and see Luke."

"Goodness," said Antonia, "Aren't you meant to preach at me?"

"You'll be hearing enough of my sermons in the next few days."

Still she looked at him unbelievingly. "Or even tell me to make an Act of Will? Geraldine says what I'm making is an Act of Won't."

"I'll dispense you from Acts," Francis said, "until tomorrow."

He drifted away from her exuberant gratitude into his own reverie. He was there before she had shut the door behind her. Drumnair, he thought, was at its old tricks. What *was* it about the place? He looked at a pattern, already visible. The pattern had begun when he said Mass this morning. An errant marker in the missal had turned up before his eyes a familiar passage, nowhere related to Corpus Christi. A mere chance; a thing that often happened; but the passage was this:—

The man Gabriel . . . flying swiftly, touched me on the shoulder at the hour of the evening sacrifice. Words of the prophet Daniel; words that had once held a magic for Carus Black. (Carus saying "We shall call our first son Daniel.")

And then, the boy with the look of Carus. And now Antonia, not knowing whom she quoted. Carus, in the last letter before the long, long silence, the silence that was still going on, had written "Every time I looked at God, Geraldine got in the way."

Well, perhaps it wasn't a pattern; (he disapproved of them;) just three little signals coming from nowhere. And storms in this house were not so much proof of a pattern as proof that Geraldine still lived here. Always she had brought darkness down on her own head.

Was this all that her fighting courage would ever do for her? He had seen her fight her parents when she was twenty; to break their hearts (they said) by marrying Tom Courtney. A mixed marriage, on a background of doom and disorder; two faiths, two families, two countries at virtual war. But her father and mother had, presumably, kept their hearts intact; to be broken six months later by her reception into the Church. Very much her own doing, that conversion; none of Tom's doing. Lazy, charming, drunken Tom might well have preferred her to keep out. ("She's caught the Faith like a fever, hasn't she, Father?") She had come in, as one might say, with a flaming sword; and laid about her, had she not? Used the Church as a weapon to beat Tom with?

Francis heard himself sigh. He had seen her fighting Tom, and the hideous result. He had seen her fight the evidence of suicide and fight it so successfully that Tom was buried in holy ground. She was only twenty-three then. She had fought Luke, her father-in-law, to stay on here, to bring up her child as the heir to untold, imaginary rights. ("As though," Luke had grumbled "he'll have anything but debts to inherit." What Godfrey had inherited was Tom's love of drink. And what was Godfrey now? A vagrant; a vanished liability; a signature on random letters asking for help.)

Francis glanced back to the moment of hope and happiness; three years after Tom's death. The year was 1929. The moment had come with the invasion of Carus Black, and this was an invasion that looked, at first, as though it would mean nothing at all. A cocky, golden-spoon sophisticate, used to getting his own way. A spoilt young man. A world-traveller, with money in his purse. Had he been merely a playboy, he would have joined the others. Geraldine the widow, in her strenuous obedience to the Church, had kept

45

the playboys just where they didn't want to be. And she was very beautiful in those days.

But the twenty-one-year-old pirate (Luke's word, he remembered) was of a different mind. Carus, with his vast, vulgar sports-car, his passion for riding unpredictable horses, his fortune and his freedom, had fallen in love with the Church, as with Geraldine.

Francis looked at his own part in the story. He knew what he would see; that the failure was still there, mocking him. And the arrogance still, the blow to his arrogance remained, because he had lost Carus, his chosen. Francis could still think of him as that, isolating him, stamping him; as though, after a lifetime in the priesthood, and a successful lifetime, he had sought one soul only and seen the soul escape.

(*"Master, we have laboured all night and caught nothing."*)

All he had left was the name, the flat name without conscious association, still enduring in his prayers. There was a mechanical Memorare at morning. There was a regular place on the old personal list that he was forever cleaning up and cutting down. (So many of them dead; over to the De Profundis. So many forgotten. . Who, for example, was Mrs. Price, still keeping her position between Geraldine and Cousin Martha, his only surviving relative?) At the beginning of the Canon itself, in regular, unnoticeable routine, the name persisted every day beside the altar:

"Memento, Domine, famulorum famularumque tuum, N et N. Carus Black."

Yes, he stayed where he belonged, that one, up at the top with the problem-children, the craggy customers. Francis could not remember when, saying his Mass, he had

46

first begun to divide the 'Memento Domine' in so severe a fashion. The spoken names in his head were one kind; the clause coming after embraced the opposite kind, with a sigh of relief:—

"And all here present, whose faith and devotion are known to thee. ." Thankfully at this point, he stopped pleading, lost the sense of the uphill struggle for God's mercy.

"But that one young man," he said to himself now, shaking his head,—"that's the fellow I'll carry with me to my grave. Because he did it. Not because of the *way* he did it. This has nothing to do with Geraldine. I'd have minded as much, however he came, however he went."

And why? The answer to that question remained, as ever, brightly inconclusive. Love was beyond all explanation and he had loved Carus. "And in those days I still had favourites. . just as I still had ambition." Ambition, long spent, resolved; being now "the accomplishment of works pleasing to Thee," no more, no less. The talents of a ready tongue and a skilled pen, the talents had been used. The long, slow training in patience and humility had borne some fruit. Not enough, but there could never be enough.

And these days were quietly rewarding. He was devoted to the rules of his Order; the London Priory was his home. Soon the disease in his bones would keep him very still. No more travels. But he had come a long way.

The ribbon of memory was unrolling fast; he couldn't stop it, any more than he could stop the flaring, crackling, physical pain. Himself, parish priest of Drumnair, the pet of the Courtney family, something of a private chaplain to the Manor. Himself instructing Carus; Carus serving his Mass; the keen pleasure of receiving somebody so young,

so lively, the joker with the bright intellect, the worldly rake
of twenty-one. Quite suddenly he recalled the rake's question
about gambling; Carus having returned from a week-end at
Le Touquet:

"If it was a sin to lose two hundred pounds on Thursday,
did I put myself in a state of grace by winning it all back
the next night? I'm serious. What would be the point of
confessing it on Saturday? Looks as though gambling were
the only sin you could wipe out, doesn't it, Father?"

"Gambling isn't necessarily a sin."

(The dark head, the light eyes and the crooked smile of
challenge. .) "Not necessarily, no. But if, for example, I'd
embezzled that money, gambled with it, lost it all—and then
won it back on Friday?"

"How, dear boy, if you'd lost it *all*, could you win it back
on Friday?"

"Oh—embezzled some more," said Carus.

Yet in his love of argument, he had never been one of the
doubtful starters, the hecklers, the near-converts brandishing their difficulties on a can't-catch-me note of triumph.
He had embraced the Faith with an enormous, willing hug;
almost a Chestertonian exuberance: "It's the only *reason*
I've ever known for being alive."

But he had his own specific stubbornness. Even now,
Francis believed that had Carus taken his First Communion
before the Nuptial Mass, he would never have walked away.
("For how many years, afterwards, did I kick myself be-
cause I didn't persuade him to do that?") He had received
Carus into the Church ten days before the wedding.

Quiet and bare, the moment, as always; stripped of ceremony; none present save those concerned, priest, convert
and sponsor. With Geraldine, deliberately self-effacing, un-

48

obtrusive, alone, far down the church, in the back pew. Francis remembered seeing her look up from her prayers and beckon an old village-woman who was lighting a candle, to come and kneel beside her; to join her in prayer for the young man at the altar-rail.

He could see that young man; the subdued, steadfast figure, kneeling upright, his hand upon the Gospels. He could see the godfather, the dark, narrow-faced Vicomte of this or that; a friend from the playgrounds of France; wafted here by Carus to act as his sponsor now and presently as his best man.

He could see the baptism; the shell filled with water that he emptied out upon the sleek, curled head. He saw Carus turning, all splashed from the font, with laughter in his eyes. Carus had looked towards the pew where Geraldine still kept her veiled head hidden in her hands. Once outside the church, he had become shy. The boisterous congratulations up at the Manor made him shyer still. But there was no shadow on him then.

How had the shadow fallen? What had made for the struggle, in those last days? Where had he, Francis, failed. . or where had he been deceived? He couldn't tell. Certain things had worried him, but they were small things. Carus' decision (which was, he knew, Geraldine's decision) to stay on at the Manor right up till the wedding-day, had worried him. But they had shrugged their shoulders at that. Geraldine had talked of 'conventional nonsense'; Carus had made jokes about the size of the house and the number of guests, each with the powers of a chaperon. There was one confession of Geraldine's that had worried him. . And the pale, driven look of Carus, the growing silence of

49

Carus. But he had never really known, he thought; he never would know.

He saw the wedding-day. Still as improbable, as melodramatic, as a scene in a bad film. When he looked at it in his mind now, he saw the scene entire; as if he had been an onlooker somewhere up in the organ-loft. He saw himself, robed and vested; standing between the prie-dieu and the altar-rail; the two figures before him. He heard his own voice asking confidently, "Carus, wilt thou take Geraldine, here present, for thy lawful wife, according to the rite of our Holy Mother the Church?"

And then the film turned into slow motion, with the long silence, with the gentle, unbelievable shake of the head before Carus said quietly "No, Father"; and, still in slow motion, he watched the compact, well-co-ordinated figure stepping away from the altar-rail, sleepwalking down the aisle, alone.

It was still, Francis thought, by far the most surprising thing that had ever happened to him. He was blinking upon the memory as the door opened, and Geraldine came into the room.

ii

"Yucks, kee, peugh—" said Antonia to herself. It was all her own fault. She should not have expected to find Luke alone, because he never was. But it did seem excessive on the part of God to have made the company American; two vivid, slender women in flawless suits with skirts uncreased (didn't they ever sit down?) and two silver-haired men with deep, slow voices. There was also (wouldn't you know?)

Kitty Fitzhugh,—the Horse-Borne Widow to Antonia. If a woman could be a fop, then the Horse-Borne Widow was a fop; a crackly, bony elegant with a yellowish face. She was said to want to marry Luke, which was disgusting.

Antonia's heart had failed her palpably on being told that she would find Himself and the Party in the French Room. A year ago she would have bolted. Something in today's precarious mood had persuaded her that she could face the company without a qualm.

"Worms and worms and worms," she gabbled under her breath. She was in the corner of a sofa, impeded by a cup of tea and some highly unmanageable hot buttered toast; it squelched and dripped. Her skirt was riding up, and Luke was telling lies. She glared at him. She could seldom think of him as her grandfather, not even an adopted grandfather; least of all when he told lies. He had told three in ten minutes; the lie about the burning of the Manor; the lie about the leprechaun; and the lie about riding the winner of the Punchestown Cup.

And here came the cue for all his lies about the Book of Drumnair. "Serve them right, though," she thought, "for getting him started. . *when* they let him start." At the moment they seemed to be doing—in chorus—a conducted tour of Trinity College Library for his benefit. To have picked on Luke, of all people, for this rhapsodic exposition was just their bad luck. Alas for them, Antonia thought, as they raved on; they had done the Book of Kells; now it was Durrow's turn.

"That darling little lion of St. Mark. . We went back next day and they'd turned the page, so there was quite another little animal than the lion; a kind of cow."

Overlapping prattle. *How did the monks the detail those*

5 1

scrolls those flowers those little mice those perfect never saw a handwritten script to touch it now there's an art that's lost the old satchel I just loved that old satchel I don't know why the Devil's Bit Mountain was it? . . and the skin of Luke's face drawing inward around its bones; half-angry, half-amused, the face of a falcon awaiting his minute to dive on the chickens.

The minute came. "What did you think of the cum-dach?" he asked gently.

"Come again?" said the American called Joshua.

"Silly of me—the shrine," said Luke, as if he spoke the Gaelic by habit. "The shrine," he added, "of the book."

"You mean the old satchel? Now which book did that belong to? Armagh, wasn't it?" They were doing their best; Luke wasn't; his head moved around like a quiz-master. Joshua said "Ah, now I remember. The silver shrine, the box. Book of. . hold it." He looked most unfortunately pleased with himself. "Dimma. . *that* was the one they found on the Devil's Bit Mountain. Dimma."

"A very dear friend of ours in San Francisco called her first baby Dimma. Now I wonder—did I say something wrong, Mr. Courtney?"

"Wrong?" said bloody Luke. "Oh, no. Nobody's said anything wrong. On the other hand, nobody has yet said anything right. In this particular regard, I mean. Kitty dear, I should be so grateful if I might see that assortment of little cakes."

This gave Antonia giggles. She came out of them to hear him pontificating: "The shrine of *our* book; the Book of Drumnair. Well, I suppose if you missed that, you missed the three pages also."

They had.

"Pity" said Luke. "The most moving sight in all Ireland. . with the possible exception of the Gallarus oratory." He beamed upon them. "Not that you are entirely to blame. Shrine and pages alike are very poorly exhibited. I'm always complaining about it. Poky little cases; wholly unworthy of them. What? . . Just on the right, beyond Durrow. Ah, well, very disappointing for you, to return to the United States without that glimpse."

"Tell us," they said "about the Book of Drumnair."

("Watch it, chums," said Antonia in her head.)

"Like the other books, it was, of course, a New Testament given by St. Columba to a church of his foundation. To the church that he founded here. . the ruins now known as the Friary. This is clearly proved by the three extant pages. All the experts, Mlle Françoise Henry among them, have attributed the workmanship to one of the four scribes responsible for the Kells Gospels."

(True enough, so far, Antonia admitted, but you're giving the wrong lecture, aren't you, Luke? And they can't take it in. Goodness, who could? Hair-sides and gatherings and a conjoint bifolium when they aren't really in the clear yet about Columba and Columcille; oh I do wish you'd stop. Ho. . question coming up. . yes, I thought so.)

"But *where*, Mr. Courtney, is the rest of the book?"

"Ah" said Luke. He ate one of the little cakes and said "Ah" again. They sat reverently waiting. Entrenched behind the tea-tray, wearing his black velvet coat and all his rings, he had turned from a falcon into a gracious old dowager. "Ah," he said for the third time,—"Where is the book? That's a secret that dies with me."

What was so astonishing was that all, even the Horse-Borne Widow, seemed to believe it. How could anybody

53

believe it? Had a Courtney ever found it, he would have blazed it abroad. Even the local guide was at pains to discount the legends. There was the legend of the faithless sacristan who had stolen the shrine and desecrated the book by cutting out the three beautiful pages. There was the legend of the monks keeping day and night watch over the book ever afterwards. And the legend of its survival in a secret place. All fancy. The only fact was the finding of the pages themselves. They had rested, not far from the shrine, down under the peat, beyond the river; perfectly preserved and never explained.

And here was Luke, at it again. Successfully feeding his audience the tale that the book had survived the sack of the Friary and was here on the demesne, its hiding-place always known to the family. A secret handed down from father to son. (Yes, but he loved the thought of the book. It was his Grail; he couldn't, he said, live without it. Antonia thought that the childish faith should touch her heart, whereas she found it merely stupid and, on occasions like this, a heavy embarrassment.)

Now he had invented quite a new piece. He was saying that all the eldest sons were allowed just one glimpse of it when they came of age He had got that from the Glamis monster. Alone, she would have challenged him.

She did not challenge him. She was outside all this. If the company gave her a thought, which she doubted, the thought would be that the fat girl on the sofa might pull down her skirt. In the effort to do so, she let the buttered toast get away from her and it fell between her haunch and the sofa-cushion.

"Butter-fingers—" said Luke.

"Very apt," said Antonia—"You ought to have those little napkins."

This rudeness, she was obliged to admit, went with a swing. The Americans agreed vociferously; one of the women gave her a large wad of Kleenex. Luke began to complain that if there were anyone in the house, indeed anyone in the world, who cared whether he lived or died, he would have those little napkins. But now, horrifically, they were all focusing upon her, expecting her to say something else. When she didn't, the Horse-Borne Widow said "How are you now, Antonia? Better? Tell us *all* about yourself."

Luke flashed her a sympathetic glance. She said gruffly, "I'm much better, thank you."

"Back to school soon?" The Horse-Borne Widow was taking over, in a glistening, grinning wave of explanation to the others: "Antonia goes to a convent-school. In Wiltshire. She's going to become a nun . . . isn't that wonderful?"

Both the American women put on special faces for religion and said it was. One of the males cleared his throat and blew his nose in a long, clinical, detailed way, afterwards examining the results. The Horse-Borne Widow, having inflicted her message, asked brightly and tactlessly "What news of Godfrey. .? That's Antonia's brother."

"My adopted brother. At least *I'm* adopted, which comes to the same thing, doesn't it?" She really couldn't see Godfrey as her brother or as anything else. One of the Americans asked what Godfrey did. "What does he do? Oh-ho. That's a nice question. Meaning a nasty one. I could a tale unfold. . But there," Antonia added, "I mustn't make your knotted and combinéd locks to part, must I?" She gave a loud, stagey peal of laughter, with which she was delighted.

She could see them thinking "A *nun*. . ?" Suddenly she was very cross with herself and with all of it. How would it be to go? Saying "I only dropped in. ." But Luke now was raising himself out of his chair, with the aid of his silver-knobbed stick. He said to the rest, "I know you'll excuse us. My grandchild has business to discuss with me." There was —wasn't there?—an immediate relaxation, a ripple of relief; hearty handshakes, and goodbyes sounding like pleased welcomes. Then she was out in the hall, with Luke and Dana, the greyhound.

"How did you know?"

"Despite your size, you are transparent" said bloody Luke. He beckoned her into the Teak room; a small monstrosity that he used as a study. His father had kept it for trophies from the Far East, so it was full of gods and brass and elephants' feet and stuffed snakes. Luke sat in a huge, hideous carved chair; Antonia slumped down on the tiger-skin, with the dog.

"This is kind," she said.

"*Kind?* As you should realize by now, I thrive on crises. They are among the few pleasures left to me. What's yours today, Miss?" he asked, sounding like a barman, "I thought you were in Retreat at Castleisland. With my old friend the Monsignor. Wasn't that the plan?"

"Not till tomorrow. I came to ask if I could be your cook and live in the cottage."

"Dear Heaven!"

"Please, Luke, please. I cook like an angel, it's the only thing I can do and I can't go on living with a lie. I haven't got a vocation."

"Well, but, the lack of a vocation doesn't necessarily compel kitchen-talents."

5 6

"It does; it jolly well must. I beg you."

"Stop. Geraldine and that harpy Susanna between them do all the cooking I require. And more. ."

"Your lady-gardener then? And drive the car? One can learn to drive in three lessons. I saw a piece where it said—"

"Stop—" said Luke again—"Nonsense. Sheer folly. And you know it."

"Well, worms and worms and worms. And worms."

His cloudy blue eyes were fixed upon her. "Geraldine" he said "is an ass. I must talk to Geraldine."

"About me? Goodness, that would be fatal. She believes you have regular dinner-dates with the Devil."

"Just as I incline to the view that she's his aunt by marriage."

"The Monsignor took me rather calmly," she said. "I can talk to *him*."

"He's civilized," said Luke. "'Comes of his having left this country long ago. I can even read his books."

"If you ask me, he doesn't believe in my vocation either."

"Who could?"

She began at once to fight on the other side. "A year ago," she said "it was all fine and dandy. Perhaps it will be again."

"You're growing up"; said Luke, "Nothing will ever be fine and dandy now until you're my age and look back and think it was. Take that from me, my child."

She scrambled off the tiger-skin, dislodging Dana. "How can I be a child when I'm growing up? I think, for seventeen, I'm quite adult and reasonable. And if you won't employ me I'll run away to sea; and you'll all be sorry; and so shall I, with my queasy stomach. And I can't see what you're laughing at."

57

"Perhaps the adult and reasonable project for running away to sea" said Luke. He kissed her: "Run home, Miss. Make a good Retreat and then come back and raise hell; that's what I used to do. Meanwhile, pray for my project; I want to sell these people—they're publishers—my memoirs."

"Your memoirs? Not the Book of Drumnair?" she asked naughtily.

He froze. "I don't care for jokes about the Book, Antonia; you know that."

"But you like spinning yarns; don't you? What about that seeing-it-on-twenty-first-birthday thing? You got it from the Glamis monster, didn't you?"

"I admit," said Luke, "to plagiarizing the monster. I get carried away."

She stared at him: "Do you honestly believe in it? Not the monster—the Book? Still?"

He nodded solemnly.

"But *here?* Hidden? All this time?"

He paused, took his ridiculous tin of cigarettes from the pocket of the velvet jacket and selected a Russian cigarette with a straw tip. "I think," he said, "that if anyone could ever prove to me that there was no Book, I should die immediately."

"Luke. . why?"

Now he looked very old and astonishingly truthful. His shoulders drooped. He said "I don't know, Antonia. Good-bye."

She crammed on her ski-ing cap and walked out into the rain. She felt more desolate than before. Silly and childish to appeal to Luke, who was, she knew well enough, on nobody's side. Except his own. She couldn't really blame him. Didn't that apply to everyone? Herself included.

As she came round the corner on to the terrace, she cocked an eye toward the drawing-room windows. Creeping near, she could see Francis and Geraldine seated at the chess table. She stepped back and moved on contentedly through the sluicing rain. She splashed across the back yard, heading for the carriage-house. It was her established hide-out.

Though it was falling to pieces, the carriage-house had, she thought, an endearing elegance, with its clock set in a graceful spire, its arch leading through to the stables. Treasures lived here. Behind the door on the left of the arch, an old painted carriage; behind the right-hand door, the harness-room. There had been a time, before Antonia's day, when this was converted into a playroom for the child Godfrey. Long since it had become a repository for unwanted things.

The junk of the years had cluttered it gradually. You could still see the shell of a room; faded curtains at the windows, rugs on the floor, a coke stove. You could sit on the implacable horsehair sofa unless you preferred the leather armchair lacking a castor, exploding here and there with cracknel-puffs of brownish wool. You could play the upright piano. You could explore the shelves of the glass-fronted cupboard. On these, there lived an entertaining miscellany; paper fans, birds' eggs, china ornaments, lumps of quartz carefully labelled, a lot of little brass brackets, a French clock with no hands and two slim pieces of polished wood that had come off something.

Skied above the piano were two pictures; a Sacred Heart of formidable impact and G. F. Watts' 'Hope.' Antonia had rescued them from the stack of dead pictures beside the wainscot. They were the only pair whose rusting wires still held them safely and they almost matched in size. There were bookcases round the walls; little rickety sets of shelves, filled with schoolbooks, old maps, pious manuals and the complete works of C. N. and A. M. Williamson. The table with the striped horse-blanket for a cloth held an oil-lamp. Antonia had polished its brass, trimmed its wick and imported a can of paraffin without detection. This room was quite her favourite place to be; much more sympathetic than her bedroom. Freedom lived here. She burst open the swollen door with a nudge of her shoulder.

Somebody had got here first. In the grey light made by the rain and the dust on the windows, she saw him standing with his back to her; he was examining the contents of the cupboard. A young man, wearing a sweater and corduroy shorts. Obviously one of the tourists who sometimes wandered beyond the 'private property' notices. He had startled her, all the same. She heard it in her voice, asking much too loudly, "And what can I do for *you?*"

He turned; he looked her up and down, taking his time. "I just came in out of the rain," he said, and smiled.

The smile brought Antonia to a halt in the doorway. She stared at him. She thought, "Well, here you are."

He had happened. She had hoped that he wouldn't; she had hoped that he would; she had despised the whole issue; she had been awaiting it with furious impatience. And here it came. She had no fault to find with him, save that he wasn't quite tall enough. By all other standards he was the most acceptable young man she had ever seen. This face, with its light eyes, its neat nose, its wide, well-shaped mouth, was the face that would never look her way. There was also, (naturally) the fatal air that put him still further out of reach. It was the air of careless composure; she found it somewhere in the tilt of his head and the lines of his body. It could mean nothing but doom.

This sort she had seen before, but far off; riding a perfect horse; driving a long car up to the doorway of the Nellon Inn, with a girl beside him. Oh yes. No doubt at all. Alas for it. This was the fellow; the *Prince Lointain,* on whom she had frequently spied in her imagination when she was supposed to be meditating.

She didn't know for how long she stood at the doorway, falling in love. The young man said gently, "Oughtn't I to be here?"

"Oh goodness me, yes."

"You look so surprised."

"Well, I am" said Antonia. She threw her ski-ing cap on the table and began to tear off her raincoat. As he came courteously to help her, she saw that he was wet through; drops of water running off his hair, the neck of his shirt and his sweater quite sodden.

"Rub yourself down with this," she said in a fierce, commanding voice. He took the threadbare antimacassar obediently.

"Didn't you have a mackintosh or *anything?*"

He shook his head. "I tried to shelter in the Friary; then I wandered up here."

"You just came in on an estate-pass?"

"Yes. And got thrown out." He looked much amused by this.

"Well, you're on private property, you see. There *are* notices," she said apologetically. "Who was it? Geraldine?" She couldn't understand where the joke was, but he was still grinning as he said "Yes, Geraldine. 'Think I'd better call her Mrs. Courtney in future." He went on mopping with the antimacassar.

"I'm Antonia Courtney. How d'you do."

"How d'you do."

"Have *you* a name?"

He looked more thoughtful. "Well, suppose I told you I was Daniel Black—" he said, watching her, waiting apparently for a reaction. She repeated "Daniel Black."

"You don't know the name?"

"I'm afraid not. But it's nice," said Antonia.

"It'll do," said the *Prince Lointain,* a little loftily. He rubbed his hair.

"I hope you won't catch cold. Have a mint lump?" She seized the sticky bag from the top of the piano. It should—shouldn't it?—be a silver cocktail-shaker, full of Dry Martinis. (It was. She made it into that. She weighed just eight stone, she wore a brocade dress of great beauty, or on the other hand, a pair of superbly cut slacks; she was pouring the ice-cold cocktail into crystal glasses.)

"God bless you" said the young man, with surprising vigour. He took a cluster of mint-lumps, distorting his face. "O Glunch" was what she understood him to say.

"No *lunch?*"

"Glno Glunch."

"But it's after six."

He looked at his watch and nodded. Having finished the mopping-up process, he draped the soaked antimacassar over an empty parrot-cage; which she thought rather clever of him. He was still very wet.

"*Why* no lunch?"

He shook his head.

"Where are you staying?"

"Nowhere," he said, shifting the burden from one cheek to another.

"Oh *do* explain. Please."

With a crunching, crackling noise he disposed of the peppermints. Then he smiled at her. He said "I'm afraid there's a lot I can't explain about me, Antonia."

"Are you in trouble? . ."

"I would think so." There was something impressive about the quiet tone, and the fleeting, adult smile. He seemed to depart from her altogether.

She heard herself burbling, "—Not that I want to pry—but it can't be *that* bad. And anyway, whatever you've done, Geraldine will always feed the hungry. She's tough, but she *does* abide by the book of words; if you see what I mean. Let me take you over there,—now—get you something to eat."

Daniel Black blew her a kiss. "You're very kind. But she'd raise hell."

"No. I promise she won't."

"She's forbidden me to come to the house. She was in a rage—shaking all over."

"Oh, she shakes," said Antonia. "Pay no attention. I suppose you were on a pet flowerbed or something—was it the one with the prunus tree?"

"I was in the Friary."

"The Friary? Then she couldn't—"

—"Yes, she could. And not because I climbed on the wall. It was something to do with my father. I didn't understand a word. But, take it from me, there'll be hell."

"Then I'll go," said Antonia.

"If you tell her—"

"Tell her—pooh. Shan't even see her. 'Won't take a minute. For my size," she added, "I have quite a fine turn of speed."

Baffled, thunderously excited, she plunged across the wet cobblestones to the kitchen door. The kitchen was empty; Geraldine's preparations for cold supper set out on the table. No time to lose. And no time to show off her cooking skill. Antonia scudded to and fro across the stone floors. She cut ham-sandwiches of huge proportions; she sliced a cheese in half; she robbed the vegetable-rack of six ripe tomatoes. In the pantry, there were two bottles of ginger-beer for her especial use; she had paid for them. These joined the rest, in a paper carrier-bag. (There were seven paper carrier-bags on the hook, because whoever did the shopping always forgot to take the last one, and they cost threepence a time, which went badly with Geraldine.)

Antonia was just running out when she thought of dry clothes for her stowaway. Appalled by her own courage, she went up the back stairs to Godfrey's room. Not a tremendous risk, really; his door was only a yard from the back-stair landing. But if Geraldine ever knew. . . There she stopped thinking.

As she opened the door, the chill of the deserted room was like a wind in her face. The room was very neat, very bare. A sentimental Madonna and Child, Della Robbia blue and white, hung above the bed. Nothing on the dressing-table but family photographs, set there by Geraldine. Cupboards and drawers alike were terrifying models of tidiness; she felt as though she were stealing from a men's outfitter. She grabbed a shirt and some socks. She helped herself to a yellow sweater. She stood, intimidated, before the ranks of trousers and jackets hanging in a profound, almost audible, smell of mothballs. She took down grey flannels and a white rainproof golfing-jacket, quite new. Shoes? These were so alarming in their liquidly-polished row that she compromised with a pair of old mocassins. "His feet, as I recall, are much bigger than Daniel's anyway. . These will do while the others dry 'Better get all his things over to the boiler-room as soon as there's a chance." She had forgotten to be frightened.

Suddenly, as she came to the stairhead, she heard footsteps on the front landing, Geraldine's voice:

"Who's that? You, Antonia?"

"Not now, it isn't," she muttered. She was down the stairs, out through the kitchen door into the rain,—safe. By an odd scruple of understanding, Geraldine never came to look for her in the carriage-house.

Daniel Black had returned to his examination of the cupboard. He was squatting in front of it, apparently finding the random collection of some interest, for his nose almost touched the glass. "It isn't locked," said Antonia, setting her loot upon the table, "You can get anything out you like."

"I'm looking for a china model of the Eiffel Tower. Quite small. It's got 'Souvenir de Paris' on it in gold letters."

"Well, it's there. . second shelf at the back. . . Hey," she said "How did you know?"

He didn't answer; he had it in his hands; he looked at it caressingly, then blinked in a bewildered way.

"You can have it, if you want it," said Antonia.

"Oh lord no—rather not. It isn't the sort of thing one would want, exactly. ." He stopped; "That sounds unkind. Perhaps it didn't hear." He patted it affectionately and put it up on the window-sill.

She watched him, enchanted. "You do that too. . Get sorry for *things*. . I'm always sorry for—"

6 5

—"Stop." He shut his eyes. "That's important. . Someone else said it. About a wallet, an old wallet. Wait." She waited obediently. "No good," he said, "It's gone—blown away."

"I know that too. . Something you just begin to remember—then don't. Sort of flashes," said Antonia. "I rather think they're a proof of reincarnation. Which is heresy, of course. Look—here's wads of food; and some clothes to wear till yours are dry."

He sprang to the table; he began to wolf the food, saying "You *are* kind—" "You're an *angel*" and "Nicest girl I ever met" between mouthfuls. She stood, watching him. She poured the ginger-beer into a pink flower-vase with handles.

"You have some too," said Daniel Black, "Loving-cup."

When she gave it back to him, she met the full, merry stare of the light eyes; she saw that he was determined for her to meet it; but he wasn't laughing at her; she was used to being laughed at when young men employed this kind of stare.

"Hullo," said Daniel.

"Hullo."

"This is fun, isn't it?"

"Is it?" she said in a growl of a voice, despising herself heartily. He became dreamy again, thoughtful:

"At least," he said "I know where I've seen *you*."

"Me? Where?"

"Outside the church, this morning. 'Know what I thought?"

She said "Sure. You thought What a fat girl."

"Wrong," said Daniel, "I thought 'She's my friend.' And now you are."

Antonia found that she could only snap "Better change

6 6

your clothes. I'll turn my back." Grabbing from the nearest shelf a book which proved to be "Carrots; Just A Little Boy" she stood reading it upside down. Behind her she could hear him chortling and chuckling.

"What's so funny?"

"Everything. Eating and undressing both at once and you reading—oh—I don't know—just got giggles."

"Tell me how you knew about the Eiffel Tower?"

"I can't. On the subject of me—anything to do with me —I'm no use to you. You've been warned."

"What's the mystery? Are you in the Secret Service?" asked Antonia. This brought more giggles. Then he said "You can turn round; I'm decent now." He was pulling the yellow sweater over his head. It suited him. He looked less Olympian with his curled hair all untidy and a bitten tomato in his hand. He finished the tomato and put on the white golf-jacket.

"Damn' nice clothes. Thank you. Whose are they?"

"Godfrey's. He's Geraldine's proper son. I'm just adopted."

"Godfrey. . Now that," he said, "rings a bell. A little boy called Godfrey."

"Not so little. He's about thirty-seven. He doesn't live here any more. He got away."

"Leaving his clothes behind him?" asked Daniel, with another giggle.

"Oh, that. ." She scowled; she felt mean, telling him. "It sounds silly, but in fact it's sad. Geraldine buys clothes for him, in case he comes back. . Parcels come from Dublin; one sees the tailors' labels and one always knows. But she doesn't talk about it. On the other hand, she doesn't try to conceal. . 'doesn't mind if one passes her on the stairs, carrying them

6 7

up to the room. Just smiles and goes on—daring one to say a word. So of course one doesn't. She can do that about anything. She always sends for the new London telephone-book in case his name's there. It never is. Those slippers are too big, I was afraid they would be."

"It's all magnificent," said Daniel Black. "But what will she say?"

"Goodness, she mustn't know."

He threw himself down in the lop-sided leather chair. "You seem to be taking a hell of a risk all round; don't you? Tell me some more about you" he added, embarking on the cheese.

She couldn't believe her ears. Young men, might they rot, liked only to talk about themselves. She began to feel as though her temperature was going up. Perhaps it was. (Careful, they said, after pleurisy.) "But I'm not *interesting*. People of seventeen can't be—nothing to tell—" she wailed.

"Oh, have a bash," said Daniel Black. He finished the cheese. She sat down on the horsehair sofa. There was a moth-eaten scarlet rug folded up in the corner of the sofa. She spread it over her lap, draping it to hide her legs.

"The only thing I can think of is that I'm supposed to be a nun and I can't face it."

Young men, hearing this, either turned facetious or went into a stupor of total bewilderment. Daniel Black managed to look lively, serious and understanding all at once. He also seemed to have grown older.

"A nun. And live to the glory of God."

"One's supposed to be doing that anyway," said Antonia.

"I know." His eyes now looked surprised at what his mouth was saying. "I *know*—" he repeated. He went into a private, questioning silence for a minute before he smiled at her and said, "Well as it happens I'm quite glad you can't be a nun." He had come back into his own image.

She needed a weapon against this. She said violently "I haven't lost my Faith, so don't you go thinking I have. No, indeed. It's the best and the most exciting and wholly delicious thing in the world. But—" here she put on brakes, so as not to say "But Geraldine's spoiling it." She substituted "Well, it is. So there. It's. . . *'my hope, my entire assurance, my riches, my delight.'"*

"Go on."

"The torrent of pleasure, the richness of the house of God." She could never get it by heart and she halted, with Daniel's voice urging her: "Say some more."

"I keep forgetting."

She saw him put his hand over his eyes; he muttered under his breath for a moment. Then his voice grew strong: *"My refreshment, my refuge, my help, my wisdom. . .* No, wait. 'Comes before that, the line I want." He sat up, pointing at her triumphantly. *"With love and delight, with ease and affection, and with perseverance unto the end."*

"Yes," she said, "My favourite, too."

They sat gazing at each other in silence. Daniel Black leaned forward; he put out a hand, to hold her fingers lightly in his. He repeated "With ease and affection."

The strokes of a gong hammered out, across the yard, echoing, booming. They brayed on, while Antonia swore; she knew what they meant. Within easy distance from these windows, standing on the back-door step, Geraldine was summoning her to lay the table for supper.

Friday   May 29th

CHAPTER ONE

At first Daniel was quite sure that he was awake and not dreaming. He saw the queer room in the carriage-house, the things of last night. The oil-lamp, the striped horse-cloth on the table, the piano and bookcases, became clear, touched with dusty sunshine. He could feel the unyielding sofa beneath him; a hairy blanket tickled his chin. And he knew that he must get up, to look for the treasure. He didn't give it a name; there was just the word blazing in his head. You could walk to the treasure so long as you didn't stop to think.

He was dressed before he knew it; and then he was on the bridge again, looking up across the green sward to see the Friary waiting for him. It made long shadows on the grass. The two gable ends of the chapel, slim, grey, pointed, were like pointed, praying hands. He saw the sun shine through the empty windows. He was skimming towards them. This time he did not disturb the big hares at their game; they leaped and danced unafraid; he went on exulting, the friend of the hares.

The sun was dazzling now; all the stones looked alight; in the cloister someone had cut down the weeds and he was glad, because he could see the figure on the tomb. He skimmed on, through the arch. He found himself standing just where he had stood yesterday, on the sunlit grass floor of the refectory, with the sky for a roof. He looked up at the embrasure. Antonia had got there first. She was sitting up there, hugging her knees. She said "There isn't room for both of us, I'm too fat," laughing down at him.

"Did you come to look for the treasure?" he asked. Antonia shook her head, still laughing. She said "I don't know where it is. But *you* know."

A second later, staring about him from the horsehair sofa, Daniel thought, "It couldn't have been a dream." It was too near, too precious. Then as its magic validity trembled and went, he knew it for a dream. He did not know why the echo of it let him lie here with joy pouring up inside him. He was very uncomfortable and rather cold. He burrowed into the tickly blankets.

Yesterday began to return, every picture of yesterday, Antonia most vividly. And before that? He fought to remember, but the cloud-curtain was down. Behind yesterday the fog still hung. "So I've still no memory. Yesterday is all I have." Curiously, it seemed enough. He felt entire indifference towards all the days that must have come before it; towards the problem of himself. It was comforting to know no more than this. But the very last memory, last night, here in the dark, brought him out of the blankets and on to his feet in a hurry. "Of course—" he said to himself, "I can't stay."

He had fallen asleep, waiting for the rain to stop; he had awoken to the beam of a torch flashing in his eyes. Muzzy with sleep, he had watched Antonia light the oil-lamp and draw the curtains. All this was dreamlike now, not sharp and clear and vivid as the dream of the treasure. . just a blurred light and a voice that whispered: "Still pouring, so I brought horse-blankets. Oh, and Godfrey's razor—and my best toothbrush, I've only used it once. . Try to keep awake and listen for a minute. . I'll leave the back-door unlocked. . downstairs placey on left as you go in. I'll bring breakfast; nobody knows but us."

74

He could just recall mumbling "What about Geraldine?"
Antonia, he thought, had said something reassuring about
Geraldine; at this moment he couldn't remember what it
was; nor, he decided, would he believe it if he did. That
white face of fury and the shaking hands haunted him. He
looked at his watch; it had stopped. He wanted to leave a
note for Antonia; he couldn't find a pencil. He wanted to
dress in his own clothes, but they had vanished; at least his
shoes were still here. He felt stiff and achy, putting on Godfrey's clothes again. The shoes were damp. He creaked
across the yard, trying to guess at the time. Early, at least.
A misty sun. Nobody about. The clock in the kitchen had
stopped too, he observed, as he stood beside the sink,
scraping with the razor. His search for pencil and paper ended
with a miserable ball-pointed pen and the back of a grocer's
bill.

He wrote "Don't bother about breakfast, you're bound to
be caught. Will get some now and come back." Remembering his dream, he added "I'll wait for you in the Friary."
This note he placed on the striped horse-cloth, with the
lamp holding it down, before he left the carriage-house.

Yesterday, he had dodged his way in from the demesne
by a back gate that opened into the stable-yard. Now he
slipped around the side of the house and came out onto the
terrace. He had to. A fierce curiosity drove him.

Yes, he said to himself, yes; he recognized it all; the
brown stone façade with its twirling ornament, the dour
portico, the enormous, solemn-looking windows. He knew,
just before he turned his head to find it, the angle that the
old wing would take as it slanted away, with the shape that
the little tower would form against the beech-trees.

"Oh monstrous house," he thought, surprised at his own

7 5

adjective, not really disliking the house. Then he wheeled; he was in full view of the windows and it was time to be going. But the sight of the prunus tree in the round flower-bed just beyond the lip of the lawn, stopped him short. "The prunus. . *That* prunus. Antonia said something about it, didn't she? But I couldn't have known."

The imprint in his mind was quite clear. There he saw a three-foot stick of a tree, with its little clump of earthy roots, and a fluttering label tied to its neck, lying just at the edge of that flowerbed, waiting to be planted. Here, now, the prunus towered twenty feet high; the tall, red-purple branches glittered, swayed, held their lashing triumph. The tree, he thought, the tree, and there were far, furious thunders behind the cloud in his head. But as he tried to hear them, they sank to silence. Just a tree, that had grown tall. He went, not looking back.

He felt safer when the drive had taken him down through the rhododendrons, and the woods had crowded in again, hiding the house. He went on, out of a gate with a PRIVATE PROPERTY notice that seemed to shout at him, on towards the bridge, by the path of yesterday. When he saw the Friary he felt a new tenderness for it. Today it belonged to him, because of the dream. (And this was true also of Antonia. . because of the dream.) Now the river, and the swan on its nest; now the big final door in the curved wall, and the village-street rushed on him, quiet and wide in the misty sunlight. The flags still flew.

A piebald horse came clopping by; the driver stood up-right in the cart, with two milk-cans behind him. He waved to Daniel and drove on up the road that led to Limerick.

The Nellon Inn looked sound asleep; the street was his alone; he walked down past the yellow cottages. Though he had breakfast in mind and still the six shillings in his pocket, he found himself halting, looking across to the church. The church beckoned him, a solid grey block, much restored. Alone and tranquil, without the crowds of yesterday. Over the wall the sycamore branches leaned, heavy with their leaves. The churchyard was empty. He walked across the street, lifted the latch of the gate and went up to the door. It yawned softly open.

He found that he stretched out his right hand before he guessed what the hand was seeking; when his fingers touched the water in the stoup, he knew. He crossed himself and went down on one knee.

There were colours in this grayness; the blaze of stained glass; gold haloes repeated in the carved wooden Stations; a silver ripple along the white altar-cloth; two candle-flames glowing. At the foot of the steps, in the Sanctuary, the priest's chasuble made the shape of a bright shield. He stood alone there. Just one figure knelt in the first pew; an old woman with her head veiled.

Walking up the aisle, Daniel saw what he must do. Here was a priest saying his Mass without a server; so it was for him to serve the Mass. He seemed to be two people at once. There was one person saying "But how can I do this?" and another hurrying in through the Sanctuary gates to do it. As he arrived on his knees with a thump, the priest bowed down to speak the Confiteor.

It was the second person in command now; the person who could do this; yet who did not dare to stop and think, to look ahead. Every time he thought he would forget, his voice, in one saving second, remembered for him. Could he trust it to carry him on?

"*Ostende nobis, Domine, misericordiam tuam.*"

"*Et salutare tuum da nobis,*" Daniel said.

He saw the priest go up the steps, watched him bend to kiss the altar, then move to the Epistle side and begin to read the Introit.

"*Kyrie Eleison.*"

"*Christe Eleison.*"

Yes, this was in line with other things that had lately happened to him; something that he perfectly knew, though he was unaware of remembering. The automatic recognition went on; now the saving second brought him up from his knees, took him to the altar; his hands, already instructed, lifted the Missal and carried it to the Gospel side. His right hand moved to his forehead, lips and breast, making the sign of the cross three times. Then as the priest began to read the Gospel, his own knee bent before the middle of the altar; his feet took him back to the other side. He found that he was glancing over his shoulder, to see that the cruets of wine and water were there on the table against the wall, beside the Sacristy door. It was all of a marvellous familiarity. While he served the water and the wine, he began to look ahead a little, to be safe.

He saw the Chalice lifted. The words "*Veni, Sanctificator*" came to his mind before the priest spoke them. He brought the other water, the bowl and the finger-bowl.

"*Lavabo inter innocentes manus meas.*"

When the priest turned from the altar to face the church, saying "*Orate, fratres*" and then turning back, it was the voice of the old woman in the front pew that took up the response just ahead of Daniel. (Familiar, too; as if he had been slow on this particular response before.)

"*Suscipiat, Dominus, sacrificium tuum. . Ad laudem et gloriam. .*"

Kneeling, through the secret prayers and the Preface, he had time to look at the bell, placed ready on the step beside him, and to see that the bell was new, different. There used, surely, to be a little one that you lifted and rang. Now there was a big round bell with a stick to strike it. He gave it three strokes for the Sanctus and bowed down. His anxiety had become no more than the normal concentration, the need to watch the priest; concentration of a soldier following his leader.

The magic silence began. The priest stretched out his hands over the offerings.

"*Hanc igitur.*"

One stroke of the bell.

Then the silence deeper than silence.

"*Qui pridie quam pateretur. .*" *Who, the day before He suffered.*

And the priest bending low. ("But who am I? What am I? A pair of eyes watching, two hands that know their duty, and no more.")

"*Hoc Est Enim Corpus Meum.*" *This is My Body.*

And now, the boy thought, there is no me. It is, I suppose, my hand that raises the hem of the chasuble, my other obedient hand that strikes the bell. But me. . ? I have forgotten what little of me I had to remember.

ii

He was aware, as the familiar ritual came to its climax, that the sense of nothingness had gone. He was no longer a cypher, a blank before God the Host, God in the Chalice. He was foundering in himself again. After he had

79

spoken the second Confiteor, he realized that the Communion was not for him. He didn't understand why. The refusal in his mind, the shunning gesture, surprised him. The priest had the ciborium in his hands; *"Ecce Agnus Dei"*, lifting up the small Host. *"Domine, non sum dignus,"* seemed all too true. The priest was turning his way, expecting him to remain on his knees and hold the silver dish beneath his chin. Dumbly he shook his head. He rose and carried the dish down to the altar-rail. He saw the old woman's face raised, her shut eyes and open mouth; the waiting tongue; he envied her. "Why couldn't I?" he wondered. He was still wondering when he followed the priest into the Sacristy.

This was the first time that they had looked each other in the face. Though the look that Daniel met was kindly, the impact was like the impact of Geraldine. A face that he recognized, a face grown older. It was an owlish face with a neat little beak of a nose. The name flashed at him; Father Francis. But the purple silk triangle below the collar meant (didn't it?) that one would call him Monsignor now. In any case, considering the effect of his greeting on the angry lady by the Friary wall, he decided to keep quiet. The priest was giving him a good, long look. Friendly? Cross? Difficult to judge. In silence, Daniel took the vestments from him.

"Well, thank you very much. Forgetting my manners," said the dry, academic voice that he had expected. There was now so much curiosity in the bright eyes that Daniel could do nothing but stand still and await the question.

"Didn't I see you up at the Friary,—yesterday afternoon?"

"Yes, Monsignor."

"You seemed to be getting what in my youth was called

8 0

a wigging. From Mrs. Courtney. . . Dear me, and so shall I," he said, looking at his watch;—"No time for a Thanksgiving either." He grabbed a soft black hat from a hook on the wall. "I want to speak to you, my son; but not here. I have to take cover. She'll be arriving any minute."

"Mrs. Courtney will?"

"For the Eight o'clock. Always ten minutes early" said the Monsignor, plucking open the outer door. Daniel dashed after him. "Excuse me, I don't want to see her either—and I'd be awfully grateful if you could tell me where to get breakfast. Cheap," he added to the scurrying swaying back. The Monsignor was obviously too lame to make such a speed.

"Get it for nothing, child. Only hurry. There's the car now. Don't look; I always think if one doesn't look, one isn't seen; something of an ostrich point of view," he added, whipping open the Presbytery door and almost colliding with a younger priest just inside it. This was the same priest whom Daniel had seen yesterday, talking to Antonia. He was large and fair; he smiled at them sleepily: "Good morning, Monsignor. Your breakfast's all ready for you."

"Enough to feed my starving server?"

"Surely."

"Well, that's good. People," said the Monsignor, hanging up his hat as the younger priest went out, "are highly unreasonable." It was an observation, Daniel thought, that had a ring of old Mr. Courtney; who would not, however, have added "Meaning myself." He was still panting a little; he led the way into the dining-room. "There is no reason, after all, why I shouldn't say my Mass at a later hour. As Geraldine arranged. Most thoughtful of her,—a car ordered too." He sighed. "But I *like* to say Mass early; I always have, I always will. So there it is."

"Will she be angry?"

"Pained,—more" said the Monsignor. "We understand each other. 'Very old friends. . And she is a person of great character. Did you get a chance to look at the church? Or had you seen it already?"

"No, Monsignor."

"Well, it's all of her giving. I doubt there's another church in all Ireland so well cared for. That modern stained glass is unique. And the Stations are good, too. The ivory crucifix above the Tabernacle; heaven knows what she paid for it. Almost as beautiful as the one in Farm Street. Dear me," he murmured, "The more one thinks of;—Chalice, vestments, all Geraldine. And she doesn't stop there. I mean— one might expect the lady of the Manor to arrange the flowers, but *not* to scrub the floor. . . Indeed, yes. . Done it for years. She used to do it when I was parish priest." He sat down at the table.

This room, with its crucifix on the wall and the statue of the Virgin by the window, was not new. Daniel felt entirely light-headed. Silently he brought another chair and seated himself. Silently he met the look in the bright eyes. When the housekeeper carried in the breakfast, the Monsignor bobbed up and said a rapid grace. After which he took the knitted cosy off the teapot.

"I like to be quiet while I'm eating; do you mind? Another unreasonable quirk, perhaps." Daniel, hollow with hunger, found it reasonable. He ate the scrambled eggs at a careful speed, keeping pace with the Monsignor. He was debating the last piece of toast when the dry, academic voice said "Take it. And now—well, I'm very much interested in you. As you probably realize. It isn't—I assure you—a habit of mine to stare so rudely. . Yes, rudely. But you remind me so much of a boy I used to know that I feel I'm dreaming. Your name wouldn't be Black, would it?"

He hesitated. "I'm pretty sure it is. But I can't be certain. 'Begins with a B. all right, because that's on my watch. And according to Mrs. Courtney, I'm Carus Black's son Daniel."

He couldn't fathom the expression on the priest's face as he repeated, "According to Mrs. Courtney. ."

"That's what she said. In the Friary. And if you'll forgive me, Monsignor, I have to go there now."

"One moment. You're being a little mysterious, surely. Who are you, according to *you*?"

He thought that he should explain. He came up against his own reluctance, and a picture of Antonia waiting for him. He said again "If you'll forgive me, Monsignor." He held out his hand. "Thank you very much for my breakfast; it was a life-saver."

The dry, cool hand held his in a vigorous clasp. "Thank you" said the priest imperturbably, "For serving my Mass." As Daniel reached the door, he added, "And—possibly—for a great deal more than that; since we're talking of life-savers." Bewildered, Daniel turned back, but the profile, content and dreaming, seemed to have no further need of him.

iii

"That's quite enough. You'll be ready, please, by eleven o'clock."

"I can't be," said Antonia. She stood her ground. Geraldine was seated rigidly before the looking-glass. The curtains of this great, sad bedroom were, as usual, half-drawn. In the glass Antonia could see only a shadowy, frozen face reflected. The voice was thin:—

"The drive takes an hour and a half. Reverend Mother is expecting the Monsignor and ourselves in time for lunch. . I told you—"

—"You did. It isn't that."

Silence. The still figure sat staring at its reflection.

"Please. I've been awake half the night. And I'm sure I got the right clue at Mass."

There was another silence before Geraldine said, "The Mass—may I remind you—isn't a crossword-puzzle. Are you trying to tell me you refuse to make this Retreat?"

"I don't refuse. It isn't 'won't'. It's 'can't'. I mean that, Geraldine."

Not a word. (It was infuriating; it was the strongest card she ever played.)

"I'm terribly sorry. I do understand how it'll hurt you." And, dear Lord, she thought, why do I have to hurt Geraldine? At a moment like this, all the kindnesses, all the care that she had known since she was a baby, stood up to shadow her with guilt. So many things. .

"Run along and pack, Antonia. You know how slow you are."

"Struth—"

"That expression, as I've already told you, is an abbreviation of 'God's truth' and therefore a blasphemy."

"Meaning He'll be cross."

"What else do you expect?"

Antonia clutched the door-handle. "*There!* . . that's the whole thing. . the whole thing!" She fought for words. "It isn't the way it ought to be; any of it. You make it all wrong for me, don't you see? There's a way I like it and a way *you* like it. You turn it into a martyrdom and a misery. You don't want 'the torrent of pleasure, the richness of the House of God.' You want rules and regulations and fun-spoiling and—and—future torments. And an angry God forever looking down. Like that one-eyed yellow idol to the north of somewhere-or-other in the Reciter's Treasury in the carriage-house."

There was the longest silence yet. Then Geraldine said, using her soft, pussy-cat voice, "If I were you, I should put on the grey tie-silk. You look so nice in it."

"I'm *in love!*" Antonia shouted and slammed the door. She went galloping down the back-stairs. "Burned my boats, that's what I've done, burned my boats. . And he may not have waited. He couldn't know we go to Daily Mass. It's after half-past nine. And why *did* I say all that to her? It's true. . but I needn't have said it. Oh worms and worms and worms." She clutched the piece of paper in her pocket, the grocer's bill, sanctified by his handwriting. "Please let him still be there" she said; she dived for the boiler-room. She picked up his clothes; "Done to a crisp," she muttered, feeling the warm, crackly surfaces. She dumped them in the carriage-house. Running fast down the drive and up to the bridge, she tried to make a plan of action. "I can ask him to stay here—wait for me. Even if Geraldine drags me to the convent by my hair, I can always run away."

As she crossed the bridge, she could see him waiting, the yellow sweater bright against the grey stones of the chapel wall. Now she was shy and, having waved abruptly, kept her head down, looking at the grass. She thought about her appearance. The paisley-patterned blouse and the linen skirt were fine, hanging in the wardrobe. She had been pleased when she put them on. But now she had a suspicion that they made her look bigger than ever.

He came to meet her. They stood face to face.

What a long way to have travelled, she thought, looking at him; and with someone who knew nothing of the journey. Despite his grin of greeting, he wasn't the companion who had walked through the night with her in her head. He was a separate, unattainable person. When he said "Hullo. Everything all right?" she found that in twelve hours she had managed to forget the exact note of his voice.

"All right? In *our* house?" She gave a shout of self-protecting laughter. He laughed too: "I mean, Mrs. Courtney didn't catch you?"

"Oh, she's caught *me* for keeps," said Antonia, "Not to worry. She doesn't know a thing about you in the carriage-house." ("And I don't, today, know a thing about you, Daniel Black. You look more contented, more settled; more grown-up.") She added rudely "You don't suffer from delusions, by any chance?"

When his face changed, becoming vulnerable, she was sorry. "I only mean I did some research last night. At supper. I tried in the most diplomatic, wormlike way to make her talk about you—tell why she'd thrown you out. She wouldn't utter. I led around to it by every sort of arpeggio; said I'd seen some odd-looking types hanging around. . heard noises in the trees. . asked how soon we were going to ration the estate-passes? Not a word. She just let it all lie. 'Behaved as though it had never happened at all.'"

"It happened," he said.

"Ah, well. . She's the cagiest woman in five continents, —or are there six? I'm never sure. And after that she settled down again to play chess with the Monsignor."

86

"He's nice," said Daniel Black, "I served his Mass. And we had breakfast at the Presbytery. And he wanted to know—" He cut off the sentence. "Come and look," he said, grabbing her hand. She stayed still.

"What did he want to know? Why do you stop like that?"

"Oh, Antonia. ." he said, and then "Please trust me."

"Well, of course I do. Did you tell him you were in trouble?"

"No."

"He could help, surely."

"I shouldn't think so." This was said on a note of gay indifference that made her feel shut out.

"You're as cagey as Geraldine. Anyway I wish I'd known he was saying one at seven. I'd have got up earlier. She wasn't half in a tiz when she found out; she was trying to cosset him. And then I had to go and lose my temper and bawl at her," she mourned.

"You did, did you? Why?"

But she refused to think about it, saying briskly "I do think it's disgusting that women aren't allowed to serve. We got that miserable Paddy Hickey. I can do it much better than he can; the answers, I mean. 'Silly clot missed out on the *Suscipiat.*"

"So did I," said Daniel. . "Come along," he added, tugging impatiently. Though she liked his holding her hand, she was too much aware of it; she thought that somebody ought to let go soon.

"What are you up to, my little mystery-man?" It sounded ruder than she meant, but she was in fact taller than he.

"We're going to look for the treasure."

"Come again?" said Antonia, in imitation of Luke's American.

"I dreamed about it, so it's got to be there. You were in the dream."

"I was?" She couldn't believe it. Now he didn't seem to notice her stunned silence. He was swinging her hand, looking about him. "'Wonderful dream," he said, "Till it stopped. But it's back again. How perfect this place is. Don't you love living here?"

"Truthfully, no. It's too sad."

"Sad? It's like the Garden of Eden." He pointed upward. "See that heron? He'll come down on the water. Watch. They have the best flight of all, I think, herons."

"*Were* there them in the Garden?"

"Oh I'd imagine so," said Daniel Black, still watching the bird. "There; down he goes. . . Why don't you like Drumnair?"

"Nothing against Drumnair. It's pretty enough. The Courtneys have always cared for it, made it pretty. But I think the ancestors must have had more fun—or more money. Drumnair's all right," she said darkly—"If it wasn't for the Manor."

"I like the Manor."

"Try living in it," said Antonia. Daniel appeared to be deflected from his treasure. He stood obstinately, waiting for her to explain.

"Bloody old mausoleum. We rattle around; and it's entailed so nobody can sell. 'Must admit, Geraldine's tried everything. Nuns, orphans, retired priests—she had an idea about lepers, but it didn't happen; I think there weren't enough. Then it was distressed gentlewomen, provided they filled the religious requirements. It always goes wrong. Luke used to let his half to Americans at one time. Now he's home for good, he wants to convert it all into a very grand guest-house for some more Americans. He spent days working out what the structural alterations would cost. He stopped when it came to three thousand pounds before he even got to the bathrooms." She sighed. "Oh, Daniel, England's much nicer. At least Wiltshire is. English country is. Don't you think?"

He didn't answer; he frowned; his eyes were cloudy, puzzled, seeking. Then he shook himself like a dog. He said "The treasure's waiting."

Guiltily, pursued by time and Geraldine, she let him lead her. Something of his magic now seemed to follow their footsteps in the grass, to fill the Friary. When they stood in the quiet, sunlit ruin of the refectory with their own shadows at their feet, she thought that the place had never touched her heart so piercingly before.

Daniel dropped her hand, pointing up to the embrasure. "See where it's broken? I kicked those stones off yesterday. And there's where you were sitting—in my dream."

"Can't imagine anything better calculated to bring it crashing to the ground—" she said gruffly.

"The treasure's in the wall. At least I think it must be. There's a shaft going down through the middle."

"A shaft? Come, come. This ain't a mine."

"I found it after the stones fell off. I was just going to explore when Geraldine started yelling at me."

Antonia said warily, "What's the next move?"

"I'm going up."

"I shouldn't if I were you."

"It's solid beyond the break. All the way to the corner. I tested it. Excelsior," said Daniel, and ran up the steps, quick as a cat. She watched him swarm across the wall, with a foothold here and a hand-hold there, until he had hauled himself up into the safe corner. The jackdaws flew out over his head. On hands and knees he crawled as far as the new break; once there, he lay flat, plunging his right arm down into the boasted shaft.

"Wow," he said "It's here all right."

"Truly?"

"Truly." He was busy dipping for it. After a while, he rolled over, changed arms and began again. Then he tried to get both arms down the shaft. Finally he sat up and wiped his hot face on his sleeve.

"Treasure-seeker out of luck," he called down to her.

"What goes?"

"Well, it's a box; a heavy metal box; but someone's boxed in the box. I can shift it, but I can't get it out. Walled in all round, that's what."

"Are you pulling my leg?" she asked severely.

"Why should I be? Come and see. It's only about two feet down."

Antonia hesitated. Not, she said to herself, from any fear but the fear of looking a fool. "It's absolutely safe," Daniel's voice urged her. "Room for us both—all we have to do is keep off the broken bit. I'll get over while you take a peek." He wriggled back into the corner and sat holding the ivy as though it were the two ropes of a swing. "All yours—" he called.

No retreat. "Keep your thumb on it, St. Anthony," muttered Antonia. The steps were easy enough. She reached the top step. Here, just on a level with her forehead, there was the break in the parapet. She steadied herself with an arm across it.

"And what plans have you for me now, Mr. Black?"

Daniel giggled. "All I ask is *not* haul yourself up that

way. Swarm round. Your next foothold is the jutting-out piece. Right foot, see? Left foot *there*. Hands on the parapet. When you get to there, it's easy." He let go of the ivy with his right hand, leaning out and down:—"You just grab hold. I'll give you a bit of a lift and Bob's your uncle."

Antonia looked at the two footholds; she looked at the kind hand, at the beloved face, sweaty and laughing in the sunshine. She said darkly, "This treasure had better be good."

"Look, darling, you don't *have* to do it."

It was the word "Darling" that precipitated all. Ignoring his instructions, she grabbed on to the broken sill and heaved herself up. It held; she was there, with scraped palms and scuffed knees; she stood swaying in triumph, bestriding the hole. Only for a second. Then there was the shaming creak and crumble beneath her full weight and she jumped wildly outwards. It was all mixed up; a torrential crash behind her, a bumping fury of stones at her heels, the yell of frightened jackdaws flying off; a dust-cloud dimming the sun. A bed of stinging-nettles, for good measure, as she landed. She lurched out of the nettles, toppled over and lay on her back, laughing helplessly.

There was a good deal of dust to be swallowed, but she went on laughing. The arching shadow that leaped down beside her through the dust, turned into Daniel.

"Are you hurt, Antonia? Are you hurt at all?" The voice was frantic. She blinked up into the face of distraught kindliness.

"You-aren't-laughing," she panted.

"I can't think why you are."

"Fat girl breaks Friary" she explained, "It's a newspaper headline."

"Are you *hurt?*"

"Too well cushioned, chum. And I jumped clear. Must have looked worse than it was."

"I thought you were buried and killed."

"Wrong order," snapped Antonia. She sat up. "Goodness," she said, looking at the cascade of rubble. "Haven't half made a mess of that, have I? National monument, too."

"Your knees are bleeding."

"Scraped 'em on the way up. Nobody's allowed to look at my knees," she added, pulling down her skirt. As she scrambled up, he kept his arm about her waist, seeming so subdued that she pulled free and gave him a great slap on the back. "Where's your treasure *now*, would you say?"

"I'd say you'd done the trick. It must be somewhere in that heap."

"Fat Girl Breaks Friary Reveals Hidden Treasure. Come on."

Daniel didn't come on. He barred her way to the outer wall. He said "Why do you talk so much about being fat?"

"Wouldn't you—if you looked like me?"

He said soberly, "You're very beautiful."

It was too much. She had no wits for a caustic answer. He didn't seem to expect an answer. He went on staring, with the old assured tilt of his head, the look of sunny composure that had spelled doom when she first set eyes on him. He might have been judging something inanimate, a picture in a gallery, perhaps.

"I think it's the most beautiful face I've ever seen" he told her and turned away towards the broken wall.

Above their heads the birds were still circling and crying; the smoky dust had settled in the grass.

"All I have to do now is clear this—bit by bit—till I find

it," he announced in quite a different voice, "Shouldn't take too long." He peeled off Godfrey's sweater and rolled up the sleeves of Godfrey's shirt: "What I'd like you to do, please, is keep watch They may have heard that crash from the house. And if Mrs. Courtney shows up, I'm sunk."

"So am I," thought Antonia. It no longer seemed of the slightest importance. She said "Okay. I'll patrol and give you a whistle if anyone comes. Then you duck into the refectory and I'll draw them off with some beguiling tale."

For a moment she watched him toiling like a navvy, before she loped away. She took up a strategic position under the chapel arch. Here she sat down on the turf, keeping a watch on the bridge and the dividing paths. Only her eyes saw them; two camera-lenses doing their work, while she herself was off and away, somewhere among the rainbow-lightnings in her head, somewhere close to the sky. "Beautiful. He said I was beautiful. 'Are you hurt? Are you hurt at all?'" She went on and on saying these things; she began to hurt inside, under her ribs. It was like pleurisy again, only much nicer.

A shout of "Got it!" returned her to earth. Taking a last careful look for spies, she walked round the walls to the rubble-heap. He was crouched down, tearing up handfuls of grass to scrub at his prize. "All dust and cobwebs," he said —"Must have been there for years."

Antonia squatted beside him; she watched his square, busy hands.

"Fun" said Daniel.

Though she echoed "Fun," this was somehow disappointing. She did not know what she had expected; perhaps an ancient brassbound chest; here, emerging under Daniel's ministrations, was a large metal box, rusted and mouldy, but unmistakably modern. He seemed very pleased with it, scrubbing away. Now he began to wrestle with it. "Quite heavy. . Either the lid's jammed with the rust, or it's locked . that *looks* like a lock, doesn't it?" He set it down. "How the devil can we get it open?"

"And how the devil," she said "did you know it was there?"

"Well, but—the dream." He broke off; he began to frown; then the glowing grin came back. "When you come to think of it," he said, "It's no odder than anything *else* that's happening to me."

She had just wailed "*Why* can't I know what's happening to you?" when the fatal sound came; the sound of a car's engine racing; then the scream of brakes. It wasn't Geraldine's habit to drive so fast. But there the car stood, at the foot of the glacis, and there she was, climbing out in a hurry. She was followed by Luke.

CHAPTER TWO

The morning had begun badly for Luke Courtney.

Spying upon his mood with his coffee, the old man decided that both were, if possible, worse than usual. He sat up in his enormous bed, wearing his tattered silk pyjamas and a kind of woollen stole. He sighed and snuffled. The English newspapers, a day old, were spread out around the breakfast-tray. He went on ordering them, reading them, loathing them, from year to year. He snuffled at the picture of a young man, chairman of a T.V. programme, whose yearly salary had been raised to twenty thousand pounds. There was a brief editorial referring to the significance of private enterprise in the ability to earn "this by no means negligible sum."

"*By no means negligible!*" screamed Luke. It did not sound like that, because his teeth were in a glass in the bathroom. He mumbled other hated phrases: "Not without interest"; "No small influence"; "No mean performer." He bundled up the newspaper and dropped it over the side of the bed, on to Dana the greyhound. He drank some more of the beastly coffee and thought about yesterday. Yesterday had gone on too long. After midnight, by the time he had succeeded in ridding himself of those American publishers and their wives.

Like everything else that happened to him, they had been tiring, disappointing and quite unnecessary. He hadn't written his memoirs; nor ever would. It was an illusion brought about by a literary friend from Donegal. This friend had assured him that he would be paid a huge cheque in advance and given a ghost-writer,—with a typewriter. That was how all current figures got their memoirs written. Nobody had to be able to write to get his name on a book these days.

But the publishers, after drinking Luke's drinks, eating his food, and tiring him to death, had never as much as mentioned a ghost-writer. On the contrary. They had made him talk too much. They had compared his life (so it seemed to him now) with those of all the great Irishmen. They had gone off declaring that this had been "a wonderful meeting of minds." (For a meeting of minds, said Luke meanly to Luke, there would—surely—have to be more than one.) They were, they said, convinced that on the receipt of a draft synopsis and six opening chapters (did it take *six* chapters to open a book?) they could 'finalize' (God have mercy) the proposition.

Well, well. Or rather, ill, ill. (He felt like echoing Antonia's cry of 'Worms and worms and worms.') The only diversion among their last remorseless researches had been the family-albums. Luke, in turning up the 1929 album, had found some snapshots of Pippin Black with Geraldine. One showed them planting the little tree,—a prunus as he recalled,—on the eve of the wedding that never took place. Because of his lunchtime encounter with the boy who looked so much like Pippin, he had lingered over this album. And a third glass of port had persuaded him to tell the wedding story. A most ungentlemanly thing to do. His guests had swallowed it, with the port, in raptures. They had said it would make a movie and it must go into the memoirs.

No need to have told it at all. But this was Geraldine's effect. Sooner or later, in any company, he would begin to talk about her with a lack of charity that stunned him. Why? Sometimes he thought it was because she was so thin. (He had a horror of thin women. . Isabelle, his wife, had been abundant all over, silky curves like an expensive eiderdown. And there had been others, not wives, who were like that.) Sometimes he blamed it on Geraldine's fanaticism; ten minutes at the Faith, and she could send him hustling into heresy. Sometimes it was her martyred, obsessional housework that drove him mad. (He had never, after all, *asked* her to empty his chamber-pot) Sometimes he went back over the years to her treatment of his son Tom. Poor Tom. (Poor Tom's a-cold.)

More usual, he thought, to blame a wife for driving her husband to drink than away from it. But he had seen the young Geraldine turn Tom into a teetotaller. Poor Tom the teetotaller, unable to play the new role, had blown his brains out. (Yes, he had. No question of an accident, though she had achieved this cheating of the Church most bravely.)

Now he could hear his own voice crooning on to the Americans. "A courageous crocodile. That's Geraldine. Pippin Black was the only one who got out before the jaws snapped. Oh, and Godfrey, I suppose. She appears, of course, to find the adopted child inedible. So poor Antonia must be swallowed by a convent instead. . yes, the girl you saw at teatime. A *nun*. . . I ask you? I shall step in, of course. Where Reverend Mothers fear to tread. . Not that it should be necessary. Nor is it new. Antonia couldn't have been more than five when Geraldine began training her to be a saint. 'Made the wretched infant go about in a blue butter-muslin shift, with bare feet. What happened? Well, she trod on a nail, among other things. I refer you to the Monsignor for the end of *that* story."

They had laughed. They had said that Geraldine sounded like a character in a movie. And, at last, they had taken off, in their huge, cream-coloured absurdity of a car, tail-finned so that its backside looked like a juke-box, all red glass and winking whorls of light. And he had gone to bed with a headache. He had had horrible dreams about the Book of Drumnair turning into the Glamis monster. With tail-fins. He had found it at last under a willow-tree beside the river, and as he had stooped to the prize it was only this finny monster after all. A dream-crowd, dressed in mediaeval clothes, had laughed uproariously while he tried to catch it. Then it had slithered into the water and swum away, winking its fins. A nightmare.

Oh, the dear Book, the shining thing that would, one day, be found in all its glory, so that the searchlights of the world would come swinging this way and the name of Drumnair would rank with Kells. . As a child he had believed; and he still believed. The child had seen a promise of magic, here on the demesne, hidden and safe and waiting for him; peat or turf holding it fast. The vision endured, though his years and his studies had given it more detail. He could see it perfectly. Encased, perhaps, in a satchel like the Armagh satchel; though, strictly speaking, such a satchel would have been made to hold the shrine and not the book bereft of its shrine. He saw every page alight and agleam, the illuminated marvels on the vellum that would (they said) last through eternity; richer in colour than the Kells Gospels, more varied in device· *"Aflame, more fine than glass."*

His Book. Everyone else had forgotten about it. He alone remained faithful. From time to time, across the years, he had found another bibliophile who liked the legend Not often. A few ignorant but imaginative persons, visiting the

Manor, had caught his fire. (Pippin Black was one of these. Pippin, God bless him, had put in much work on that hopeful peat-cutting project, beyond the river. .) Not any more. Nowadays he just went on spinning the magic tale in his head and telling the great lies for fun. But there would come a day. .

He picked up another newspaper. It was dull. No airline disaster, no unparalleled traffic-chaos, no floods washing out holiday camps. (Perhaps a little early for that one. .) However, part of a wall had fallen on a woman-shopper in Oxford Street. He read on, past a caption advising him to "pinpoint your figure with these pencil-slim lines." He turned to the book-reviews. He read "Miss Grout's prose has a wry, arresting way with it while her oddly alfresco judgment is not without compassion" and then he upset his coffee in his bed.

Howling for help, clanging on his large brass handbell, he was not appeased when old Susanna came at once. She said that Mrs. Courtney wanted to speak to him urgently.

"I *will* not speak! Not till I'm dressed, she knows that. Pull off all the bedclothes quickly. Take them away. Bring some more. Get that bestial breakfast-tray out of here. Take the dog. Take a message. Well then, say I'll be down in a little while. Oh dear, oh dear, oh dear, how horrible everything is."

Hurrying with his bath, he considered selling the Americans the Manor instead of his memoirs. Given the right kind of lawyer, that tiresome little matter of the entail should be surmountable. "Entrails to entails, dust to dust," he said aloud, experimentally, as he dried himself. Under the entail, his absentee grandson Godfrey must inherit.

"If Godfrey would only come back and look after things,"

he thought, ". . come and help me. Brighten the place up too, wouldn't he? That's what it needs No young ones here any more; the young ones always move out. Godfrey's kept his liveliness, I'm sure. And I've no objection to a drunkard, provided he pays for his drink What did they say I was, last night? 'Land poor.' *What* an expression."

With his usual tremulous fervour, Luke finished dressing. He fluffed up his two wings of white hair, fluffed them down again and decided that he was still remarkably handsome. No wonder he had been greatly loved. But why did nobody love him now? "I should be adored, and endowed, and protected at all times from tedium. I should have a valet. I should have a proper bed-table for the breakfast-tray, with little legs on it. You'd think somebody would give me one. . Now *those* were presents," he muttered, peering at his cufflinks "What would be nice," he said, selecting a cane from the blue-and-white china umbrella-stand beside the door, "would be to hear that somebody I had quite forgotten, somebody for whom I once performed an unique service, had left me a very large legacy."

It was at this point that Geraldine crashed his door open. She said "The Friary's falling down."

"My dear child, it was bound to. Why not? I could only wish the Manor would follow its example. What am I expected to do? Rebuild it—stone by stone?"

She stood, staring at him with her fixed, Medusa stare. (Head all tied up in one of those rainbow turbans, as usual. You'd think her jaw would drop if she left them off. . Ridiculous make-up. . One could still see the bones of her beauty showing through. La Belle Dame Sans Merci, with eyes like aquamarines. . Pippin said that.)

"The boy's there again, Luke. I saw him prowling; I know I did."

"What boy?"

"Doesn't matter. He is an enemy," said Geraldine.

Was she losing her reason? One had seen it coming, hadn't one? Well, this at least might serve as a crisis, though he wished that she wouldn't hurry him so. Nor,—for the Friary —did he feel as greatly detached as he sounded. Feathering shakily down the stairs, he said "If this is some local hooligan, why not call Francis in? Power of the Church. Much more effective than mine."

"I haven't told Francis. He must rest before we go. He was up much too early."

"I" said Luke "was up much too late."

As she whirled him down the drive, he rocked and swayed in his seat. He should, he thought, have remembered to bring Dana; a barking dog was a good weapon. Geraldine wouldn't utter. He kept murmuring, "Ridiculous. How can I handle a bunch of hooligans? Really, you have no consideration whatever." As they reached the bridge he said "What *are* you talking about? There's the Friary—quite intact."

"It's the refectory wall."

"Is *that* all? My dear child, the same thing happens in Oxford Street all the time. Crushed women are a quotidian occurrence."

She slammed on the brakes. Now he saw the heap of rubble. Of all the absurd fusses. . And there was Antonia, sitting on the grass with a boy. He looked, this boy, like the reincarnation of Pippin Black, from yesterday. He was, undoubtedly, the same boy. "My long sight, at least, is still trustworthy," said Luke. Geraldine went flying across the turf and he followed, groaning a little for the purpose of the act. "I am not," he thought, "in that loathsome newspaper language, wholly uninterested."

The Monsignor's room overlooked the river. It was the best spare room, with the four-poster and the writing-desk. He knew it well. He paced from the desk to the window, saying his Office. His eyes took in familiar things; the old gilt and crystal flower-vase, a vase that he remembered always standing just there on the corner of the desk; it was filled now with yellow lupins. The painted German panel on the wall, part of a reredos. The green velvet curtains, faded in streaks, one curtain sagging loose from its rings.

Francis finished his Office. He packed the last of his possessions neatly into his suitcase and shut the lid. While he was doing this, he heard a muffled explosion, not far off; somewhere in the demesne. Perhaps a tree falling. Presently there was the sound of a car roaring down to the bridge. These sounds did not really penetrate. Nothing could penetrate his pouring, private happiness, stronger than the sunlight, making him feel as though this sun was shining through his bones.

It was true, the impossible thing. Carus, his chosen, had not failed him after all.

God's gifts came like this He saw his own long-unanswered prayers as an endless ladder that he had raised and climbed, putting each rung ahead of him wearily, hopelessly. And now, after thirty years,—without warning,—he was up on the last step, shouting his thanks into the face of the Lord.

"How did it happen? Has Carus himself come back to the Church? Or has he given his son the faith he lost? It *must* be his son." He saw again the boy's face; a curious calm, a secret happiness. What was he hiding, this one? When he had lingered over admitting his own name, there was about him a look of seeking serenity; the look of a blind man moving to his place in a familiar room.

O *Deo gratias*.

The last thing that Francis wanted was to disturb the mood of shining peace, to let it be interrupted, invaded by talk; least of all by talk with Geraldine. Yet what else to do? It didn't surprise him that she had known since yesterday, recognized Daniel at once, challenged him beside the Friary wall, and then kept silent. Her silences were as much a part of Geraldine as her nose.

He cocked his owl's head on one side, studying his own dilemma.

"Naturally she knew him at once. It is likely that she knows a great deal more. I can, for example, be tolerably certain she knows the name of whatever industrial kingdom it is that Carus reigns over nowadays. If she does, will she tell me?" He would so dearly like to write to Carus; not, he thought, to have his hope confirmed; this happiness had no room for doubt in it; but to ask for the story, to be told why the boy was here.

Impossible to think, as he would have loved to think, that Carus had sent Daniel to him as a messenger. ("*The man Gabriel, flying swiftly.*") "He has no notion that I'm in Drumnair. Unless, perhaps, he thinks I've never left it. No, no. . fanciful, sentimental, ridiculous. He has probably forgotten my existence." Standing at the window, he looked down at the river, where the yellow iris grew; all summer was on the river and the trees. In his mind, this place had put off its mourning.

"I should like it always to be now; to stand forever at this window, with the prayer on my lips and in my heart," thought Francis. And at once the little glimpse of eternity went. Time-the-present was here instead, with its question-marks stretching before and behind.

"Suppose that he has sent the boy, as a messenger, not to me but to Geraldine? And she never gave him a chance to deliver the message?" This wouldn't explain Daniel's hesitation about revealing himself, but, whatever the cause of the hesitation, she had, most typically, jumped on it and so deprived herself of hearing the one thing that would give her pleasure. (Here he recalled an observation of Luke's: "Geraldine, of course, will forgive child-murder, sodomy and blackmail provided they're committed by Papishes.")

Francis looked at his watch. Almost time to be going. He said his prayer of thanks just once more, standing at the window, and went out.

As usual, old Susanna had left the carpet-sweeper planted squarely outside his door. There was a pail, too. He was just negotiating these when he heard the front-door slam and a volley of voices sounding through the hall. Angry voices, he noted, as he came along the passage, carrying his suitcase. That was Antonia, yelling "Damned if I will!" Somebody must have stepped on one of the dogs at the same moment. Now a loud cackle of laughter—Luke. Then the furies again. So much for the mood of shining peace, Francis said to himself. He came to a diplomatic halt on the landing just beneath the stained-glass window. He set down his suitcase. He leaned on the rail.

"Straight upstairs, Antonia; change and finish packing. We leave in twenty minutes."

"Worms! Worms! Worms!"

"Take it easy, darling."

"Quiet, please. This is none of your business; I've said that once already, have I not?"

"At least three times, Geraldine, in my hearing; not that anyone seems interested in what I—"

Here Antonia interrupted Luke; she bellowed "Get it clear! I'm *not going!*"

She stood close to Geraldine,—enormous, flashing, dominant. She also looked as though she had been rolling in a dust-heap. Behind her, Luke elegant in his grey alpaca suit, leaned on his cane; his morning tremors were jerking his white head up and down. Daniel stood placidly, a yellow sweater tied about his neck by its sleeves, a box under one bare, black arm. He was even dirtier than Antonia. The quiet, authoritative voice came surprisingly from this chimney-sweep.

"Listen to me, Antonia, please. I said *listen,* darling. Don't fight this. Off you go. I mean it. And don't worry. I'll be waiting when you come back."

A hush came on them. Francis saw Geraldine turn to the boy, with a sudden stiffening of dignity; it was a slow, careful movement as though she were balancing a weight on her head.

"As for you—" she began; then broke off. She was looking him up and down:—"Is that *your* sweater, may I ask?" Without waiting for an answer, she twitched it off his neck. As Antonia and Daniel both began to speak at once, she clenched her fist as though she would strike the boy in the face.

"*All* Godfrey's clothes. Every one of them. Is that it? All right. I don't want to hear when or why or who—*will* you, both of you, be quiet! *At* once!"

"Well, no, if you'll excuse me," said Daniel, "I want to apologise."

"It wasn't him—"

"*He*, dear child" corrected Luke.

"Up you go, Antonia. Run along, darling, I'll take care of this. Please."

"Mr. Daniel Black" said Geraldine "kindly understand that you do not give orders in my house."

"I am only asking her to do exactly what you want her to do, Mrs. Courtney."

"I think," said Francis, "that I should like to know what's happening."

"She'll tell you!" Antonia shouted and was silent As Francis came down he saw the two ragamuffin figures rush into an embrace; then Antonia, in tears, crashed blindly past him, and up the staircase. Oddly, he found his entire impatience directed at Geraldine; who stood now with the yellow sweater over one arm, her hand on her hip, looking at him with cool malevolence.

"What—" he asked her, "is all the fuss about?"

"I wouldn't call it a *fuss*, Francis."

"Merely a mort of ill-feeling," said Luke, giving him a large, vulgar wink.

"I do see about the clothes," said Daniel, "and I'm awfully sorry."

"Suppose we go into the drawing-room?" said Francis. He led the way. The sunshine, through the wide windows, was dazzling. It taunted the room; it pointed up the damp-stains on ceiling and wall; the dust on the chandelier. It made much of cracked paint, of shiny, departing patterns on velvet and brocade, of worn places in the tapestry.

Looking at Geraldine, Francis was unpleasantly struck by the same ravages. Below the bright turban, above the swathes that hid her neck, he saw a futile mask of make-up, with imprisoned eyes. She looked an angry old woman. She halted just inside the door and leaned her back against it. Luke went on, steering for the blue chair with the fringed footstool, that was placed beneath the portrait of one of his ancestors. The chair that Carus liked, Francis remembered inconsequently. Luke sat down, hands on the top of his cane; his old eyes blinked at the sun, but he seemed mightily amused, nodding and smiling.

Francis chose himself a hard, backless Empire stool in front of the window. Daniel, moving up beside him, still giving off an aura of serenity, stooped to set his box on the floor. Francis didn't look at the box; he heard it bump on the parquet as he watched Geraldine. She inclined her head towards him, graciously inviting him to speak. When he didn't, she said "Please don't think we're going to make you late, Monsignor. We shall leave as soon as Antonia's ready."

"Thank you. Time, perhaps, for a few explanations?"

"Precisely," said Geraldine.

"What *she* wants to know," said Luke, "is where this—ah —embryo Pippin has sprung from, and why he should think himself entitled to make what I believe—in the current re-volting idiom—is known as a pass at Antonia. I," he added peevishly, "just want a screwdriver, or some such imple-ment. Bring the box over here, Pippin. ."

"Stay where you are, please," snapped Geraldine. She was transfixing Daniel with her stoniest glare. Daniel, Francis saw, met it with a little crooked smile. Luke said "Oh, *really*, Geraldine. . You'll observe, Francis, that the lad, in reducing the Friary to ruins, has recovered a large deed-box which may contain valuables."

Francis looked down at the box; he looked again, an old memory suddenly stirring, coming alive, cutting across the moment of now and the voice of Geraldine.

"Both the Monsignor and I are waiting for your explanation. Speak up."

Daniel strolled towards her. "There's only one important thing, Mrs. Courtney. I love Antonia and she loves me. I'm going to ask her to marry me. I'm absolutely serious, and I don't care how long I wait. Do you understand?"

She neither spoke nor moved. Luke had cupped his hand quickly around his ear. Leaning forward, he exuded the attentive delight of a man watching a good play.

Daniel repeated, "Do you understand?" At the enduring silence he merely shrugged his shoulders and went on. "I want you to be clear about it because it really is the only important thing. As for my coming into the demesne, that was a matter of an estate-pass, same as anybody else. I know I've caused trouble. But the Friary wall was an accident and I feel a bit better about it since Mr. Courtney's said it was bound to happen sometime. I'll help with the work to get it up again; I'm extremely strong. That's the next thing. The clothes are something else again. I oughtn't to have taken them—or made them dirty, scrambling about on that wall. And I'm sorry I did. I'll have them cleaned right away."

He paused, watching her face. He now began to look as comfortable, as compact as his father (and Francis thought, every bit as obstinate.) "Could we go back to Antonia for a minute? I'm all for her going into Retreat; she mustn't break her word; and it will do her good. But the idea of turning her into a nun,—can't you see it's spoiling God for her? And that, if you'll pardon my saying so, is just plain idiocy."

"Daniel." It gave Francis the purest pleasure to speak the name.

"Monsignor?"

He liked the disciplined movement, the ready eyes. He said, "I take it that you don't expect a ruling on those two questions in these ten minutes?"

"Trust a priest to spoil the fun," said Luke. "'first time I've enjoyed myself since 1939."

"I don't, of course. But it had to be said," Daniel explained, as Geraldine stepped away from the door, opened it and went out, shutting it behind her without a sound.

Francis followed. He caught up with her halfway across the hall. She was, he admitted, in perfect control. She faced him with a smile, with light, laughing eyes and a voice of silken sweetness.

"There's no problem here, none at all," said Geraldine. She bent over the bowl of pinks and nipped off a dead bud: —"Just a matter of putting a telephone-call through to his father."

"So you know where to find Carus. ."

"Nothing odd about that." She was still smiling. "He's the Chairman of B.C.M. One sees these things in the papers." She moved tranquilly away across the hall, to the little

1 0 9

table in its alcove under the stairs. "Lucky—" she said, "Having the new London directory." He saw her lift the section from its place beside the telephone. Leafing through it, she gave him a glance that was almost roguish. "What's on your mind, Francis?"

"And then. ?" he asked in return.

"And then? Oh, I see. Well, then I simply tell him to come and remove Daniel."

"You know he *is* Daniel?"

"Don't you?" she said sweetly, picking up the telephone.

"I think he is, yes. But would you mind waiting one minute? There's something I want you to know."

"Hullo. . Now, I want you to be very quick about this call, please. A personal call. ." She added "Sorry, Francis. But you can tell me in the car. Our time's running out. ."

So it was, indeed. Francis thought of the Retreat; of his introductory sermon to be preached at four o'clock. He hadn't looked at his notes. Castleisland, the Convent, Mother Paula,—the whole purpose of his journey, seemed extraordinarily remote. So, at this instant, did his true life; his room in the Priory, his tranquil days. (All his own fault. He should never have trusted Drumnair; its power had come sweeping in; and he must leave the house, beset and beleaguered, knowing that he would not see it again for years; perhaps never see it again.)

At the telephone, Geraldine was saying "Thank you. Thank you *so* much. I'll hold on."

Francis went back into the drawing-room. Daniel had carried the box over to Luke's footstool; he was kneeling on the floor, stabbing around the edge of the lid with a penknife. When he saw Francis he jumped to his feet.

Luke said "Ah, Francis. I hope you won't leave before we find the doubloons. Take a seat, now. There may be millions inside. It seems to me I've heard such a tale. Somebody who was after hiding up his money at the time of the Troubles." This rush of brogue in the mouth of one who claimed to despise his ancestry, and who had, for years, made a point of cultivating what he called "classical speech" diverted the Monsignor. Then he took a fresh look at the box. He was sure that he had never seen it, yet it had some strong significance. What . . ? Another trick of Drumnair . . ?

He remembered.

"Looks as if we'll have to take a hammer and a chisel to it," Daniel was saying.

"I shouldn't." Francis' voice sounded as abrupt, as harsh to himself as it must sound to them. Luke blinked at him.

"Shouldn't take a hammer and chisel? What do you suggest? A crowbar?"

"D'you mean not open it at all?" said Daniel quickly.

"That is what I meant."

"Oh really" Luke said, "Are you crediting it with sacred origins? A holy deed-box? Church property? I cannot believe your return to the—ah—hills of home can have so rapid an effect."

"You would be surprised," said Francis wistfully, "how rapid the effect is."

Luke stamped his foot. "You might," he said "be that young booby Father Barrett, telling me to say my Act of Contrition aloud, you might indeed."

"I haven't asked you to say anything, Luke. I'm only suggesting there might be something quite—quite unexciting inside the box."

"Support your statement."

"I can't." ("And those words are truer than you guess.")

"Well, well—a minor miracle" said Geraldine at the door; she beamed, waiting to be asked what the miracle was; then added, "Through to London in five minutes." At the word "London," Francis saw Daniel wince and screw up his eyes tightly as if he were trying to remember what the word meant. He didn't seem to hear Geraldine's voice.

"It's you I'm talking to," she said sunnily.

Some of his glow seemed to have left him. He turned an anxious face to hers.

"I want you to promise to stay here until I come back. On your honour, please."

"Oh, that's easy; doesn't require a promise. I shall stay here anyway." But he still looked troubled. "Thank you" said Geraldine, gracious and smiling. To Francis she added, "I had to leave a message. It will be delivered today."

"Mrs. Courtney?"

"What is it?"

"May I go up and say goodbye to Antonia before she goes?"

"You shall say goodbye to her as soon as she comes down. I'm going up to fetch her now. Luke, dear, that's such a very *dirty* old box. Would it be too much to ask you—" She went out.

Some of the shadow stayed on Daniel's face as he turned to Francis. But his voice was calm. "It looks as if we shan't meet again, Monsignor. Will you give me your blessing?"

He knelt down. It was with a return of the sunlit happiness that Francis spoke the words, traced the sign and tapped the boy on the head.

Standing under the portico, Daniel watched the car drive off. He waited after it had gone out of sight. He shut his eyes, studying to keep and hold Antonia's face. She had looked at him as steadfastly as he at her. And all would be well. "*And all shall be well, and all shall be well, and all manner of things shall be well*" he said aloud to the garden. He had no idea whence the words came. He stood there, thinking them hard; gazing at the prunus tree; the light wind still shook the red-purple branches. He tried to think of another prayer, but he had, ominously, forgotten them all. For the first time since the beginning of this adventure, melancholy was creeping upon him.

London. London. London. Like the beat of a menacing tom-tom behind the cloud-curtain. Worse, it was coming through; in pictures of familiar streets; in certainty that the city had a hold on him. Did he live there? Perhaps. There was a house that he knew; and a white room; the sound of ice clinking in a glass; the half-seen face of a woman with dark eyes, who smiled at him before she vanished. "Irna" he said to himself but he did not know who Irna was. He didn't want to know. The name stayed. And the look, the feeling of London stayed. It wouldn't go away. One edge of the safe curtain had lifted. He shivered violently.

"My poor Pippin." The voice of old Mr. Courtney was a Godsend. "All alone, sighing a lover's sighs?" He had the box in his arms; at his heels the red setters and the greyhound were frisking abundantly. "Courage," he said "Courage. She will return. Indeed, when one thinks of your combined talents for demolition she may easily breach the convent walls before her time's up. As for your future," he nodded benignly. "Well, take it from one who knows,— Geraldine will always consent to the marriage rather than let the girl live in mortal sin. I suppose you *aren't*. . ?" he asked, sounding hopeful and excited, "I understand that young people nowadays—"

—"No, sir," said Daniel—"Among other objections we haven't had time."

The answer appeared to please Mr. Courtney.

"Well, my advice, dear boy, is to get her with child. A sound local custom and the shortest cut to parental permission Come along, now. We're going to my part of the house; I think you'll like it. What a wonderful morning!" he said, leading the way. "I do like to see a little action about the place. I'm quite prepared to forgive what you two children have done to my poor old Friary. If, that is, the box really yields some solid reward. Can you imagine why Francis took such a pessimistic view?" He halted in the middle of the paved courtyard that spread fanwise around the older wing. "Priestly prudence, eh? Priestly bossiness. What was it he said, exactly?"

"That there might be something quite unexciting inside."

"The old owl. If it wasn't worth finding, then it wouldn't have been worth hiding. H'm? Besides, it's heavy. You shall carry it now."

And here, Daniel thought, was the best of the Manor. He was temporarily consoled. He knew the octagonal hall of mellow stone, the cobweb-thin flags hanging against the sunlight, the mullioned windows and the carved staircase. He looked contentedly about him.

"For proper ceremony," said Luke, "we will conduct our

operations in the French room. I'll collect some newspapers. For once they'll come in useful. You get the tools."

"Where from?"

"Go straight out of the back door. Given luck, you'll sooner or later observe a moron with a face like a ferret, smoking a cigarette and doing nothing whatever. The name is Paddy Hickey. If he isn't there you'll have to rummage in the toolshed yourself. Next to an obsolete privy. You can't," he added, "miss it."

There was no sign of the moron in the derelict stable-yard. Dan prowled, opening the doors of stalls with no horses in them, finding a big dusty garage where a big dusty car sat disconsolately on a bed of straw He had to read the name before he knew what make of car it was; a Hispano-Suiza. Traces of yellow paint; a rusted metal stork on the bonnet. The condition of the car saddened him. So did the condition of the tools, when he finally located the right shed. Choosing a hammer and the biggest chisel, he came to the knowledge that he liked tools and knew how to use them. "I can always get a job" he thought, "Any old job. Antonia and I can run away from them all. I'd like a job on a farm, I think."

London. London. London.

There it was again; he couldn't get away from it It was running after him, shaking the cloud-curtain, getting through. But it wasn't only London, this time. It was voices, words:—"We want you to choose, Dan, it's up to you to choose." Who was the tawny man, giving him a cigarette, telling him to choose? And who was the woman? He couldn't see her; he could only hear her bright, steady voice saying . . what? . . something to do with a birthday; his own birthday, and the presents; he saw their pretty wrappings on a table with some coffee-cups. Where was that room? It wasn't the white London room; there was a garden outside.

"No, don't hug me, Dan. Remember? We're never sloppy, are we, Dan?"

But that wasn't only on the birthday, was it? That had been going on for ages. Like all of it. They had hounded him, for ages; these people, whoever they were. .

"Please, God, don't let it come back. Please, please. Don't let me remember. Don't let me go back."

Fish on Friday. Sorry on Saturday. Funny. It was meant to be funny. They were always being funny about God.

But if I don't look. . if I hold on to these things in my hands, to the hammer and the chisel, if I stare at that cobweb on the wall, at the sun in the yard, I'm safe. The words of the Mass came suddenly:—*Domine, exaudi orationem meam. Et clamor meus ad Te veniat.*

He was out of it; he was walking across the stable-yard, carrying the tools; the sun was on his head, Antonia was in his heart. The discordant jangle of terror faded, was gone.

"You have been a very long time," said Luke. He had spread out a great carpet of newspaper in the middle of he floor. The dogs wandered about, sniffing. The French room didn't play the usual Drumnair trick; it was quite new to Daniel, with its silver-gray colours, its delicate furniture, its multitude of mirrors.

"All this came from Paris. . from my house in Paris. Thank God I had the intelligence to get it out in '39, before those unspeakable Teutons moved in. 'Cost me a fortune. And, talking of fortunes, give me that hammer."

"I'll do it for you," Daniel said. He went to work, with Luke and the dogs for audience. For a minute or two it was fun. Then it stopped being fun. This was a new sort of sadness. Every blow that he struck, every hopeful cockling of the lid, as the tool bit along the rusted edge, became more horrible. "I don't like this," he thought, "I don't like this."

"Splendid, splendid," Luke hissed above his head.

("But it isn't splendid at all. Why not? Am I being sorry for the box?") With the next grim, reluctant blow, he drove the chisel upwards; it went through; he had cut a deep gash under the metal lid, just at the lock; working the chisel out, he felt the whole lid move.

"Bravo!" cried Luke. "Now you ought to be able to lever it right off. What are you waiting for, Pippin? Hurt yourself?"

Dumbly, he shook his head. He picked up the chisel again. Yes. Now he could slide it in quite easily under the jagged place and work all around, without using the hammer. It was done. The meek, battered lid gave way, its rusted hinges broke softly; it fell off, on to the newspaper.

For a moment he thought that Luke was right, that his own dream was right, that here was the treasure. He lifted it out. It was wrapped in a fold of green baize and this looked promising. Before he had time to unfold it, Luke's shaky, freckled hands snatched the bundle. The hands picked at the cloth and flung it aside.

What was it, after all? It looked like an ancient satchel; he saw dark, embossed leather, so old and hard that it might well be wood; he saw a glint of black metal; a hasp? Whatever the thing was, it had been broken. One whole corner was hacked away, raggedly, leaving chewed edges. From this gaping hole, as Luke raised the satchel up, there rained on to the newspapers a shower of crumbly scraps. They looked like dark brown leaves. (Something hideously familiar here; something that rounded off his ignorant sadness perfectly; as if he had known.)

He could hear Luke panting. He could see the old hands tremble on the flap of the satchel. It wasn't as solid as it looked; it cracked right across. Luke lowered it carefully. First tilting it, then pawing gingerly inside, he brought out handfuls of. . what? Paper? Leather? It was all nibbled and torn. The stains, the discolouring made it quite unidentifiable. But Luke handled it as though it were precious stuff. Something kept Daniel from speaking while the old man laid the last handful gently down. He peered into the empty shell. He laid it aside and creaked on to his knees; he began to pick among the tattered pieces.

"Magnifying-glass," he snapped, without looking up. "Oh, God have mercy, on my desk. In the Teak room—straight across the hall. And get the dogs out of here." His head was jerking like a pigeon's.

He was still on his knees when Daniel came back with the glass. He was breathing fast; he was muttering, "There. . and there. . and there." He selected a fragment, held it under the glass, held it up to the light; then rubbed it gently between finger and thumb. He went on doing this. "See?" he said, handing one of the larger fragments to the boy. Daniel cradled it in his palm; he could make out a trace of script, a dimly-coloured initial showing through the brown leaf. He wanted to ask what it was. But now Luke Courtney might have been alone; he returned to the mutilated satchel. He examined the broken corner for a while before he went back to the fragments. It seemed to go on forever, this matter of separating them, holding them under the glass, holding them up to the light. As he crawled and panted in the sunshine, his white hair swung forward on either side of his tragic, devoted profile. The white head shook; the hands became busier, the eyes went on steadily searching. Every little piece was studied, examined, laid down upon the paper as reverently as though it was, in fact, a treasure.

At last he was done. He said in a tired voice, "Well, that's that. It can't be anything else." He sat back on his heels, just as Daniel was sitting. He gave a lop-sided smile: "So all we have is the cumdach, . . and those three lovely pages. . . This," he said, stretching out his hands over the fragments, "is the work of rats. Vellum lasts through eternity, you know. But not if the rats get it. They gnawed through the satchel. . . You can see the marks of their teeth. Appropriate, in a way. Yes, appropriate. . The rats have eaten the Book of Drumnair. It's gone." He gave a cackle of laughter. Then his eyes misted over.

Through the cloud-curtain Daniel saw dancing words and pictures. Cumdach; the Shrine. A casket, with a silver cross on it, a rock-crystal set at the centre of the cross. Where was that? When? He was looking at the shrine through glass; he was reading a printed label stuck under the glass. Now the words formed on the label: THE SHRINE OF THE BOOK OF DRUMNAIR.

Luke's voice broke the small vision. He said "Oh, Pippin, why did you have to find it?"

"I'm sorry. . I'm sorry."

"Help me up, there's a good boy."

The shaking hand pressed hard on his shoulder. Luke stood still, leaning on him with full weight, now using him as a crutch, moving forward, pointing down with his free hand.

"But *this*" he said; he shot out one foot and kicked at the box. "What about *this*? Eh? Eh? This. . and the cloth?" He seemed to be waiting for an answer. "Don't you see? Ah, use your wits, can't you? Who the devil found it. . dug it out, wrapped it up, and put it in the box?"

Friday Evening May 29th

i

Carus Black looked at his watch. His good temper, one of his more reliable possessions, was slipping. He was bored with the flight, exasperated by the twenty-four-hour delay, driven mad by the woman sitting next to him. He began to compose a letter to the airline. The letter would suggest that payment for travelling De Luxe should include a guarantee against neighbourly conversation.

The woman was well-dressed, enamelled and smug. She had the kind of English voice that smacked upon the ear; the flat, upper-class voice. She was given to sudden high peals of laughter because something was quite *absurd*. . Now she was retailing a conversation with the president of a bank in New York. For this purpose she found it necessary to contort her face and make sharp, sing-song sounds through her nose; in the belief, apparently, that she was reproducing an American accent. She used the expressions "Say," "Mebbe" and "I reckon" to show that she knew the language too. It was doubtful, Carus thought, that the Bank-President would recognize himself.

"But of course I like some *individual* Americans very much. Don't you? We stayed with a charming family in Boston. Now *there*. . Don't you find. . ?

Carus Black looked moodily out of the window. Occasionally the break in the cloud-floor cheated him with a glimpse of land far below that proved, when he looked again, to be only a shadow on the sea. This—like the woman—had been going on forever. Soon the captain would be paying him another visit; and the woman would bask again in a reflected glow of V.I.P. treatment. Carus began to twiddle his tongue around the new gap in his teeth, on the left side of the upper jaw; an enormous gap; he wasn't used to it yet. It ached; it did more than ache; it symbolized; it threatened; it was the shape of things to come. All his life he had had sound, splendid teeth. And now the American X-rays proved that every one must go. (Back to New York for that little job; just as soon as he could make it, the dentist said.) It was a melancholy thing, the thought of the gums and the bone working underground against him for so long. How long? How many years since that retributive attack of trench-mouth in Paris? Twenty-five at least.

But if you began to think about your body, said Carus to Carus, you might as well pack it in. Justice, after all. The doom-prophets had been warning him, it seemed, since his twentieth birthday. "By the time you're fifty—" they used to say. Quite a while since they had stopped saying that, of course. He was fifty-one.

And small wonder that the envelope was wearing out years ahead of its time. He couldn't really resent the fact that old men of eighty read without glasses or swam in the Serpentine. Had he driven any single car in his succession of expensive cars as he had driven his body, he would think himself pretty stupid.

Yes. If you had consistently overworked, overplayed, overlusted; if you had smoked forty cigarettes a day minimum and drunk the midnight out since you could remember,— well, the answer was that you had bought Carus Black at fifty-one.

Still handsome? Well, almost. Grey curly hair, light eyes with heavy lids, a crooked smile. Middle-sized; a little too thick and massive-shouldered for your height. Although, in this, the eleventh month of the water-wagon, people were telling you that you had lost weight. Was the wagon worth it?

Carus, brooding upon the question, thought not. Staying away from drink for so long made him feel like a tight-rope walker who could, at any minute, choose to leap down. Not yet. Obstinacy held; and vanity. His surface looks were improved; the eyes brighter, the skin a better colour.

Below the surface, the ill-used body was still sending in its statements of account. Unattractive statements, too; from the haemorrhoids to the heartburn that came with the morning cigarette. Never having argued about a bill in his life, Carus paid up stoically in this kind. He tried to keep silence about the horrid little handicaps.

Just now and again some bright remembrance of his youth, time returning by way of an old snapshot, a tune or a scent, would make him murmur reproachfully in the words of a poet whom he had once loved,

> "You promised I should always be
> the partner of Persephone."

But nobody had ever really promised him that.

And wasn't he, compared with most of his friends, compared with a wider circle than these, a lucky fellow? Had he ever, indeed, been anything else? No. His only lack was a pedigree. Who cared about that? He had developed a habit of saying "Common chaps like me. ." in a drawly Oxford voice. It went. Anything went, if you had inherited a fortune and trebled it. The death of his two highly indulgent parents when he was eighteen had been the beginning. He was already, by the time that the yachting-accident removed them, a little conscious of their class. Dad owned a ship-ping-line; Mum was an ex-Gaiety girl with some unfortunate public habits when plastered; putting soup-plates on her head, for example, or trying to dance with the waiters Maybe she was dancing with the engineer when the explosion in the boiler-room occurred. Why not? He could think of her more tenderly now. His middle-age carried him along in a jog-trot mood of compassion. He was on good terms with his first wife, Jennifer; with his current wife, Irna. He had fathered a son. He was Chairman of B.C.M., the firm that made the best British cars on the market. He had no trucu-lence in politics, no racial prejudices, no particular views —he supposed—about anything important. And he was a busy man. Lucky fellow. .

By this time the lucky fellow had explored the gap in his upper jaw so thoroughly that it hurt too much to go on. His neighbour asked him, for the third time whether he thought they *would* be at Shannon by six-thirty? Or whether —ha-ha-ha? It was *too* absurd, wasn't it, that with all these sputniks, luniks and jets, nobody had yet discovered a way of dealing with a little thing like *fog?* Didn't he think so?

Carus thought of saying "Oh, fog off" and substituted "Mind if I go to sleep for a bit? I've got toothache." She became kind at once; she offered him a drink from an ele-gant gold-topped flask; she even apologised for chattering. "Can't win, can you?" said Carus to Carus as he shut his eyes.

His thoughts began to shape into the fuss-routine, asking him a number of questions that couldn't possibly receive an answer yet.

"What about the car?" "Did Dan get your cable?" "Is he just hanging around without a clue?" The fuss-routine was habit. At the end of any transatlantic flight, a high-powered programme could be waiting; waiting and shot to pieces by the delay. This time, for once, there was nothing of the kind. All that waited was a brief holiday with his son.

Daniel would be there, at Shannon, with the car. Since the car was on order from the B.C.M. showroom in Dublin, Carus had cabled the boy to sign for it and let the Dublin chauffeur catch his train back. A priority cable from Newfoundland; bound to have got there. Dan, who was a sensible chap, wouldn't be in the least put out. Probably he had enjoyed having the car to himself today. He was a skilled and a safe driver.

He was a good boy; reliable in every way. "Which, when I think of myself when young, is all the more remarkable," said Carus to Carus: "Jenny's blood showing up there. And Jenny's influence. Look how she's worked. . 'Made the best possible thing out of what might have been a disaster. Something of a triumph for Jenny. ." Yes, here it came again. Whenever he tried to look at his son, he would find that the boy's upbringing got in the way. The boy himself was lost behind that devoted network of planning and strategy. The boy was almost invisible; a polite, shadowy stranger.

Carus had, they told him, a talent for people; a flair; a gift for sizing up character.

"Can I size up Dan? I wonder. . At least I know the kind of thing he *wouldn't* do: crash the car: get drunk: seduce a virgin. . Nothing subtle about him; he's Mr. Solid Worth; all his instincts are sound. What else? What does he really want out of life?"

Well, that—according to Jenny and Irna, according to Jenny's second husband, Bryan Loomis,—was the sixty-four-thousand-dollar question. Wasn't it? Would Dan decide to come into the firm of B.C M., under his father's wing, or plump for Oxford? Carus couldn't, he decided, join the other three in their sense of urgency. He would like Dan to choose B.C.M. But the important thing was that the boy should make up his own mind.

"Maybe he has, by now. . Maybe he'll tell me." Here he cocked an eye to the prospect of being alone with Dan. It was, as Jennifer's last letter reminded him, a little acidly, a little reproachfully, the first holiday that they had ever taken alone together.

Why the acid reproach? Only an overtone, of course; he had caught it; no one else would. On the surface the letter was friendly as could be. Nothing would ever induce Jennifer to haul down her bright, determinedly-sensible flag.

"Truth of it is, I've always left the boy to her. And she looks on this as a kind of grab. He's always been more hers than mine."

Which, of course, was as it should be. Jenny, with her obsession for facing facts, would not, even now, hesitate to admit that he had only married her because she was going to have his child.

A wartime marriage, between Wing Commander Carus Black of the Air Ministry and his bright, brisk young clerk, —the one with the good eyes and the bad legs.

"*What* an ass you were, weren't you?" he said to himself. A scrupulous ass, at least. A kindly ass, he hoped. He didn't want to think about it now, but it seemed somehow in order as he kept his eyes shut and the aircraft droned on. The marriage in his recollection resembled this pain in his jaw, an infinitely tedious, nagging thing; to be borne until you could bear it no longer. He would have got out, eventually, of course; making over-generous provision for wife and child. He would have had to get out. But it didn't happen like that. The relief, when it came, stunned him. Finding that Jenny was unfaithful had felt like winning at roulette.

He would always remember the moment of confession. That long, listless fellow from the B.B.C., with the liberal views and the tawny hair, drooping awkwardly against the mantelpiece, while Jenny explained; brave, bright and intolerable as ever; he could hear the clacking voice:

"Bryan and I have fallen in love. And the *first* thing we have to talk about is Daniel."

"Ouch" said Carus, aloud, so that his neighbour came up with the gold-topped flask again.

"No. . really. . I'm quite all right, thanks."

When he shut his eyes he couldn't help seeing Daniel, small and stubby, with a toy gun in his hands, asking "When's Mummy going to marry Uncle Bryan?" Oh, it was all so truthful, so matter-of-fact, so damn' civilized, from the very beginning. Now he saw Jenny seated on the sofa between him and Bryan, holding a hand of each, saying "The security of a child is its most precious possession and we mustn't —ever—jeopardize that. We must all be very good friends."

"And what's so astonishing is that we are," Carus thought. "It's worked out. One must give Jenny marks there."

He gave her marks for including Irna in the close, comfortable circle that surrounded young Daniel. In fact she had managed to turn their unorthodox, ill-matched group into a happy family. Yes; marks all round.

To judge the effect of his marriage to Jenny, he had only to look at his marriage to Irna. He had raced to the opposite pole. Away from the slapdash untidiness, the delicatessen mind, the psychological approach. Irna was a near-society beauty, something of a comedy kid. She was the person who now ran his luxurious home-life with entire efficiency.

He began to talk to Irna in his mind; he could hear her answers easily.

"Irna—just why have I laid on this Irish jaunt with Dan. will you tell me?"

"Well, darling, because he's *there*. Hitch-hiking with his old school-chum. All very opportune. Isn't it?"

"I don't know. I feel rather an ass for suggesting it, somehow. 'Not the sort of thing we do."

"You mean not the sort of thing Jenny *likes* you to do. Dan's crazy for the idea."

"Think so?"

"Certainly he is. And as for Jenny, we all know what's on *her* tiny mind. . She's sulking because you weren't home for his birthday."

"I couldn't be. The deal in Cleveland ditched it—you know that."

"Ah, but Jenny had the birthday all set. She wanted this sickening family-conference and cards-on-the-table and Dan to make his choice."

" 'Got to come sooner or later," he said—"hasn't it?"

"Darling dopey,—there *isn't* a choice. Dan's going into B.C.M. Oxford's only Jenny's and Bryan's pipe-dream. . I mean, it's plain idiotic. It's just *not on*."

"But, look,—it's up to Dan, after all—" he said feebly, and heard an echo of Irna's laughter before he turned off the imaginary dialogue. All very well for Irna to underline Jenny's disappointment about the birthday. Jenny had said much the same about Irna, hadn't she? They had perfected, over the years, a two-way technique of buck-passing.

With a wary glance at his neighbour who was now, merci-fully, engaged with the *Reader's Digest*, Carus sat up. He took two letters from his wallet. The first was Jennifer's:

Brimpton Bells Guest House,
Sussex.

. . No use pretending we aren't all disappointed about the birthday-news. We are. Irna particularly; I've just spoken to her. She felt—as Bryan and I felt, that this was the perfect moment for our 'round-table discussion' with Dan. Now we'll have to let it go. It mustn't happen without you. Still, I realize that you would have got home had it been possible. You've never let home-brewed matters interfere with work, have you? I said just that to Irna. . And I do understand.

Irna says that of course she'll come down for the birthday; so we shall be a gay little party and she'll drive Dan back to London that night. He leaves for Ireland next day. Carus, I still don't know *why* Ireland. Of course I'm not worried about it, but I think it must mean something to Dan that he doesn't himself realize. He simply leaped at the idea. Both Bryan and I find it all the more puzzling since we've met the lad he's going with—one Tim Russell. He came over to tea yesterday. Such a dull, reactionary type of boy, who's besotted about early Christian monuments. 'Last thing I'd have thought would appeal to Dan. It will—of course—take him away from an important week in his reading; Bryan's most disappointed. But I stand by my policy of non-interference. I've been thinking about that. Do you know,—I don't believe I've ever *forbidden* Dan to do anything? Something of a record in nineteen years and I can't help being proud. . Still, perhaps if you'd been here you could have persuaded him that he hasn't really earned this rather pointless holiday. Particularly now. Every day I feel it's more vital for him to make his choice. Don't you? But I know I can trust you to keep our "rules" and use no persuasion-tactics when you have him all to yourself. ."

There was more of this, with the overtones sounding. Carus skipped it and read the second letter. Typical of all Dan's communications, whether verbal or written: brief, agreeable and straight to the point:

Dear Carus,

that sounds an awfully good idea. If you'll let me know your flight-number I'll be waiting for you at Shannon. Having a car will be wonderful. 'Expect I'll have walked my legs off by then.

Love,
Daniel.

Carus put away the letters; he never knew why he kept them. His eyelids began to droop. He was trying to remember how it felt to be nineteen. He must have looked much as his son looked now. Everybody remarked upon their likeness. He couldn't see it. He could only see himself at fifty-one.

What sort of birthday had it been for Daniel?

He must have been nearer to sleep than he thought, for presently he was looking at another boy instead, in another place and another time and a sudden voice flew up like a bird to scream *"But you're going back!"*

Startled, Carus opened his eyes. The aircraft was rocking,

bumping. The forward panel flashed FASTEN SEAT BELTS. They were over Shannon.

His neighbour smiled at him. "You looked," she said, "as though you were having a nice dream."

ii

All airports were alike to the Chairman of B.C.M. Here was the same smooth priority-machine set in motion; the touching of caps, the "This way, Mr. Black"; the flash through the Customs and the porter picking up the luggage. As he came through the barrier, leading the field, Carus looked for Daniel. A chauffeur in uniform sprang forward. "Mr. Black? Good evening, sir. I'm from the Dublin office. I've got your car outside."

Carus gazed at him. "Good lord. . have you been here since yesterday?"

"Quite all right, sir. They announced the delay at once so I went and got myself a bed in Limerick. I phoned the office, sir."

"But where's my son? What? Oh nonsense. I told him to connect with you—sign for the car. Damn it, this is idiotic. 'Mean you haven't seen him at all? . . Oh, honestly. How long have you been here now—this evening?"

"Just about half an hour, sir."

"Damn it—" said Carus again, aware that he was tired and jittery, and very angry with Daniel. "Even if he missed you yesterday, I don't see how he could today. Have a look for him, will you? Boy of nineteen—dark hair—middle height. Probably got a rucksack with him, he's been hiking."

"Certainly, sir." He endured the rest of the driver's speech, telling him exactly where the car was, punctiliously giving him the registration-number. Storming up to the Airline counter he met, behind the wooden bulwark, a poster-pretty colleen wearing a silly peaked cap. Now there was the V.I.P. treatment again, the recurrent "Mr. Black"; and now his cable to Daniel lay before him unopened.

A dead stop. He realized, after a moment, that he was temporarily more worried about the driver than about Daniel. He went out through the barrier again and found the car; a sleek, decisive new model, with the man pacing beside it. "I can't see a sign of him anywhere, sir, I'm sorry."

"I'm sorry too. 'Can't make out what's happened. I won't keep you. Get a taxi into Limerick—Get on your way. ." He slipped a flurry of notes from his wallet, saying "Rubbish, you've been kept hanging around far too long. No, nothing you can do, thanks." He strode in again to the meaningless hall, faintly compensated because he had done the right thing by the driver, with a hundred per cent overtip for good measure. All such emergencies were easy for him; born rich, thought Carus, you were born wise. But where the devil was the boy?

He now had the ground-staff enjoying themselves, calling Daniel over the public-address system, commiserating, combing the place for a possible message, making brisk, show-off enquiries. "This way, Mr. Black, please. . You'll be more comfortable in here." Pickled wood and plushy chairs; an excess of ash-trays. "Just lift the receiver and ask for the number. . Can't we bring you something while you're waiting?"

"Ginger-beer," said Carus, after the longest hesitation in eleven months. He took a Drynomil with the ginger-beer while he waited for his call to come through. He despised these pills and had developed the habit of watching for their effect, being usually more pleased when they didn't work.

"My darling—" said Irna's voice. "Hullo. Welcome home. Except you're *not*, are you? Where are you? Everything all right?"

"Apart from a twenty-four-hour hold-up and the fact that Dan isn't here, everything is perfectly fine."

Irna said something to somebody else, that sounded like, and probably was, "More ice—", before she joined him again.

"*Dan* isn't there? Why not?"

"Search me. I was wondering if anything had gone wrong that end," said Carus. "If a message had missed me somewhere along the line."

"Oh darling, *no*. I've got his postcard; wait. You can wait, can't you? Not in some hideous box with coppers?"

"No, dear, in the head-boy's private office, as you might expect."

He drank the rest of the ginger-beer. Irna's voice returned: "This is from some wholly unpronounceable spot. . Bally-something. Posted. . 'day before yesterday. 'Wonderful fun all the way. On to meet Dad tomorrow.'"

"Dad? I wasn't aware that he ever called me Dad," said Carus.

"Darling, what's *that* got to do with anything?"

"I don't know. . Blast him. If it wasn't for the delay—which means he's had a night and a day to kick his heels about this place, I wouldn't be so damned annoyed."

"Oh, darling. . he'll turn up any minute. Delays always make muddles. I do see it's a cracking bore, but not to worry," said Irna, "Jennifer rang up at lunchtime; she'd heard from him too. Nothing *can* have gone wrong; it never does with Daniel He'll be there. How are your piles, darling?"

"Under control," said Carus.

iii

Replacing the telephone, Irna looked around her white drawing-room and found that its atmosphere was changed, invaded by the call from Carus. The young man seated in the corner of the sofa (exactly where Daniel had sat, eleven days earlier, on the night of his birthday) raised inquiring eyebrows. The young man was Peter Anthony, the director. He had red hair and a cheeky, clownish face.

"Only my beloved stepson making some kind of a non-sense—most unlike him," said Irna.

"Can't make out why you call him your stepson," said Anthony. (He had met Daniel here and liked him. Carus remarking on it, she had said "Oh darling, Peter's a lot less queer than his reputation." Carus, grinning, had asked her how she knew that.)

"Well, but he *is* my stepson. Isn't he? What d'you want me to call him?"

Peter said, "I'm sure one can't have a mother *and* a stepmother. Or, if one can, it must be highly up-mixing."

"Nobody could be *less* mixed-up than Daniel," said Irna crisply. "As Jennifer puts it, he's had four parents since he was eight."

"Personally, I found two more than enough."

She let that lie; she went on:—"Father—mother—step-father—stepmother. . all the best of friends. In fact, we're a damn' good team." Here she became aware that she was echoing Jennifer. Peter continued to look sceptical. She knew that the moment had somehow slipped; she wouldn't, now, ask him to read her First Act. Daniel had intruded upon her only other devotion, the professional theatre. Of the two devotions, Daniel was, in any case, the more rewarding.

"I grant you it may sound cock-eyed," she said. "But it works. We've gone all out to make it work, for Dan's sake. He's utterly sweet, that boy. You thought so, didn't you?"

"I found him sympathetic, yes."

"And he's going to be a big success in B.C.M. I know it. Carus knows it too, which is what matters."

Peter said, "B.C.M.? I thought he was going up to Oxford."

"Oxford? He told you Oxford?" She heard the shrillness in her own voice. Peter raised his eyebrows again:— "Seems to me that's what we were talking about. I remember telling him it was one of the few intelligent time-wasters."

Irna thought about it. "I'm sure he didn't say he *was* going. He probably told you he had the chance. So he has. But it would be ridiculous."

"Why ridiculous?"

"He hasn't that sort of brain. . I hinted as much to Jennifer when I was down there for his birthday. Couldn't do more than hint, of course. 'Honour bound. Just a throwaway line while we were doing the washing-up." She saw the moment clearly in recollection; the two of them at the sink. Jennifer was hopeless at washing-up. . and hideously stingy with the dish-towels. Jennifer had, naturally, ignored the throwaway line; she had simply said "That's not clean," handing back a fork that was perfectly clean.

"Why the sigh?" Peter was asking.

"Don't know. . Thinking about Dan's birthday makes me sort of sad."

Peter said, "Possibly because of the washing-up."

137

"I think because it was Sunday. I *do* wish there was some way of getting Sunday abolished."

She saw him look at his watch. "All right, Peter, you run away. You're bored. . Yes, you are. I can feel it."

"How does it feel?"

"As if you'd suddenly put on a mackintosh. Do go."

He was brilliant; he was the fireball of the Stratford season. ('Macbeth' set in Kentucky; 'Twelfth Night' in London of the 'Twenties; 'Antony and Cleopatra' in Delhi, period 1900.) He was just one of the people whom she could always collect, by way of her looks and her husband's money. She didn't really want to sleep with him, though she would—of course—raise no objection. She wanted him to read her First Act. Of the many First Acts that she had completed, it was easily the best. He was saying, "But you had something you wanted to discuss with me. You said—"

"Never-mind-not-any-more-all-over-ups-a-daisy" cooed Irna, with intent to madden. "Bysie-Bye—" He rose, a chunky young man with a grievance. He made a conscientious effort to embrace her and she moved tranquilly out of reach. Another one gone, she thought, hearing the slam of the front door. She looked at herself in the glass, saw the dark, baffled beauty of her face and laughed.

She seldom fooled herself for long. However often she might make these little darts away from frustration, they were doomed; the First Acts along with the social ploys, the hobbies along with the lovers. At thirty-nine, she knew what the trouble was. Marriage with an older man who had ceased to be exciting for her and who had failed to give her a child. Quite a simple trouble, really. Sexual love between Carus and herself was over, finished; without the sequel of companionship setting in. That was nobody's fault; they both

138

put up a good act, she thought, but in truth they were lonely with each other. She neither knew nor cared if he slept in other beds. He showed the same friendly indifference toward her secrets. Sometimes she thought that she only stayed with him because she hadn't, yet, fallen truly in love again. Sometimes when she wanted to hate herself, she said that she only stayed because of the money. But then she came to Daniel in her mind. The one person with whom she wasn't lonely, with whom she always had fun. The image of Carus in youth,—the Carus whom she had never seen. Lately he had taken on another likeness,—the one that she could find in the old photographs—the sexy, playboy look. Dan had grown up quickly in this last year.

She saw this image now,—the boy seated in the corner of the white sofa, on that Sunday night. He was wearing his best clothes, the charcoal-grey suit and the white shirt. She watched again the tanned, glowing face. He was unwrapping his special birthday present. Always she had given him one special present, away from the rest. This time it was a black sealskin wallet, with the initials D.C.B. in gold. It had pockets for passport and tickets, for sterling and foreign currency; a splendid thing. In his pleasure there was a touch of awe, as though he were thinking about the price. Then he began to change his possessions devotedly from the old wallet to the new. Afterwards he said "Now I'm sorry for this one. Who can I give it to?", patting it with a silly, fubsy kindliness that touched her heart.

"We'll find somebody. . One of the lift-boys here, perhaps. Meanwhile—" as he fondled the new one again— "Rather the right thing for an up-and-coming chap in B.C.M.,—no?"

He raised his head, the dark curly head; the look he gave her was level-eyed, guileless; Carus with a difference. Perhaps Carus had once looked at people in this trustful way. "Is that it, Irna? Think so? An up-and-coming chap in B.C.M.?"

Remembering the rules, she said "Darling, it's for you to decide, of course. But you've enjoyed it, haven't you? Looking at it all? Seeing how the wheels go round—sitting in on the job?"

The light grey eyes, the eyes of Carus, were solemn. "Well, yes, I have. But I've only been playing at it. . For a few days at a time. . Haven't I? Just strolling around the sales-room and driving the cars and being taken to lunch. . It's all been a bit of a romp."

"Not as much of a romp as you imagine. Carus planned it that way."

"I know he did. But—"

—"Listen. He wouldn't have taken the trouble if you weren't the kind of guy you are,—see what I mean?"

A pause. "No, Irna. . I don't see. I don't know what kind of guy I am. How does one know?"

(He was so sweet. .) She said "One can take it from me. You're a personable young man; a gentleman; you're unself-conscious, and you mix well. That's awfully important. As you've seen already, there's quite a heavy social side to B C.M."

Another silence; then his voice dropped to a mumble:—
"What about Oxford?"

"Oxford? It's there, too, of course. If you'd rather. Your name's down; it's up to you."

Silence again.

"How's it going, Dan? You enjoy it? Bryan's coaching, I mean? Fun? As much fun as the B.C.M. romp?"

Perhaps she should not have asked him that. He said "Bryan's a damn' good coach," sounding stiff and loyal.

"I'll bet. ." said Irna. "You're a lucky fellow, you know. As a stepfather, Bryan can give you a lot that Carus can't: and vice versa. On the academic side, Bryan's got it all." She was forever fighting her prejudice against the tawny, listless Bryan; it was, she told herself, of Bryan's making. His deliberate idleness, his silly cracks at big business, his cult of worldly failure; these were so obviously a retort to Carus.

"Just one thing he hasn't got," she said to the boy on the sofa. "And that's a flair for people. Carus has. He sizes people up in no time flat; and he gambles on them—just the way he does when he plays chemmy. Quite extraordinary. You'll see it when you come of age for casinos; he's *always* right. And at the minute, darling, he's gambling on you."

As neat an exit-line as any. Patting Dan's shoulder, she followed it up with "Bed, I think. . . After twelve and you're leaving at cock-shout."

She went up with him to his room. She had taken pains with it; there was a divan bed, a good solid writing-desk; enough shelves, enough cupboard space. And, of course, his own bathroom; Irna couldn't really understand about houses with only one bathroom. His bleak little bedroom at home, on the top floor of the guest-house run by Jenny and Bryan, worried her too. (Lovely to have him here all the time, once the B.C.M. job was fixed. Week-ends at the guest-house, oh yes; always. But these luxurious quarters would soon turn into home.)

Carus said so often "Dan adores you." She remembered

the eight-year-old with the big eyes, staring at her across the table, the first time,—giving her a sudden glorious smile. In those days he was still calling his stepfather "Uncle Bryan." He had used her Christian name from that first day. Always, she had been glamorous and exciting for him; and a chum as well. Was it self-deception to believe that he was closer to her than to anyone;—Jennifer included? No, it wasn't. Jennifer held him off. Jennifer's idea of motherhood was a cross between the functions of a social worker and a psychiatrist.

Standing in the doorway, she watched him unpack a top layer of needs for the night. The rucksack was an old one of Bryan's.

"Is that really all you're taking? Darling, *bliss* to be young and travel light. . I can't any more. . Dan,—what made you want to go off on this trip all of a sudden? I don't mean to pry," she added. "But you took us by surprise, you know that."

He grinned at her. "Yes, I know that."

"Secret?"

"Not a bit. I was just thinking I'd rather like to go off somewhere,—and when Tim Russell turned up and talked about Ireland"—he paused, unfolding a pair of pyjamas. "Well, it sort of beckoned."

"It'll be tough sledding, won't it?"

"I don't mind."

No, he wouldn't mind. Not only because he was young, but because he was used to it. Jennifer and Bryan had one pet place in Cornwall where there was an outdoor privy. Dan, loyal as a dog, had never said a word against it, but she had seen his wide-eyed reaction to the expensive holiday jaunts with Carus and herself. A twinge of jealousy now because, this time next week, she would not be with them. Just Carus and Dan alone.

"'Shan't be awake tomorrow when you go, darling. Car's ordered for eight. So I'll say goodnight and goodbye now. Have a lovely time. And you and Carus look after each other, eh?"

The embrace need have been no different from their other embraces. But for a moment, with his arms about her, she thought of him as a man, a man very dear to her, and she held him close. She leaned back, saw the Carus look in his eyes, laughed and kissed him on the lips.

Alone now, pouring another drink, Irna knew what she had meant when she said to Peter Anthony "Thinking about Dan's birthday makes me sad." That was why. The one little sensual moment had left a shadow of guilt behind. It wouldn't lift until she saw him again, until they could be as they were before, in the old, easy relationship. Perhaps she was taking it too seriously. Perhaps it had meant nothing to him. She hoped it had meant nothing. One might be a stinker, said Irna, but one wasn't that sort of stinker.

iv

Jennifer was putting the flowers on the dining-room tables and Bryan was fetching the wine. They served wine with both main meals at the guest-house. It was one of the touches in which they took pride, like the free copies of the New Statesman.

A warm evening, for the end of May; an amiable view through the dining-room windows; the shaggy lawn, the garden-chairs set round the sundial, the herbaceous border beginning to flame with untidy colours, the Sussex downs on the skyline. Since it was Friday they had almost their full quota of guests. They could hear the lazy, comfortable chatter from the lawn.

Their guests were their friends, and this, thought Jennifer, confirmed the success of their project. The same people, intellectuals, liberal thinkers, writers, talkers, came again and again. They were a family; they enjoyed one another's company; they enjoyed the sprawly freedom, the food with its casual, continental flourishes. Above all, they said, the place had atmosphere. There was no profit in the guest-house, but somehow Jennifer and Bryan kept scraping along.

When the telephone rang, one of the guests, Mervin Duff, the anthropologist, answered it. He yelled "For you, Jenny! Personal call from Ireland!" on his way back to the garden.

Jennifer was irritated. Carus, of course; Carus being lavish; and sentimental; thinking it a good idea to telephone because he and Daniel were together. He would put Dan on to talk to her; and then they would do the same for Irna. More probably, they had talked to Irna already.

The telephone was in Bryan's office at the back of the hall. The voice of Carus sounded tired, unusually cross.

As she listened, she began to be afraid; she rebuked herself stoutly. It was just the effect of him; the hangover from fear, the old phobia operating; the feeling that the floor was thin under her feet.

Once, Carus had been able to do this to her every day. Now, though the feeling came rarely, it was still sharp. It was a sense of inferiority, mixed with terror. Inferiority was, she knew, a myth. Gone were the days when she would say, and believe it, "Socially, of course, Carus is a cut above me." It wasn't true. It never had been true. That Olympian manner of his came merely from money, from mixing with the worthless upper crust of this world and knowing the ropes.

As for the terror, this was understandable to her now; an emotional terror, a deep psychological reaction. (Her old father-hate repeated.) From the first moment of their meeting, Carus had sent out danger-signals, hints of a secret life. *"I took one wrong road a long time ago, and I've been taking them ever since. ."* It was the earliest of his observations that she could remember, and somehow the worst. He had never explained about the wrong roads, though he had made it easy for her to feel that she was one of them.

Now she heard his tired voice saying morosely, "It's so unlike Dan. 'Can't help thinking he must be in trouble." She fought that: "Nonsense. He *must* have left a message for you. They simply haven't found it. You know how inefficient people can be."

"Not when I'm about, they can't," said Carus.

"But he was waiting for you in Limerick. He's *there*. His card from Limerick came this afternoon."

"Then what the hell's he playing at? I don't propose to wait forever in this God-forsaken airport."

Wildly, Jennifer hunted for a rational explanation. She found it. "Now look. . here's what must have happened. He didn't go to Shannon yesterday. He telephoned first from Limerick to check the arrival-time. . Sort of sensible thing he would do. . Once he heard the flight was delayed that long, he went off by himself somewhere. . That explains why he didn't get the cable. And now he's just a bit late.

Hitch-hiking—thumbing lifts—anybody might be late. Particularly in Ireland."

Silence from Carus, palpably thinking it over.

"Isn't it the obvious answer?"

"I suppose it might be."

She said, "I'm *sure* it is."

"All right," said Carus, (so gloomily that he made the words sound like "All wrong.")—"Here's what I'll do. I'll get these people to book me in at an hotel, wait for him a few more minutes; then if he hasn't turned up, I'll leave a note telling him where I am. And I'll call you—"

—"There's no need to call me. If I don't hear from you, I'll assume all's well." She rang off briskly. When she had finished the flowers, she returned to the kitchen. Chopping chives and parsley, she said to herself "Don't be a fool, now. Dan's in no trouble. He wouldn't do anything silly; he never does. 'Only shows how little Carus knows the boy.'"

But she was too well-adjusted, she thought, to flatter herself that she knew Daniel simply because he was her son. He was remarkably easy to know. An extrovert, an out-goer, with no hidden depths. She had rarely seen him in a 'down' mood. He had been steady all his life; a placid, chuckling baby; a gay, noisy little boy, who sometimes lost his temper in a good round rage, but never sulked. So far, she had watched him through adolescence without a qualm. She recognized all the dangers here. She wasn't, she knew, one of the myopic mothers; she was neither possessive nor starry-eyed, but a devoted student of psychology.

She thought back to Daniel's birthday; still something of a landmark in her mind, though Carus, by his abscence had postponed the important 'round-table' discussion. It had been a good day, all the same, a happy day.

She remembered Irna's arrival, at the wheel of the latest B.C.M. model. Irna, looking enchanting as always (—it was the face of a doe, with the huge dark eyes and small features—) bringing presents that were de luxe and prettily-wrapped, like herself. Long ago Jennifer had learned to reject the sentimental pang that came because the presents from Irna and Carus were so much more elaborate than hers and Bryan's. Daniel had guessed at the pang. In the earlier years he had taken trouble to say an extra word for the cheap, home-wrapped presents as though he liked them better. Realizing this, she had set to work on herself. And worked well. If Carus and Irna had bought him a yacht for his nineteenth birthday, she would have taken it calmly.

And Irna was really rather a darling. It had come as a surprise to Jennifer to find that she could like somebody so entirely frivolous. At the beginning, she and Bryan alike had entertained grave doubts of the exquisite creature. Nowadays Bryan said that Irna was the only living example of that wholly false legend, the tart with the heart of gold. (This was one of their more private jokes.)

Lining up the earthenware soup-cups on the trays, Jennifer realized that she was listening for the telephone. Foolish, when she had made a point of asking Carus not to call her again. What a long time Bryan was taking in the cellar. . She wished he would come.

Standing at the sink, rinsing the lettuces, she was reminded of Irna; Irna helping her to wash up after the birthday lunch. Nobody, she thought, washed up as badly as Irna, but one always tried to be restrained and grateful. Irna had dropped one of her little hints, (as well as a saucer.) She could hear the voice now:

"Darling. . *not* wanting to needle you about Dan—and

what we laughingly call the choice. . but, well, I know what I think and so does Carus."

To which blinding glimpse of the obvious, no reply had been necessary. And the hint itself gave her no anxiety. Not only because Oxford seemed to her the inevitable choice, but because neither Irna nor any one of them would dare put pressure on Daniel. That was the agreement all round; a solemn pact.

Jennifer began to mix the salad-dressing. She worked deliberately at the task of keeping a calm, level-headed view. She clung tightly to her own explanation. She tried to picture Dan arriving, late and apologetic, at the airport; Carus rasping at him in a moment's fury and then snapping back into his usual good temper. Once again she applauded her own sound sense in letting the boy have these few days alone with his father. It gave some point to Dan's otherwise meaningless expedition: "Now that Carus is such a big shot, he gets so little time. It's good for them both."

She had said something like this to Daniel on that sunny birthday evening. (Irna waiting beside the car; the boy with his arms held out to her, then lowering them quickly as he remembered that they didn't, by her own ruling, hug or kiss any more.) She had patted him on the back; she had made her usual speech, telling him not to write unless he felt like it: "Letters are a *bore*, unless one has the impulse." He had turned away with the compact swing of his shoulders that reminded her of Carus. The physical likeness was complete. (But, oh, what a different fellow lived inside. Mercifully for Dan and for all concerned. .)

There was no steeling of the heart when saying goodbye to him. She had perfected the work of non-attachment; their relationship was balanced, adjusted, right. And the secret of the achievement lay, she realized, in the fact that she had never let herself down. As he drove off, turning to wave, she had known a threefold happiness; happiness in herself, happiness in Bryan, happiness in the boy.

Here was Bryan now, in the kitchen doorway, waving two wine-bottles. The faithful happiness returned at once.

"Sorry I was such an age, darling. The Spanish supplies are running low again. Time we entertained some teetotallers for a change."

"You can pour this teetotaller some sherry."

Bryan took down their special bottle from the shelf. It was a part of the kitchen ritual. They both said "Skoal". Then Jennifer said, "Carus just called from Shannon. Dan hasn't turned up."

Bryan listened, his face thoughtful. Having heard it all, he said "Oh you're obviously right. . He just didn't want to stick around. Anybody but Carus would see that. He never expects anything but the Yes-Sir-No-Sir treatment. Don't worry, Jenny."

"I'm not worrying."

Bryan began to carve the cold beef with his usual exquisite precision, not hurrying at all, though supper was late already. Moving delicately, he set the slices on the plates. He was a graceful creature. Always conscious of her own sturdiness, Jennifer took pleasure in his length of limb, his lazy manner.

"There's a cloud on you, all the same" said Bryan. "Don't let there be; Dan's all right."

"Of course he is. Everything's always all right in our family," she said.

"Thanks to you," said Bryan.

149

"It was just Carus. . You know how he takes me now and again."

"By God, I do. ." He spoke with passion. "It's the one thing I can't stand. How many times have I told you you're twice the person he is? I mean—I've nothing *against* Carus —not any more. He's just an amiable, tired tycoon. But that he should get *you* down—you, with your brains and your guts and your absolute rightness about everything—" He snorted over the last of the sherry.

She couldn't help being pleased when Bryan spoke up like this. She stood, in a glow of comfort and security, putting dabs of cream on the cups of cold tomato soup.

Then Bryan said "Well—Carus has got it coming to him this week, I shouldn't wonder. ."

"What did you say? *What?*"

His silence strung out. Once again the floor felt thin under her feet.

v

"God, what a fool—to let that out," Bryan thought. Hurriedly he said "I mean, if you ask me, Dan's all set to tell him he's choosing Oxford."

"Why are you so sure?" she snapped.

"'Hinted as much—on his birthday."

"When?"

"In the afternoon. We drove over to Barcombe with those typescripts of yours—remember?"

"What did he say?"

"Jenny—darling, why the inquisition?" He tried to sound gently injured.

"You know I hate secrets. Why didn't you tell me? If it's true, of course, I couldn't be happier" she said; she looked far from happy.

"I'll swear it's true."

"Then you'll please tell me exactly how he phrased it. *And* I want to know why you've kept quiet until now. ." She set her hands on her hips, her feet a little way apart. She was like a brown terrier, squaring up to him.

He tried "Let's dish out the supper first, darling. We're running awfully late." Still she stood firm: "You're hiding something. . You *never* do. Bryan,—you didn't tell him—?" He caught her roughly in his arms and kissed her. Holding her close, he said "Oh, Jenny. . would I? Look at me, now. . . *Would I?*"

After a moment she said "No. I trust you utterly. I'm sorry. But I don't understand—"

"I'll explain. Just a hint he threw out, that's all." He picked up the first tray.

It was a relief to get away from her, to shout "Soup's on!" through the dining-room window, to chatter with the chums as they came straggling to their places. Even on a cold-supper night, Jenny never ate the first course. She liked to get ahead with the savoury and the coffee-machine.

Taking his place between Deirdre Stubbs, the child-psychiatrist and her husband, who wrote about birds, Bryan went down into a lonely silence. The jolly voices rose He felt anything but jolly. Perhaps, if the telephone rang, if Carus came through to say that Dan had turned up at last, he would feel better.

Would he, though?

No use pretending that the boy meant as much to him as

151

a child of his own would mean. (Poor darling Jenny; four miscarriages; then no more hope; and he could never get it out of his mind that this was the fault of Carus.) He was, he told himself, devoted to his stepson. If only Dan didn't look so much like Carus,—Carus before he thickened up with success. If only he himself could have fathered a son by Jenny; a son who wasn't like Dan; Dan was such an ordinary, English boy; Bryan had met many of them in his old tutoring days. Good-tempered, athletic, at ease with country things; no scholar, no dynamiter; leaning towards an outdoor life, with no notion how to get it.

Despite all his own teachings, he had to admit that Daniel remained an old-fashioned type. There he could blame Carus, too. Naturally Carus had put his foot down on the project of a really progressive school. But Bryan could flatter himself that the chosen public school was the least reactionary of all. (Shorts in summer; current-affairs and facts-of-life discussions; no compulsory church.) Bryan was fond of quoting the line, "Sour authority's ancestral show." It summed up for him the enemy of youth, the enemy of all mankind.

Now Deirdre Stubbs was leaning towards him, saying quietly—"You're not worried about the boy, are you, Bryan?" The guest-house grapevine was highly efficient. Just who had listened to the telephone-call,—who had told, he didn't know; but it was always like this and, as a rule, he had no objection. He heard himself drawl "Why should I be worried?" before he began to embark with vigour upon Jenny's explanation.

They were all helping themselves to their cold plates from the sideboard when she came in. As she took her place at the second table, she blew him a kiss. She looked happier now. The bright, trustful face gave him a sudden clue to his own behaviour.

"Am I ruthless? Single-minded? Yes. Where Jenny's concerned, I'm both. I'd rather kill than see her hurt."

He went on watching the brown head, the eager profile. There was so much about her that he admired; her lifelong fight for detachment, her climb away from her own origins, her raw honesty. So much that he loved. After twelve years of marriage, his body was still enslaved to hers. (Lord, how jealous Daniel could have made him, had the boy been a demanding child, or Jenny a doting, son-eating mother.)

"I say, Bryan—" Alvin's voice cut in—"If you don't want your beef, I'm on for a second helping."

"All yours," Bryan said.

"Lost your appetite, ducky?"

("No, just my honour. . . Oh snap out of it, can't you? You're making too much of it. You'd behaved so damn' well about this Oxford-B.C.M. tug-o'-war—till then. Till the birthday. And it was all Irna's fault, let's be clear about that. .")

He was clear about that. Irna had begun it. Here in this dining-room. They were alone together, just for a few minutes, clearing up after the birthday feast; dealing with the clutter of gay wrappings, the coffee-cups, the remains of the fruit and cheese. Irna and he had shared the same situation for so long that there was a rapport between them. (Being married to the other two partners, Irna said, made for strange bedfellows, if he saw what she meant.)

She had given him one of her grimaces, wrinkling her delicious little nose, saying, "*Well*,—no family conference.

One thing to be grateful for, eh? A Munich— A breather. Hostilities postponed."

"Hostilities?" His own view, kept conscientiously hidden. . "Funny word. . Why hostilities?"

"Dear Bryan. . old smoothie." Laughing, she had lifted the tray. "I feel exactly as you do, chum."

"And how do I feel, Mrs. Crystal Ball?"

In the doorway she had turned skilfully, balancing the tray:—"Come off it. . I want to sell him on B.C.M. You want to sell him on Oxford. What's more, I bet you've had a bash already."

It wasn't true. He hadn't. Under Jenny's direction, the four months since Daniel left school had been scrupulously free from 'selling' by either side. Still, that little dart had gone under his skin. A threat to peace. He had realized, as Irna swung off towards the kitchen, that she would have Dan to herself all the way to London, and after. Here came his last chance of getting in ahead.

"*Mushrooms on toast—oh, goody, goody, goody!*" With a start, Bryan realized that Jenny had let Aelred Robinson, the 'cellist, help her carry in the third course. She hadn't summoned him at all. Anxiously, he watched her; yes, the cloud was on her still.

But she couldn't know; not possibly.

Now he was back at the car with Dan. The drive to Barcombe had been his chance, the only one.

He saw the boy's surprised face: "Coming too? Don't you want to sleep after that wonderful lunch?"

"No. I'd like the drive—like to say Hullo to Paul and Rebecca."

Their talk was vivid in memory. Dan talking about the

two articles that Jenny had written, sounding amused rather than respectful:—

"'Read those?"

They were random essays; for the random broadsheet that Paul and Rebecca Branch liked to print on their own press at Barcombe Mills. He had said Yes, Jennifer always let him read them.

Daniel saying: "First time she ever let *me*. ."

"Salute to your approaching adult status. Good, aren't they?" He had found them brilliant; two short attacks on the Church of Rome, entitled "Fish on Fridays" and "Sorry on Saturdays." Jennifer had flashes like that sometimes.

"Well but, Bryan, I didn't get the point. Why can't people believe what they like? What's it matter, anyway?"

(Despite the little spurt of anger on Jenny's behalf, Bryan had recognized a seed of his own sowing. Agreeing with Jenny that the imposition of arbitrary beliefs made an intolerable burden for a child, he had been content with their joint policy: "We'll leave all that alone till he's old enough to make up his mind." And had he not, himself, told Daniel often that none of it mattered, that a tolerant, open view was what mattered?)

"Well, you see, Jenny's studied these things. When you've read the amount she has—"

—"Carus says picking on other peoples' religion is bad manners."

Himself thinking: "The devil he does. ." His voice murmuring, "Hope you didn't quote that to Jenny."

"Lord, no; it would have hurt her. But she seems to me to be making an awful fuss about nothing. . . Still—if it gives her pleasure."

155

"You'll run into a lot of religious polemic—pro and con—when you get to Oxford, you know."

"Shall I?" Dan's voice now offhand, uninterested. The feel of his own heartbeat quickening before he spoke again: launching the forbidden question:—

"You're all set for it, aren't you? I'd rather like to know."

Then turning to study the Carus profile, with the straight nose, the wide, well-shaped mouth, the black curls blowing.

"Not sure yet," from Dan as he continued to watch the Sunday traffic. He handled the car well. Carus had taught him.

"Nearly time to decide. This trip to Ireland—though it takes you off your reading—gives you a good chance to think—to make up your mind, away from all of us. ."

"Till I get to Shannon Airport. And Carus starts in about B.C.M."

That was startling. Consoling, somehow. Easy to drawl, "Well. . . You mustn't let him put the heat on you."

It was at this moment, Bryan thought, that he had seen quite clearly how unfitted Dan was for B C.M. Up till that instant, B.C.M. had been no more than an obstacle to Oxford. In changing focus, it had presented him suddenly with a picture of Daniel as a smooth young salesman, walking a soft carpet; clean, handsome, well-dressed; a candy kid, to be groomed for his place in the fleshy, tinpot world that Carus ruled. The world of contracts and commissions, of short drinks and long lunches; of big deals and small scruples. Jenny's son. . All wrong; utterly, hopelessly wrong.

And it was when Daniel turned the car off the main road, down the long, steep lane toward Barcombe Mills, that he had played the unforgivable card, the trump card; the card that must win.

"Pull up half a minute, old boy; pull in here. Let's have a cigarette. There's something about the Oxford project that I think you ought to know. Jenny, being the kind of person she is, doesn't want you to know. So this must be between you and me. Not a word to her, eh?"

"No, Bryan, of course not." A solemn face now, the lips puffing inexpertly at the cigarette.

"I know you've been wondering how we can afford to send you. Not being, as you might say, in your father's income-bracket. Well, it's quite simple. Nothing to do with Carus. The money's there. It's a small trust-fund. Your great-grandfather's legacy. . only legacy that ever came Jenny's way. She made that trust for you—years ago. It's meant a lot to her to be able to do that. . safeguard it for you. You can see, can't you, how it would mean a lot?"

The face quite baffled and stupid. . the voice mumbling, "But—look—couldn't *she* use the money? I mean, we're always pretty broke, aren't we?"

"Oh, we manage. . Besides, she wouldn't. This is awfully important to Jenny—to be able to give you Oxford *herself*—if you want it. Not to take a penny from Carus."

The face, still changing, shadowed, lonely with its bewilderment. The smoke of the two cigarettes curling upward in the sunshine. His own damnable words, crisply spoken: "I had to tell you; my duty, really; 'think it must help you. Nobody can make the right decision without knowing every factor that's involved." (And then, belatedly, keeping a tight rein. Just because some of it was said, he had wanted to say it all. He had wanted to say "It'll break her heart if you don't do this. And I won't have her heart broken.")

When Daniel answered, he might have been speaking

to himself. "Of course I've realized which choice you and Jenny wanted me to make."

The last lie: "No, chum. . Do get that straight. None of us wants anything except what you want. All it amounts to is that Carus makes one suggestion, we make another. I simply thought you should be clear about the financial position. I don't have to remind you we've all talked it over time and again. And always in a friendly spirit. There's no fight. Look, Dan—has there ever been a fight?"

Dan's face looking at him cloudily; frightening him for a moment because it was a stranger's face. As though he were talking to some perplexed, shadowy boy whom he had never met before. Then the moment passing. The glow and the grin coming back, Dan saying heartily, "No. Rather not. We just don't go in for fights in our family, do we?", and starting up the car again. "Okay, Bryan. I'll bear that in mind. Thanks for telling me. And of course I won't say a word to Jenny."

"And what do *you* say to Jenny? What do you tell her? How d'you explain that 'hint he threw out', eh?" Bryan nagged at himself. She would be waiting for it, any minute now. . He heard her voice crying the nightly slogan, "Coffee in the *laounge*, everybody!", the responsive peal of laughter and the racket of the chairs pushed back.

He would think of something. . He didn't know what. All he knew was, and this quite certainly, quite defiantly, that—given the chance—he would do the same thing again.

"For Jenny's sake. And that means my own sake, I suppose. It's I who can't bear her to be hurt. Oh, she's right when she says we do nothing in life that isn't for ourselves. She's always right." As he went to find her, he was thinking,

"If I were Carus I'd have called her by now—no matter how brave she'd been about telling me not to. . . Selfish bastard; he always was."

vi

Just for a moment, when he had finished talking to Jennifer from Shannon, Carus let himself be lulled. Hers was a possible explanation after all. Wasn't it? Yes; Dan could have telephoned instead of coming to the airport; he could have wandered off somewhere. He could be late.

Lighting another cigarette (How many today? Two packs gone and a third coming up. .) he was tempted to accept. They must find him rooms at the best hotel (which was it, he wondered, after all these years?) and he would leave word for the boy. He sat slumped in the stripy chair, letting his tiredness take over. A more amiable tiredness now; the Drynomil had begun to work.

There came a gentle knock on the door; a new face wearing even more than the usual deference.

"Mr. Carus Black. . I'm extremely sorry, sir, but there *has* been a muddle after all. This message came through for you this morning and I'm afraid the girl who took it down—she's new on the job—made a mistake; it's been held for a Mr. Black who's booked on the outgoing flight. He just handed it in. *Most* inefficient of us; I can only apologise on behalf of the line. ." Carus heard him burbling on: "She's gone off duty, of course, or. . . rocket in the morning, Mr. Black." He wasn't listening. He was hearing his own confident voice declare that people couldn't be inefficient while he was about. He scored an unwilling point to Jennifer.

1 5 9

Then he said placidly, "All right; these things happen" and opened the envelope.

He had to read the words on the flimsy sheet twice through, to make sure that he believed them.

MESSAGE FROM:- MR. BLACK'S SECRETARY,
                       AT HIS LONDON OFFICE.

TIME: 11.50 A.M.

Mr. Black's secretary has just received a telephone-call from Drumnair, County Limerick. Please contact Drumnair Manor on arrival; number Drumnair 12. Important message about your son.

Friday Night May 29th

CHAPTER ONE

Geraldine saw the rain begin. For a few miles she had watched it coming, the black clouds shouldering up across the western sky until the last pale streak was hidden. A grey, premature twilight. Then the spatter of drops on the wind-screen. The wipers moved forward and back, making their little moan as they cut their clear half-circles on the glass.

If she could believe the genteel-voiced London secretary, Carus Black had arrived at Shannon by now. And this, at least, explained why Daniel was in the district. One single geographical clue. But it was for Carus to tell why, in this mad malevolence, he had sent his son to Drumnair, to dig dead bones.

She drove more slowly. She was tired. But good, she thought, to be quiet, to be alone, even for a little while. This was true silence, unlike the long tension of the drive down to Castleisland, with Antonia's dark sorrowful profile at her left and Francis in the back seat, studying his notes. All the way she had felt that she was daring either of them to say a word. That precarious silence had been broken at last by Francis, saying "I seem to remember preaching a better sermon than this when I was twenty-three. Although on that occasion, of course, I *did* refer to the Pharisee and the Republican; with a certain amount of topical excuse . . But I hope you won't wait for this one, Geraldine."

"Of course I shall. I intend to stay for Benediction."

"What about your message? Your London message?"

"Ah." She had hoarded her secret complacently. "It won't be coming through before seven at the earliest."

And then the surprisingly quiet shaft, let fly by Francis: "Would you be interested to know that Daniel's a Catholic?"

She hadn't answered; it couldn't be true; she had pretended not to hear.

And she wouldn't think of it now. She couldn't. Other words were keeping her company. "Words," Carus had told her a long time ago "are the only things that can really hurt."

Antonia's words of the morning: "You like it to be a martyrdom and a misery. . You don't want 'the torrent of pleasure, the richness of the House of God.'" Thanks to her own outward armour, she thought, Antonia would never know how deep that wound went. This sword had stabbed before. The message was an old one. Now all the lights were out for her. If the words were true, then this was also true, that within her tired body there lived just the same failing fool who had always lived there.

She tried to push away that horror. She tried to set against the words some other words of today, some other images. She thought of the white nuns kneeling in the convent chapel; she saw the dark veils on the Retreatants' heads, —Antonia's head bowed somewhere among those. She saw the gold monstrance raised up. For a few minutes, after Benediction, surely, she had known peace? But then, as she stood on the steps saying goodbye to Reverend Mother, Francis had come from the chapel. His last words were "Be gentle with the boy. Be gentle with Carus, if you talk to him. But most of all, and it isn't the first time I've said this to you, be gentle with yourself."

As though one could be.

Idly, gratefully, she took in the picture of a tinker's van beside the road. It looked like a huddled beehive; the rain was putting out the smoky fire. She saw wet, half-naked children scrambling on the steps of the van; a dark boy with a tarpaulin pulled over his head, raking the red ashes; a thin brown dog running in the shadows. It was the encampment of the homeless. And she envied it. The home that waited for her held no consolation.

Three miles more. She must fight her way out of this sadness and be ready.

Daniel Black presented no problem. If he dared to mention Antonia, she need only tell him that he would never see Antonia again. (Insane, that speech of his. Comforting, —wasn't it?—to think that the son of Carus was a little crazy.) She had only one question to ask him; she knew just how to phrase it. This would disprove what Francis had told her. It must. Somehow he had managed to fool the Monsignor. She didn't know how, but she knew this boy. The child of divorce; the heir to rich worldly rubbish; the same sort of playboy as his father, beyond a doubt. How could he belong to the Church? Easy to call his bluff. (Though difficult to see the reason for the bluff; another crazy symptom?) And, after that, her business was with Carus.

It felt neither new nor strange, to have business with him. Had he not, by a chain of devil's mischances, kept in sight? Why? Why, when his name reached the newspapers, did she always find it? It wasn't, even now, a name of enough importance to appear in headlines. But it had hounded her for years; standing out from a gossip-column; bobbing up under 'Marriages'; sudden in a brief record from the divorce-courts; part of a caption that identified some grinning tycoons at Heath Row. Then there was the line on the City page,—a page at which she seldom looked:—"B.C.M. Appoints New Chairman." The doom of the name went on, though it had long ceased to hurt her. Perhaps one pain had immunized her forever against the rest. The morning in May 1940, when she was waiting for the worst of the war-news. Luke's London papers delivered to her door by mistake. And her eyes finding the notice;

To Carus and Jennifer Black. A son (Daniel Carus.)
Daniel: the name they had chosen together . . .

After that, it seemed to her, she had shut all the inner doors upon him; the process by which she had exorcized Tom's ghost and tried hard to exorcize Godfrey's. There had been the smallest flicker of interest when the divorce came; no sort of emotion in realizing presently that he must have remarried. (And no reason whatever to remember that the woman's name was Irna, except that this Irna had a way of haunting the cheap Press with some foolishness or other.)

She looked at her watch; half-past seven; and the delayed plane due at six-thirty. Would he, perhaps, be waiting for her at the Manor? So much the better, she said to herself. She had all the weapons on her side. And she had been, always, the stronger of the two.

But was she still? After thirty years?

She swallowed; her mouth felt dry. She was astonished to find herself back at a phrase out of her own youth. The eighteen-year-old Geraldine, little older than Antonia was now,—the girl still outside the Church, having nothing but herself, had talked of "one's reserve-tank." Meaning,—as far as this Geraldine could see from here, the foundation of

1 6 6

human courage, unhelped by Grace. The core of the human spirit, stripped, alone and brave.

It was there, the reserve-tank. She could think it a silly expression, but she was aware of the thing expressed. God might hide His face from her; but this was left; her own courage. She drove on.

The road curved and she saw the village street drowning in the rain, the Corpus Christi pennons soaked and limp, poor rags deprived of yesterday. She braked the car at the Southern gate of the demesne, stepped out into the downpour and swung the gates open. Now she drove up under the trees to the gaunt gray-brown silhouette of the Manor. No car waiting on the terrace. Well, if he had come by car, he could have sent it away again, back to Limerick. He could, most easily, be here.

She went up the steps, in under the dripping portico. In the hall, the aqueous gloom depressed her and she switched on the light. No, she thought, he isn't here. She began to fuss at the pinks, still dissatisfied with the jammed, spiky look of them in the bowl; as she had been dissatisfied this morning. She had a talent for arranging flowers, but you wouldn't, she thought, know it by looking at the pinks. They still showed the traces of her temper when she put them in; that was a few minutes after she had met Daniel in the Friary.

As though she had conjured him, the boy came quietly on to the landing and down the stairs. She saw that he had changed his clothes. He was wearing his own sweater and the corduroy shorts of yesterday.

"Good evening," he said. "I thought I heard your car." He smiled at her. The smile made the likeness too absurdly faithful. How dare he be so exact a copy of Carus?

167

"Good evening," said Geraldine coldly, "Any message?"

"No. I think the telephone's gone funny. It made a sort of chirrup once; I was in the drawing-room. When I went to answer I just got a lot of buzzing."

"What time was that?" she snapped.

"Oh, quite early this afternoon. Just after I left Luke." His manner had changed; he was no longer gay and confident. "Geraldine, could you go and see Luke?"

"Why should I. . and you're a little free with our Christian names, aren't you?"

"I beg your pardon. 'Point is,—he's awfully unhappy; and it's my fault, in a way. He didn't want me around. But I think he'd like to talk to somebody. You see—" here he hesitated, shadowy-eyed.

"My dear child, if you knew my father-in-law better, you'd realize that there's nothing he enjoys more than his own miseries."

"I don't think he's enjoying this one. He wants to die, he says."

"That's nothing new. And take it from me,—he dislikes me intensely; I'm the last person to comfort him. "But," she said, "I've a question to ask you."

"About Antonia?"

"Nothing to do with Antonia."

Certainly he was easy prey now. He looked frightened.

"About London then?" he asked; she could see that he braced himself for the answer. By "London" she supposed that he meant her telephone-call.

"Nothing to do with that. It's quite a simple question. About you, yourself. ."

The dark, defensive stare could not disguise his fear of this. He said in a low voice "What do you want to know?"

"Are you cradle—or convert?"

For an instant he looked relieved; then he shook his head, bewilderedly: "I don't understand."

"You don't know what it means?"

"No."

"I thought not. . How did you manage to fool the Monsignor?"

"*Fool* him. . . I didn't fool him." He stopped suddenly. "If you mean there's something I didn't tell him,—fair enough. I haven't told anybody." Increasing in truculence, he was like his father. "Couldn't you talk to me straight, Mrs. Courtney? Tell me what you're driving at?"

"Daniel, I'm wet and I'm tired, and I'm going to change before supper. Susanna will bring you yours in the spare room. Did she show you where it was?"

"I know where it is. If it's the room with the four-poster, the room that looks on the river."

"Been exploring, have you?"

He wore his insolent face again. He said, "You know, you're quite impossible."

She pointed over his shoulder. "Up you go. And don't dream of coming down till I send for you."

"After you, please," said Daniel Black. The sound of his footsteps was maddening. She did not look behind her until she had passed the spare-room door and heard him open it.

"Mrs. Courtney—"

"Yes?" He was standing halfway in, halfway out of the door.

"Are they. . is anybody. . coming for me?"

"You'll see," she said; and now his whole appearance was so deject, so lost, that her heart, in spite of her, turned compassionate. She had seen Godfrey look like this, in older days.

"What is the matter, Daniel?" she asked him gently.

He raised his head. He gave her his father's crooked smile: "Oh, I couldn't tell *you*. . Not now."

The words slapped her in the face. But she had, she thought, deserved them.

"Are you sure you couldn't?"

"Quite sure."

He looked even younger, wearing his own clothes. This thought came to her in a moment of detached observation before he went in and shut the door. After he had vanished, the thought was still there.

So young. How could anybody be so young? Here she was again, even at this precarious minute, transfixed by the simple, physical signs of youth, as though they were phenomena. It was a routine, this. She could not remember exactly when the routine had begun. Obsession. An obsessive preoccupation with smooth skins, with the clean, bluish whites of eyes; eyes that could read without spectacles. It was a disbelieving, catalogue mood that listed, willy-nilly, heads of young, shining, healthy hair; young white teeth; straight legs that showed no varicose veins; the backs of young hands, unwrinkled, unblotched.

The absurd envious spying went on; from day to day. She couldn't, now, look at anyone of Daniel's age without seeing the place where,—more than Paradise—she longed to be. Within that physical envelope, there lived a king; a person so damnably lucky that she was shaken by exasperation because he didn't know it; never would know it until he had lost his kingdom.

"Enough—d'you hear?" she said to herself, angrily and

aloud. She went on, into her own room. The gray twilight of the rain was here too. She drew all the curtains against it; she switched on every lamp. Her nerves were jumping. She felt chilled, afraid. Was that a car coming now? Difficult to hear, from this side. It sounded like a car going round the front of the house, to the old wing. Yes. Some visitor for Luke.

She untied her head; she hung up the linen suit that she had worn all day; she put on her dressing gown and slippers. Standing in front of the wardrobe, she despised her own deliberation. She twitched out a dress that she saw as an admission of weakness, a soft, blue-green dress that matched her eyes. Flinging it contemptuously on the bed, she went to sit down at the looking-glass. Around the looking-glass, framing the centre panel and the two wings, there ran a hard, glaring tubular light. She pressed the switch; the white blaze sprang.

Thirty years. From Carus to now. That was the notion, wasn't it? To study what had happened in the time between? She wouldn't play one trick with the glass. She wouldn't narrow her eyes, nor prop her chin with hands gracefully linked, to hide her neck. She would take the reflection straight.

It was there. Geraldine at fifty-seven. The head was still shapely, the hair cut short, with a permanent wave. In this light the red, metallic glints from the dye were purple; the hair was a hard, cruel helmet. And the face. . ("Face of a very beautiful lizard, Carus said, didn't he? H'mm. . The lizard look I can still see.")

But what of beauty? She saw the wire-thin furrows all across the forehead, the heavy creases from nose to mouth, the jaw line losing itself in the droop of flesh below; then the throat, papery-skinned, corded, unbearable. Only the eyes and the pretty nose saved the reflection from a harsh, peevish ugliness. She studied the little mouth, with its downward curve, the little pointed chin with the sharp, half-moon wrinkle at the place where it began to jut forward.

She hadn't finished yet. Adjusting the two side wings of the glass, she made herself a present of her profile. The sag of the flesh below the chin made her look less like a lizard than like a chicken.

Now she permitted herself the game; played with fingers and thumbs, pulling all the slack skin tightly upward; the wishful face-lift. But it wasn't a young face, even then; it was a mask that stretched between the pressing finger-tips.

Doggedly she went to work, with cream, tissues and lotion. She ran a finger along her upper lip. Then, putting on her strongest spectacles, she took the tweezers and the magnifying-mirror; the only way to be sure of pulling out all the hairs. This evening she remembered the two single whiskers sprouting under the jawbone. Sometimes she missed those. She made the finger-test again. Not a hair left. It was time to work in the foundation-cream, to build up the painstaking disguise. Often she wondered why she bothered. She saw the faces of the older nuns today; faces that never looked in a glass . . withered-apple faces, shiny noses, hairy chins.

"More sense, after all," said Geraldine.

But when the work was done, when she had spread the blue stuff on her eyelids and reddened her mouth, she was encouraged. She played the tricks again. Turning off the tubular light, she darted her head, narrowed her eyes, rested her chin on her hands. By the time that she had put on the chiffon dress, arranging the scarf-collar to hide the poor neck, the truth was beginning to fade.

Deep in absorption, she gave a shudder and a start when somebody rapped on the door. She shot up from the dressing-table, crying ridiculously, "Who wants me?"

Susanna appeared; Susanna saying that it was after eight o'clock and should she lay a place for the young gentleman? "Is he not well, then, poor soul?" was her reaction to the supper-tray. Reassured, she stayed to talk; admiring Geraldine's dress; wanting to hear about the convent, asking for news of Sister Theresa, who was a relation. Geraldine cut mercilessly through the prattle: "Please go down, Susanna—just till I'm ready—and listen for the telephone. I'm expecting an important call."

As soon as she spoke, she realized that she had ceased to believe this promise, or threat, of Carus. Today looked suddenly like a long bad dream. In weariness, she went to the full-length glass, for the final scrutiny.

At least (posing with hands on hips) she was still straight-backed and slender. The blue-green dress hung well. Hers was, she reminded herself a little grimly, the same boyish thinness that had been fashionable in the 'Twenties. She had (in the menacing phrase) kept her figure.

And now she was sick of all this. "I've painted my face and dressed myself up—for what? For an evening alone, with Pippin's mad child upstairs. But *certainly* he's mad" she flung at somebody, possibly Francis, who had dared to contradict her in her mind.

("Be gentle.")

One moment later, she heard the sound of the bell. Not the telephone, but the front-door bell, ringing loud and long. As she reached the stairhead, she was calling down to

Susanna—"I'll go—I know who it is," and she was halfway across the hall before she thought "But how ridiculous. . why should I want to let him in?" She laughed. She opened the door.

CHAPTER TWO

It wasn't as easy to die as Luke had hoped. What he wanted, more than anything, was to be found dead, in an elegant position, of course, and decently dressed, on the sofa in the French room. With the ruins of the book still scattered on the floor. The wanton indifference of all those in the other wing (he multiplied them automatically, made a stony-hearted mob of Geraldine, Susanna and the Pippin-boy) would be disturbed by the sound of Dana howling. They would come. They would break down the door; he must remember to lock it. And they would be very sorry; and spend the rest of their days in remorse because they had all been so beastly to him. His preparations for death were complete by five-fifteen. He made his Act of Contrition, lay down on the sofa and waited for his broken heart to stop beating.

What happened was that he went to sleep. He awoke to find darkness in the room; he had, of course, drawn the curtains. He heard the noise of the rain outside. The first thing that struck his full consciousness was a pang of fierce hunger. He remembered refusing his lunch. And this reminded him that the Horse-Borne Widow (Antonia's name for Kitty Fitzhugh still stuck, despite all chivalrous attempts to forget it) was coming to dinner.

He sat up and turned on the standard lamp at the head of the sofa. He looked at his watch. No wonder he was hungry. He climbed off the sofa, being careful not to look at the wreckage in the middle of the room. Somebody was knocking. "Come in, come in," he called peevishly. At the third knock he yelled "I said come in, fool!"

Through his deafness, a plaintive bawling informed His Honour that somebody would seem to have been locking the door. "I can't imagine *who*—" Luke grumbled, taking refuge in the sort of lie that he used to tell as a child. He unlocked the door. Here was Michael, looking as usual like a boiled baby. He was doing duty as butler for the second night in succession; he was in fact a waiter, a regular off-season import from the Nellon Inn.

Obviously, Michael had been affected by yesterday's Americans. He carried in an over-generous tray of bottles. He followed it up with a large bucket of ice. Then he brought two plates of elaborate hors d'oeuvres, a little lop-sided and squashy from their ride. "We had these made up for you at the Inn, Mr. Luke. I was thinking—"

—"I know what you were thinking. That if a two-hour session of drinks again preceded dinner I should be starving. I'm most grateful. I happen to be starving now." He snatched one plate from Michael and sat down again, balancing it on his knees. "But we shan't need all that—" he said, with his mouth full, looking at the bottles: "Sale or return, I trust. . The Horse-Borne. . ah, Mrs. Fitzhugh—takes sherry. What's the matter now?" Michael had, belatedly, become aware of the miserable exhibition on the floor.

"Don't touch it, please. And above all, don't talk about it. It stays there,—understand? And if the—, if Mrs. Fitzhugh arrives while I'm washing my hands—" (he was torn between the needs of his appetite and his bladder) "please ask *her* not to touch it. Thank you."

Gazing at himself in the glass above the wash-basin, he

thought that he looked handsomer than ever. He had acquired a tragic, Henry Irving, expression. And why not? He hovered before the glass. The long sleep had resulted in some creases on his velvet jacket. He had chosen the plum-coloured one, to die in. The black, though more suitable, was less becoming. He pulled at the jacket. He straightened his flowing tie. Hurrying back to the hors d'oeuvres, he found Kitty in the hall. Dead punctual as ever, not a national characteristic. Elegant as ever in a short black dress, not the national wear. She had put on her cultured pearls, a good string. She had put on a little rouge; it helped her skin. Very fine bones. A fine-looking woman; if only she were a little fatter. Why, when he groaned to God that nobody cared whether he lived or died, did he always forget Kitty?

"I'm afraid," he said as he took her hand, "that you are to be the first witness of my life's tragedy. Please prepare yourself for a shock." With a faultless gesture, he flung open the door of the French room. "On the floor," he snapped, since she was obstinately searching the room at eye-level. Lacking, sometimes, Kitty.

"Lord save us! What's all that?"

"That *is*—nothing. If you asked me what it *was*, I could tell you."

"What was it?" she asked obligingly.

"It was the Book of Drumnair."

After a long moment, wherein she stooped over the mess, she said "So you were right after all." This surprised him so much that he shouted "*Right?*" and skidded on a rug. Her hand caught his elbow, steadying him. "I mean," said Kitty Fitzhugh, "that you were the only person who ever believed it would be found."

Luke received this comment suspiciously. It wasn't what he had expected. Was it comforting? Did he want it to be comforting? As he decided that it was temporarily indigestible, Kitty said "But *where*? How?"

"If I may pour you a glass of sherry," said Luke, in his grieved-ghost voice, "I should like to tell you the whole sorry tale."

"But of course. I long to know."

"Thank you, dear Kitty." Reaching the sideboard, he began to rehearse his opening sentence. How about "This is the work of devils"? Not bad. Here he was deflected by some happy squeaking and crunching,—by the swish of Dana's tail against his leg. The fool Michael had transferred both plates of hors d'oeuvres to the low coffee-table and the dog was eating them. It had cleared one plate completely. By the time that Luke had rescued the second plate, smacked the dog and brought the sherry, he had lost his opening sentence.

"Now. . where shall I begin?" he asked wistfully, and then the front door bell rang.

He started screaming. "Michael! Michael! Tell whoever that is to go away! Do you hear me? Of course he can't hear me,—he's in the kitchen."

"Still, he can hear the bell," said Kitty, "You're not expecting someone else?"

"Of course not. I couldn't bear to see anybody tonight. Only you—" he added, remembering his manners.

She put her hand on his arm: "Just stay where you are, then. I'll tell Michael." The bell was pealing again as she went out. He waited, drinking his sherry. Presently the small warmth in his oesophagus began to console him,—even for the prolonged voices in the hall. Strange. . . They seemed to indicate that Kitty herself had admitted the anonymous poltroon. They were still talking, the voices. His insatiable curiosity reared up. He was on his way to the door when it opened. "I'm sorry, Luke," Kitty said "but this seems to be urgent."

A man followed her in; a man of middle height; something truculent, Napoleonic, about him. Luke saw grey hair with a curl to it,—a pale, frowning forehead, saw this in a flat blink of detachment before the man smiled at him. The light eyes and the crooked smile sent the moment flying.

"Pippin—" Luke said.

The smile widened. "Haven't heard *that* name in a long time," said Carus Black. As he grasped Luke's hand, Luke was shocked to see him grown so old. Well, not old, perhaps; but horribly middle-aged; stocky and prosperous-looking. Rather disconcerting, this.

"My *dear* Pippin—" He wanted not to seem disconcerted, "It's a pleasure, it really is. Have you come for your boy?" And that reminded him; he couldn't help glancing down at the sad shambles on the newspaper. Pippin Black didn't follow the glance. He stood with shoulders hunched, saying "Was it you who sent the message?" (Why had he developed this thrusting manner, this hoarse voice with the near-American accent? Kitty's voice made a pleasing contrast.)

"Mr. Black found a message waiting for him at the airport; a message from here."

"'Been trying to call you. 'Tried again from the Nellon," Carus croaked—"Your line's on the blink."

"On the *what*, Pippin?"

"Out of order."

"That" said Luke, "is the only merciful dispensation on the part of the instrument, wouldn't you say—?"

—"Where's my son?"

The poor fellow sounded hoarser than ever; and he looked desperately tired. He croaked again "Where's my son? Tell me. Is he all right?"

"Very much all right. Oh, very much indeed. In radiant health and spirits. The boy couldn't be better. Apart from wrecking my life's hope and setting this whole dilapidated endroit by the ears—what's the matter, Pippin?" He saw sweat come out on the pale forehead. He saw Carus hunch lower, like a bull about to charge. He didn't charge. He swore. Not a word that Luke would have used before a lady. Then he laughed. "I apologise, Mrs. Fitzhugh. Sorry, Luke." He wiped his face. "I'm tired," he said "and not one thing that goes on makes the smallest sense. Where's Daniel?"

"Over with her, I imagine."

"Her?"

"Geraldine."

Carus said "Why?"

"A pertinent question; she'll have an answer, no doubt. It was she who sent the message, come to think of it. Haven't you seen her yet, Pippin? Why not? Frightened?"

"Luke dear. . Wouldn't it be kind to offer Mr. Black a drink? He's been flying the Atlantic since the day before yesterday."

"Heaven! I thought they did it in five hours now. My poor Pippin. . What will you take? We have everything here." He moved to the sideboard, making ample gestures.

The visitor said "No, thanks. I'm only here to find Daniel." Then he said "What have you done to this room? Different. ."

"Entirely; since your time. My loot from Paris." Pippin nodded absently: "I'll be off next door, Luke. All apologies." A grin brought back the boy from the past. "And you're right, of course. I was scared of tackling Geraldine. Even—" his tired voice trailed suddenly; the hand held out for the farewell dropped to his side. He had come to the edge of the newspaper-carpet. He stopped there, looking down, seeming to grow smaller.

"Luke wants all that left untouched, please, Mr. Black. It's something very important."

Silence. Luke, turning back from the sideboard, became aware of a change in the temperature. What was happening? Pippin, paying no attention to Kitty's words, went down on one knee and picked up the mouldy metal box; he knelt, turning it over in his hands. His head sunk lower between his shoulders until he seemed to have no neck at all.

"You found it," he said in his hoarse scrape of a voice. He lifted his head, staring at Luke accusingly. "Where's the lid?"

"The lid. ."

"It had a lid."

Luke said vaguely "Oh. . . yes. . . There. We prised it off." Before he could say another word, Pippin's rage roared on him. "What the hell were you up to? Breaking down the wall? You'd have to break down the wall."

"Precisely" said Luke, "Your son did just that. But how do *you* know?"

"About this?" Carus asked as he set down the box. "Why wouldn't I? I put it there."

It seemed to Luke that the room paled and receded; that everything in the room was now two-dimensional, cardboard-thin. "Perhaps I really am dying," he thought:

"Serve them right, all of them." He felt his head begin to shake up and down.

"Well, well," he heard himself saying, flatly, without inspiration. "So you put it there. That was a nice thing to do."

"It was meant to be." The hoarse voice was a whisper. Pippin was down on all fours now. He put out a hand to pull the broken lid towards him; he fitted it carefully on to the box. Then he picked up the satchel. Wavering on his feet, Luke saw him copy with every movement his own movements of the afternoon. He examined the satchel's broken corner; then he turned his attention to the poor scraps. All the time Kitty was moaning—"You're not to touch. . *please.*"

"Let him," said Luke.

Pippin looked up, wearing his slanted smile: "I swear it's no worse; any of it. Except for the break in the satchel-flap. That's new."

"I·did that."

"Well, there's no other change. This is what I found; it's exactly as it was. Preserved. Good solid box, of course. Paid a quid for it in Limerick." He scrambled to his feet. His eyes were pleading. "Luke, you'd have hated it then, too. You know you would. That's why I put it back,—bricked it up again."

"When?"

"1929. Same old year—" said Pippin,—"'Year everything happened. I was climbing around the Friary,—kicked some stones off the refectory wall—found a hole—and the poor, chewed-up old satchel at the bottom. Once I'd gotten it out I knew what it must be."

"And didn't tell me."

"You see why not," said Carus, "don't you?"

182

Luke sat down; he felt Kitty's hand on his shoulder; but he could only look at Pippin, middle-aged and pleading: "I couldn't bear to leave it. . Thought it would crumble right away. . Got the box. . 'Took a hell of a time, all of it. I used to work in the dark, with a flashlight. If any of you had happened to take a night-walk to the Friary, I'd have been sunk."

"Luke, dear. ."

"Hush. Kindly hush. This is between us." He puzzled his way through his whirling wits,—back to this morning. "Pippin—did Francis know too?"

"Oh, sure. I told him in the Confessional. He" said Pippin gloomily "approved."

"He would. . Yes. . I see. You thought it'd break my heart, eh? Protecting me, eh?" But this was somehow false, and it took him another minute to remember why. Pippin was saying "I thought you need never know."

"Ha!" Luke had got it. He pointed a quivering forefinger. "Then why did you tell Daniel?"

CHAPTER THREE

In the half-light, Geraldine found him hard to see. He had stepped back as she opened the door. Behind him there was the grey, lashing garden; before him the lamplit rain made a nimbus of thin, bright wires. Then the misted figure came forward, moving slowly and heavily. She thought "But you are old, too. And that's a thing I hadn't imagined."

"Hullo, Geraldine," said Carus. He added, "I believe you're expecting me."

("Not this you. And not this truculence, either, damn you.") She said "Yes, indeed," looking at his hair, at the pouches under his tired, slitty eyes. Oh, a very tired, very cross little man. And not looking his best in the wrinkled grey suit whose jacket was splashed with the rain.

"What goes on?" he snapped.

"That's what you're here to tell me," she snapped back. It made him laugh; a short snarl of a laugh. "Oh bloody funny," said Carus, "Let's keep at it, shall we?" He straightened his tie. "I apologise for my appearance," he drawled in a peculiar, imitation-Oxford voice: "Tough sledding, this journey. Where's the boy?"

"Upstairs, having his supper."

"Right. Which room?"

She barred his way. "Oh, no. *Oh*, no."

"What the hell d'you mean oh no?"

"You'll see your little boy just when I please, and not before."

She thought he was going to slap her face. She rather hoped he would. "If you're worried about Daniel," she said in a honey-sweet voice, "You needn't be. He's perfectly all right. Seriously, Carus; that's the truth."

"So what? If he's all right then I'm damned angry with him."

"'Curious coincidence,—so am I. And my God, I've got a score to settle with *you* So let's get it over."

Silence She held her ground. "Don't stand there making that little gangster face at me. It's not impressive. We've got to talk now, d'you see? You look very tired. I'll give you a drink."

"No, thanks. I don't do that."

"Come, come," said Geraldine.

"Haven't had a drink for months."

"Well, you're going to need one. I put the whisky out. And that's unusual in this house, as you may remember."

"I remember." His shoulders sagged; she could feel, thankfully, that she was still stronger than he.

"Why did you send me that message?"

"That's what we're going to talk about, fool" Though he was still standing fast in his humped rage, she knew that the first short struggle was over; that he would follow her into the drawing room.

"There's the whisky."

"I could use it" said Carus, "God knows."

"Well, help yourself. I'm accused of mean measures. And I'd better tell Susanna to keep the dinner back. Had any?"

"Any what? Dinner—Good grief, woman, you don't get dinner on delayed flights. . just a series of breakfasts."

She had to look back, from the door, to make certain that he was pouring himself the drink. He was.

She returned to find him in the blue velvet chair, the odd-man-out chair with the fringed footstool, that he had chosen in time past. As he rose, he kicked the footstool aside with his old, impatient gesture and lifted his glass to her. It was empty.

"Score to you, Geraldine. Mind if I take another?" He added sombrely, as he filled the glass, "Let it come on. ."

"Why the Shakespearian pomposity?"

"Don't you see—I've kept off the stuff—for a year. . almost a year." He put a thimbleful of water into it. "Good whisky. Powers, eh?" He wandered back to his chair, but he didn't sit. He tilted the glass at his lips. "Fine," said Carus.

It began, she thought, to be a different person standing there. She saw his strength coming back and his swagger. She sat still, not saying a word. Aware that she was watching her horror, her devil of devils, she still found that the effect of the brown, liquid magic fascinated her. It was like seeing the result of a quick blood-transfusion. He went at it with deliberation, too; filling up the glass a third time; then taking a pill with water before he drank again.

"Aspirin?" she asked.

"Lord, no. Drynomil."

"Never heard of it."

"My innocent friend," said Carus. "Today's life-saver. First time I ever tried it with liquor." He grinned at her. His eyes had widened; his voice was strong and lively when he repeated "Score to you. The omnipotent, implacable Geraldine. Unchanged and unchanging. Now then." He sat once more in the blue chair. As she expected, he first kicked the stool away, then drew it back with his feet. "Now then.

let's have it." He hunched forward; alight with the drink; alight and dangerous.

"Come on. Give. What's Dan been doing, aside from digging up the Book of Drumnair?"

This shook her. Incredulous, she repeated "The Book of Drumnair. . ?"

"Didn't you know? Well, it's not so much the book as the rat-eaten remains. The worthless mess I took such trouble to hide in a box. . In the Friary, years ago."

She remembered the box under Daniel's arm, Luke babbling of the treasure.

"My nice box," said Carus, "Skip it. All over now. 'No good deed that goes unpunished, is there? Poor old Luke. .'" Then he laughed. "Said I was scared of you. That's what Luke said."

She was still at the thought of the book. "It *was* really there. . . and you hid it. Why, Pippin?"

"I was sorry for it. And we can talk about the poor bloody book any time. Get on."

"I don't care for the tycoon manner."

He said "Nor do I. But you're buying it, aren't you. . ? I swear I'm going crazy."

"Like your son."

"Eh?" said Carus.

"I know all this is your fault. . provoked by you. But the boy's touched in the head. He must be. Even though you sent him here—"

"I didn't."

"What's the point of lying, Pippin? . . All right, all right. You didn't *send* him. Merely briefed him with the story—comes to the same thing. But there's more to it than that.

Whatever sort of monstrous, beastly little joke you two cooked up between you—"

—"Keep going, keep going." He drained his glass.

"It's hard to see where you stop and where Daniel begins. 'Couldn't have been *you* who told him to lie about his religion. Or was it?"

"Religion? He hasn't got a religion. His mother's seen to that."

"Score two to me" said Geraldine.

"Meaning?"

"Well, what about you? Don't tell me you ever came back to the Church?"

"You're damn' right. I never did. What's that got to do with anything—where does it tie with Daniel?"

"It simply proves he's crazy. As I said." The effect of his voice growing louder, rougher, made her speak the more quietly. "Do you know Antonia? Of course you don't. You couldn't. She's my adopted daughter. Seventeen. Your son has the impertinence to tell me he means to marry her. They've known each other since yesterday evening." Carus sat completely still, glowering at her. "Now you're getting my point, aren't you? Now you may be cured of playing obscene, ill-bred joker's tricks in your middle-age. Wait. I haven't finished. I'd like you to tell me just why you had to do it in the first place and after that—don't interrupt —you can take your nasty crazy little boy out of here. And your nasty crazy little self, too."

He jumped to his feet. Though his face kept a hint of calm in its fury, he frightened her. He raised his hands and crooked his fingers as though he were going to take her by the throat. The hands stayed like that.

"Listen, you silly bitch—" said Carus, "I'm only telling

188

you what I told Luke. That I've never said one word to Daniel about this place or anything that happened here. And now I'm going up to him. You stay right where you are." Before he slammed the door, he turned, using the drawl again. "You know, Geraldine, it's very remarkable to me that somebody hasn't knocked you cold long ago."

She heard his footsteps crossing the hall. She heard the creak of the stairs. She waited.

ii

As Carus went up the stairs, he felt enormous; huge in satisfaction, ready for anything. He was no longer tired at all. He was on home ground. The feel of the banister-rail fitted his hand; the creak of the steps was familiar under his feet; he gave a nod to the stained-glass window, curtain-less and horrible, before he turned to his right and found the door. Outside it there was a tray set down. The empty plates were neatly stacked. Daniel had eaten his supper. Why had he put the tray there?

Carus knocked, a brisk perfunctory knock before he walked in. The curtains were drawn back from the windows, letting in the long grey twilight. There was nobody here.

Oh, but there was, though, he thought, looking about him. There was a ghost here. Yes, and yes, and yes. Nothing had changed. The four-poster had the same coverlet; those were the same curtains; and the same pretty old vase, with yellow lupins in it. His room. Here had slept the fellow who would always be the partner of Persephone. The fellow who stayed awake with God and the moon; who had knelt once by this bed, saying "With hope and delight, with ease and affection, and with perseverance unto the end." And here also (though he seemed even more far and faint) there was the same young man lying wakeful, committed and trapped, not praying at all, telling himself only, "I can't. . I must get out. It's tomorrow, and I can't go through with tomorrow."

That one, he recalled, (loping across the floor, loping back across the years) had sat at the writing-desk half the night. He remembered the letters, every one of them unfinished, torn up, begun again; crumpled paper thrown on the floor.

The writing-desk had been moved. But there was, and this seemed quite in order, a letter lying on it; an envelope. He picked it up; it was addressed to 'Mrs. Courtney' and the present ran over the past with the sight of Daniel's handwriting. Squarely-formed letters, firm and strong, with a dash under the name. The flap of the envelope was tucked in. Carus didn't hesitate to open it.

> "Dear Mrs. Courtney,
> This is to say thank you for my supper, and to say I hope you don't mind if I wait in the carriage-house instead of up here. I can't explain why it's easier to be there, but it is."

He had signed it "D.B."

Carus folded the note, putting it back in its envelope. The carriage-house. . Godfrey's playroom across the stable-yard. Good lord, the carriage-house. "Don't half keep in my tracks, do you, Dan?"

Another door swung open in memory. (Had it ever really shut?) He saw the child's place. There were toy-animal curtains at the windows; scarlet rugs, shining boards and a round white stove. He saw the dappled rocking-horse; the Meccano set, the treasures in the games-cupboard. And a row of little china angels along the window-sill. In the middle of the angels, Godfrey had placed, proudly and incongruously, Pippin's latest present. Carus could see it now; a china model of the Eiffel Tower, with the words 'Souvenir de Paris' in gold lettering at the base.

The carriage-house. He could hear the echo of Geraldine's voice scoffing "Sheer infantilism," and Pippin's voice replying "Well, you see, I never *had* this; we were always on the move. It was hotel-suites, furnished flats; never any nursery."

The door in memory was open wide. Carus stood, looking through. The carriage-house. . Geraldine had no objection to his playing there with Godfrey. But she had flown into a fury on the evening she found him there by himself. This, after one of their fights. A Church fight, wasn't it? Certainly it was. All begun because he had invited two of his voyaging friends to meet his bride. And Geraldine, hearing that both had been divorced, refused to entertain them.

And then the argument. He could, he found, restore nearly all of it. Pippin talking, gaily sarcastic: "Wasn't there something about casting the first stone? Seems to me—"

—"Quite irrelevant. You haven't learned loyalty yet, have you?"

"Loyalty to my friends, darling?"

"Loyalty to the Church. Loyalty to the Sacraments. Do try to understand. If I condone—"

Here he had lost his temper: "Oh, hell's bloody teeth, is it your business to condone—*or* condemn? All right. . I'll give them lunch at the Nellon."

"Yes, you do that, Pippin; it really would be better."

191

"And kindly remember—" he had flung at her as he left "that divorce among us Blacks was an old family custom."

He had stayed out all the afternoon. Instead of returning to the Manor, he had sneaked into the carriage-house, long after Godfrey's bedtime. He could remember sitting there, wrapped in a juvenile sense of security. He had played with the solitaire-board; popping one brightly-coloured marble over another until Geraldine came.

"Oh, Pippin, I'm sorry. . I've been so miserable." As he rose to take her in his arms, she had asked "But why *here?*" He had answered. "Because it's the only really happy room" and seen her stricken face.

Carus blinked. The image of Daniel had receded, hadn't it? He found it difficult to focus on Daniel. He was Pippin, getting a sudden thirsty glimpse of the bright room over there. He was Pippin, running from Geraldine.

He put Daniel's note into his pocket. He went out, quietly shutting the door behind him; the drink and the drug made all easy. He slipped along the passage to the back stairs, and ran down as lightly as a cat, ran down as he had run before. Then he went close to the wall; the door into the kitchen stood half open; the light was on; he could hear Susanna bundling about. It was all the old games of long ago, rolled into one; his stealthy hand feeling along the passage-wall until it closed on the handle of the back door.

He was out, in the rain. The graceful shape of the carriage-house, glistened at him, spire and arch. Yellow through the greyness, he saw a light shine; the window of the happy room.

"All very improbable," thought Carus contentedly. The rain was falling more softly now; no more than a gentle mist on his face while he crossed the wet cobble-stones. He ducked under the arch and gave the right-hand door an automatic shove with his shoulder; the hinges had been a little stiff, always.

Then he was staring at a cluttered, dismally-abandoned room; a travesty of the place in his mind. All dust and dimness; the impression of hopeless, broken things crowding everywhere under bat-flapping shadows. On the table an oil-lamp flared. He saw his son.

Daniel was sitting in an armchair that tilted lop-sidedly; he had pulled it close to the table, to read. A book lay open under the oil-lamp. But now the boy had drawn back into the chair, so that the light fell short of his face.

"Hullo, there" Carus said.

"Hullo. . have you come for me?" The voice was quiet and faraway; voice of someone thinking too deeply to be disturbed. The shadow that hid the face was baffling and Carus came close. He put a hand on Daniel's shoulder. Daniel didn't say a word; but he lay back, looking up; his expression was quietly puzzled. Carus found that his own light-headedness had a lucid quality; a passion of acceptance; he was looking at Pippin, he thought, looking at his young ghost still haunting this room. He would let the ghost speak in its own time.

"I know who you are," the ghost said; the voice had become more troubled. "Wait. . Shannon. B.O.A.C. Flight One One Seven. I was coming to meet you. Yes. You're Carus; my father. You wanted me to meet you."

"What happened, chum?"

"I went for a walk, and forgot."

The excuse of a six-year-old. But he wasn't irritated; nor disbelieving. It didn't even make him laugh.

"A chap gave me a lift," said Daniel, "and we came to

193

Drumnair. And I knew it. It was like coming home. It was so easy; all of it. If it could *only* go on. But any minute now—" He had lowered his eyes; he bent his head. "Any minute now—" He began to shiver.

"What are you scared of?"

"My memory coming back. It's begun. It's on its way. 'Been on its way, ever since she said 'London.'" He shrugged free of the hand on his shoulder, he said "Oh damn it, oh damn it,—all the stuff that's moving in." He scrambled to his feet and dodged round the table. Gazing at Carus across the lamplight, he looked as though he were fighting his way out of an anaesthetic. His voice dropped to a droning whisper. "Now I don't know. . was it me? Was it you? Carus . . that's you. Pippin. . that's you. They called you Pippin."

"Yes."

"And the Friary. . and the Mass. Did you serve the Mass?"

"I used to,—a long time ago."

Hopelessly, the boy said "Drumnair's your place."

"It was, once."

"Then—don't you see—it can't be mine?" His face twisted. His head jerked back as if to a blow on the jaw. "But of course, it isn't mine. How the devil did I ever think it could be?"

iii

As the last of the cloud-curtain shredded away, dissolved, he felt as if his head had split in two. For while today and yesterday kept in sight, they made no sense. Stretching behind them there was the whole landscape that the curtain had hidden; a glaring backdrop that utterly distorted the scene; clamorous arrival of the world he knew and had always known.

He stood clutching the table, finding every detail on the backdrop. All was in place. Yes; this was the world from which he had run.

He could see himself running. He breathed again the wind of freedom blowing; that one short span of escape. He was standing on deck with Tim Russell as they came into Waterford Harbour. Exultant, thinking "I've got away. I need never go back." He saw the whole Irish journey, the random roads that led to treasure; Tara, Monasterboise and Kells. He saw Cashel of the Kings and the doorway of Cormac's chapel. He saw Tim, solid, orthodox Tim, on his knees by a wayside shrine and himself standing stupidly, praying to the air, "Don't let me go back." And the wind of freedom blowing ever less. The shadow creeping as they went westward; creeping on lake and mountainside, creeping up to the foot of the silent, holy ruins. Shadow of tomorrow walking to meet Daniel Black.

He remembered the morning at Limerick, yesterday morning, a lifetime ago. He had stood with Tim in O'Connell Street where the Corpus Christi pennons fluttered over their heads. They were waiting for Tim's bus. Tim was saying "What's the gloom about?" (Not the first time he had asked; but of course one couldn't tell him. Even if one could put it into words, Tim wouldn't get the panic behind the words. Tim was just a lucky fellow, with a faith and a family, and a girl-friend waiting for him in Tralee.) Then the bus driving off. Standing alone, dazed and stupid, realizing that he had kept Tim's map in his pocket; wondering if his wits were going. And then the walk to the Post Office, to stamp his postcard for Jennifer. Thinking as he went that only half a day remained to him; then it would be Shannon Airport and Flight One One Seven.

No escape. Ireland had looked like an escape and he had clutched at it, but it was no more than a run to the end of the tether that tripped him. The tether was stretched tight now; it held him fast. There waited only the same intolerable pattern that he had tolerated for so long. He had not said, even to himself, "I can't bear it." Only then, walking down the street in Limerick, had he seen with full, fascinated horror, how much he wanted none of it to be there.

Not only the choice; the bloody impossible choice that Bryan and Irna had thrust at him on his birthday. The choice had loomed for months. The two-way ultimatum had only clinched its urgency, shoved him nearer the brink. Bryan, triumphantly brandishing the fact of Jennifer's money, like a conjurer with a borrowed watch, was one kind of last straw. And Irna, in whom he had tried for such a long time to see a mother, a real mother, a proper, loving mother like the mothers of his friends at school, Irna had pressed close to him and kissed his mouth. And that was another kind of last straw; making him feel sick and silly. But both these things, he saw, as he walked slowly down Lower Cecil Street, had simply shown him the truth that had been there before. The truth was that he wanted it all to be gone, past, present and future.

Yes. The two partisan-groups, with their clacking, striving plans; their continued reassurances. The sense that they batted him to and fro between them like a ball. His guilty nag of responsibility to each. His obligation to be pleased and polite while they explained. (God, how they explained. The endless ache of their talking. "It makes sense, you see,

Dan." "You get the point, don't you, Dan?" "You'll like that, won't you, Dan?")

Had he ever liked any of it? He remembered asking himself this question as he stood in the Post Office, fixing the stamp on his dutiful card. It seemed appalling to say No. But that was the answer. He couldn't, he thought, hate them; not one of them, not even Carus, with his big guns ready. He just wanted them, all of them, not to be there. Most, perhaps, he wanted Jennifer not to be there. Because, after all her cool sensible rejection of him ("We're never sloppy, are we, Dan?") she had put out, with Bryan's ultimatum, a great, dragging hook to pull on his pity; to lay on him the burden of being unkind. It wasn't that he wanted to do the other thing; to please Carus. The road forked, but he had no desire to go either way. This had been quite clear to him, while he put back the spare stamps in the new shining wallet, "rather the thing for an up-and-coming chap in B.C.M., no?"

"I must think hard" he had said to himself.

And then the curtain had come down, the kindly curtain, so that he was walking in a dream in a strange city.

If only it would come down again. But he was here in the carriage-house, here in Drumnair where magic and love and God had kept him safe for a little while. That safety was over. He wasn't the fellow who had found the magic places; who had served the Mass, fallen in love at a lightning-stroke, heard the far, furious thunders sounding when he looked at the prunus tree. And yet he was. Those things had happened to Daniel Black. But he had lost his powers. There was no magic any more; no freedom. This Daniel, standing here, cursing inside his head, wasn't free. He never could be free. He was the son of Carus and Jennifer and Irna and Bryan ("four-parents-since-you-were-eight") with no faith, no happiness, no light anywhere. It had been a dream; he had lost Antonia along with the dream, because she was part of it. He had woken up.

CHAPTER FOUR

The lights of the village street came through the mist; small drowned lights and the glimpse of wet flags fluttering. The rain had stopped; all was grey and lucent. Over the trees the moon was rising.

The lorry-driver said "Which gate would you be wanting?" He sounded suspicious. "They'll all be locked, for certain. They lock the gates of the demesne, surely."

"I have a key," said Antonia,—"I live at the Manor."

This appeared to stun him. She said "Go on; up the street. I want the other gate; it's exactly opposite the Nellon Inn —a curved wall to the right. You can't, as they say, miss it."

When he pulled up, she tried to give him one of the half-crowns that had been destined for the collections in chapel. He seemed offended; the Irish, she had observed, became more Irish when offended. "Seeing you there waiting in the rain like that, whatever else would I be doing?" he asked her.

"Seeing that you were my salvation—please have it."

He shook his head: "It was nothing at all."

"Well, you have my prayers," said Antonia. She climbed down; she was cramped and aching from the ride. She was also very hungry, which at least saved her from being more frightened. The only margin for escape had been the fifteen minutes before supper. Quite a long journey, forty-nine miles. A two-mile walk; a nasty little woman driving a nasty little car; ("here's where I turn off, I'm afraid—hope you'll be all right") then the wait and the saviour lorry whose red tail-light she now watched disappear down the Limerick road.

"And don't think for a minute," said Antonia to herself as she stood beneath the wall, in the glimmering greyness, finding her key, "that Rev: Mum won't have telephoned hours ago." Since she had equipped herself with a torch (a precaution for reading under the bedclothes in the convent-dormitory) she took it out and flashed it on the face of her watch. Five minutes past ten.

"Keep your thumb on it, St. Anthony."

She opened the gate. There was just a hope—wasn't there? —that the Monsignor had done the telephoning. Even though she had broken her word and let him down, she couldn't lose the conviction that he would understand the note she left, that he was on their side, her side and Daniel's. Flashing the torch ahead, she went along the path beside the river. Her stomach rumbled. "Wouldn't say no to bacon and eggs," thought Antonia,—"Friday, wouldn't you know? (Is it *still* Friday? Can't be can it? Yes, it jolly is. .) Well, eggs and fried potatoes. In abundance. Ho. More likely bread and water for you, cocky."

She came to the bridge. She had to stop and blow a sentimental kiss to the outline of the Friary. The long twilight still persisting on one side of the sky, the moon coming up on the other side, the misty river, made it look far away.

"Wonder if he got that box open. . What was inside? A skeleton? Have to be a very small skeleton. . Somebody's baby? *Too* sad. ." She went up under the trees; great drops showered from their branches; she zig-zagged, trying to avoid the drops. Reaching the terrace, she put out her torch. The silhouette of the Manor was intimidating. The thought of Geraldine behind those window curtains shook her. Antonia stood still, irresolute, trying to foresee the worst.

"The worst would be to find him gone. No" she said stoutly, "He won't be gone. He promised. *'I'll be waiting for you when you come back.'* Well, then? To Luke? No. Up and at her, you big sissy." She took a pace towards the portico. She stopped again. "It's no good, you *can't.* . Not like this, you can't." She was acutely aware of the trench-coat bundled over the silk dress, the mud-splashed shoes and stockings; of her draggled hair; of the noises that her stomach was making. A fat, wet, untidy girl, with wind. Hardly the figure for a brave entry. "And there isn't a prayer of my getting to my room to change without her hearing the front door. Worms and worms and worms. . . I'll try the back-door." When she saw the light in the carriage-house window, she stood still. There he was, of course. Nobody else. She couldn't bear to look like this for him. On the other hand, she couldn't bear to wait. She crashed across the cobble-stones in a frenzy of excitement; a jigging rhyme kept her company:

> *"Over the cobbles he clatters, and clangs in the*
> *dark inn yard.*
> *He taps with his whip on the shutters, but all is*
> *locked and barred.*
> *He whistles a tune to the window—"*

Nice, but she hadn't enough breath to whistle a tune. She strode under the arch and set her shoulder against the door.

It was mixed up, in the way that a moment of surprise always mixed things up; she couldn't sort out the picture.

She saw the windows pale with mist and moonshine, the bright red-yellow glare from the oil-lamp; the stocky, grey-haired man who stood slouched, with his hands in his pockets. Daniel was doubled over on the horsehair sofa. He was blowing his nose with violence, as if he had a very bad cold. When he looked up she could see that he had been crying. Her first coherent thought was that he wouldn't want her to know this; her second, that the stranger must have made him cry.

"What d'you think *you're* doing?" she shouted at him. She saw a tired, friendly face and a crooked smile. "This is *our* place," she told it "See? Daniel's and mine." She was trying not to look at Daniel; the fact that he sat quite still and silent was worrying. The stranger cocked his head on one side and asked tentatively, "Antonia?"

"That's me." The word 'me' brought with it the memory of her unfortunate appearance. It cut the bluster. She just stood and glared at him.

"How d'you do. I'm Carus Black, Dan's father."

"Oh. Oh, I see. Well,—not to *know*, was I?" she barked as Daniel rose from the horsehair sofa and took her hands. He stared at her most oddly; the poor, red-rimmed eyes blinked and peered. He might be expecting her to vanish.

"I ran away. It was quite easy. God help me with Geraldine, all the same. I'm sorry I look so awful." When he put his arms round her, she grabbed him, holding him in a bear's grip. Now renewed in courage, because he clung close as though for protection, she said to his father "We're in love. Take it or leave it."

"Oh, I'll take it," said Carus Black, "Don't worry."

But Daniel was suddenly pushing her away. Undignified, clutching, she fought with him.

"No. No. Don't, darling." It was his old, authoritative manner. "Don't hug me."

"Why ever not?"

"I've got to tell you. You wanted to know. And when you know, you aren't going to like me any more."

"Aren't I just? What did you do? Rob a bank? I don't care *what* sort of trouble he's in," she said to the father— "I don't care if he stole—or raped, come to that. I don't care if he's a convict."

"How's about his being a heathen?" asked Carus Black; he had the fatal look of somebody who found her funny.

"Goodness, I'm not Geraldine, he could be a Mohammedan, what's the odds? *Anyway—*"

"There isn't an 'anyway'" said Daniel. "I'm not anything. Nothing you thought I was; nothing I thought I was."

She said "I don't get it." She was, all at once, very frightened. He folded his arms; his face was set and sad and cross.

"When I met you yesterday, I didn't have any memory. It had gone. That's why I was cagey. I couldn't remember anything."

"Oh pooh. You remembered this place. . and Geraldine; and how to serve Mass—and that little china job you put on the window-sill—the Eiffel Tower." She saw the father spin round, suddenly, with his back to them. Daniel was saying "Hush. Stop. I don't know how any of that happened. We were trying to work it out. But none of it, *none* of it , was true. D'you see?" His eyes were beseeching, miserable.

"Ho," she said in the same loud voice, "Yes, I do see. You mean loving me wasn't true—well—all right—no need to have such a *thing,* is there? I mean—"

It was Carus Black who interrupted her, turning from the window, with the china ornament in his hand. He said "Oh my dear girl, don't make such a noise. He wants to marry you."

Antonia's stomach gave the loudest rumble yet. She saw Dan's father put the ornament back on the window-sill. He looked at her steadily, no longer appearing to find her funny. He said "Well, I don't see that I can be much more use around here. I'll cover your tracks with Geraldine, chum." He nodded to them a little wistfully and she had time, standing under the arc of the rainbow, to feel sorry for him.

ii

The man who walked across the cobble-stones under the rising moon wasn't Pippin any more. He was Carus, alone. The drug's clarity lurked safely in his head. It would; it still had several hours to go. The drug, he thought, made a smooth, solid floor and the drinks put up warm, comfortable walls around the floor. In this new house of the brain, thought moved easily, fluently.

Carus walked out of the yard and lingered at ease upon the terrace. Still this curiously pale sky above the trees. He stood at the lip of the lawn, close to one dark tree that towered and shone; with a star, a bright pinpoint pricking the pallid sky, just over the topmost branches. He went down across the lawn, he looked back at the house. Its shape had acquired a forlorn dignity, by the kindness of the moon.

Carus jigged back and forward on his heels. He found the last new pack of cigarettes in his pocket and stripped off the cellophane. His lighter needed a refill (who could blame it?) but he located a folder of book-matches, relic

2 0 4

from his New York hotel. Strolling and smoking, he began to conduct the necessary conversation with himself.

"Loss of memory means only one thing. . A long pile-up of agonies inside. . Going on and on. . 'Doubtful he knew they were there at all,—till Limerick. Agonies made by us?" He tried to put the full pressure of his mind upon the truth. "Ever since he was a kid, we've been too damn busy keeping our own noses clean. . is that it? Haven't we really taken a look at the boy himself—except in his relation to us? . . 'Can't have; or we'd have seen. Tearing him to pieces, dissecting him, planning for him—with only ourselves in mind,—is that the story? Looks like it. Jenny, Bryan, Irna and me. . . oh not *me*, surely. The others called the tune, didn't they? I was the one who said all right and signed the cheques. . . but there we go again, into nonsense. I paid the piper, yes, but I never called the tune. Just took him for granted. Me, with my celebrated flair for people. Not for my own son, it appears. If I'd used one-tenth of the brains I put into any B.C.M. deal, for Daniel instead. . maybe I'd have seen him."

He threw the cigarette-end into the grass and immediately lit another. "I see him now. He's what the Americans call a simple duck. They're the ones who lose their memories, when the last straw comes. And the last straw, I don't propose to forget, was the thought of meeting me at Shannon. Then he just walked out. . . walked away. The only refuge —the mind's escape."

"He escaped to Drumnair."

"Don't try to make *that* sound like comfort, will you? So he came to my place,—so he was happy for two days. 'Living in a sort of magic dream. As if, when he lost his own memory, he found mine." Could that happen? How?

He found himself believing it could. "And now he's woken up. To what?" He saw the fat ragamuffin Antonia, with the beautiful face, and he smiled, accepting her too. "She, at least, puts some of it halfway right. No thanks to us. . to any of us.

"And now for Geraldine."

At once it was Pippin who stood here, feeling mischievous and quite pleasurably afraid. Pleasurably, because that young man had got a kick out of being frightened (see, Carus thought, his motor-racing and his choice of horses. .) The most intelligent action would be to take the back-door route again. He had kept her waiting for nearly two hours. One side of his head suggested that this was an abominable thing to do; in the other side, there was a fit of giggles.

She might, of course, have locked the back door.

She hadn't. With a last wave to the carriage-house, elegant in the moonlight, keeping youth's secret now as then, Carus stepped over the threshold. It was dark inside. He fumbled his way by a zig-zag of short passages to the green baize door that opened into the hall. The light in the hall still burned. He stood, sniffing the scent of the pinks.

Then he went on.

The room rushed upon him. He hadn't noticed the room at his first furious entry. All was as he had left it long ago; so much remembered; so much awaiting his return. On that pale tapestry the hunter still launched his spear; the lean dogs curled and pranced; the stag bounded through the trees. Over his head there hung the great chandelier; with yellowish lustres twinkling. He looked at the tall, rose-coloured curtains standing still. He found the portraits one by one. He found Geraldine. She was lying on the sofa at the far end of the room; in a little tent of light, stitching at a piece of embroidery in a frame. She didn't speak while he came down the shadowed, magical floor.

"I'm sorry to have kept you waiting."

"I thought you'd gone," she said, as coolly, as lightly as if she spoke to a servant.

"It took a lot of time." He found the small, tranquil head and face unnerving in their reminders.

"I kept dinner for you. Susanna made a savoury; I told her you'd like it."

"I'm sorry," he repeated.

"Then I went up. To the spare room. And there wasn't anybody. So of course I thought you'd taken him away."

"It was what you asked me to do, wasn't it?" said Carus. The sense of guilt was disturbing the effect of the drug. He looked at the whisky-bottle.

"Oh yes" said Geraldine. "I thought of that. I thought about a lot of things; plenty of time." She snipped a thread and added, without looking up:—"Help yourself. If you think it's a good idea."

"Oh, it's always a good idea." She didn't answer that. He filled the glass; he looked about the enchanted room again as he came back to his blue chair. "I don't believe," he said, "I'd forgotten a single thing. . . Memory like an elephant. Always had."

"Me too, Pippin. You have my sympathies."

"Sympathies?"

"I should be happier with no memory at all."

The chance words shook him. "Good God! What makes you think so?"

"I know so."

("And Daniel would agree, wouldn't he, Carus?") He

said "But a memory—as one gets older—is one's treasury—one's storehouse."

"Yes? What about the things you'd prefer not to store or treasure?"

"Those—" he said violently "are kept in locked boxes at the back."

"And if the locks don't hold?"

"You bloody well see to it that they do."

She gave a little laugh. "You're still rather drunk, aren't you? You ought to have eaten. I'll go and forage for you as soon as you've told me."

"Told you. ."

She laid down the embroidery-frame. She sat up, arranging the soft blue-green skirts carefully to cover her ankles; an old-maidish gesture, he thought.

"Not such an elephant, after all, Pippin. Let me help you. At half-past eight, or thereabouts, you went to get an explanation from your son. It's now after half-past ten. And I'm still waiting."

Carus swallowed the rest of his drink at a gulp. He felt gay, up-in-arms again. "Oh,—we took a walk," he said. "Quite a long walk."

"Really? You must be tired." She lifted her head and looked at him. The delicate movement of the head was unchanged; and the long eyes. He said "La Belle Dame Sans Merci. You're still remarkably beautiful."

"You are drunk. And you'll never see me by daylight, I promise you. This light, or lack of it, is very kind," said Geraldine. "What have you done with him?"

"With Daniel?"

"Yes, dear, with Daniel."

"I walked him back to the Nellon. 'Seemed to me" he

said, putting on his drawl, "that some few centuries back, I'd thrown my luggage in there and asked for a room. I proved to be right. So I turfed Dan into bed."

He cocked a foot up on one knee, feeling pleased with himself Score to Pippin.

"And left your car—" said Geraldine—"It didn't occur to me till just now to go and see if your car was still there."

"I told you, we walked."

"You didn't try to telephone me, by any chance? It rang and I answered and there was nobody there."

"No" he said. "I didn't telephone. . May I give myself a drink?"

"Just as soon as you give me the explanation."

"Oh, that. Well, as it happens, there isn't one." He saw the lizard-look, infinitely untrusting. "Maybe we'll get one tomorrow. At the moment, Dan's much too confused and miserable to be nagged at. Either by you or by me."

"*Why* is he. . ?"

"Well, I'll be frank with you."

"That means a lie, if anything does."

"You're wrong, darling." He put a little more water into the whisky this time. "I was going to say he's every right to be confused and miserable; and that it's our fault."

"Yours and mine? Dear, dear."

"Not yours and mine. When I said 'ours'—" he stopped. "I was referring to Dan's four parents."

"Are you sure you really need that drink, Pippin?"

"Need. . ?" He tried to weigh this up, cradling the glass. "Need. . Now wait a minute. I've several different uses for drink. I use it for fun and I use it for fear. I use it when I'm tired. And sometimes—a night like this being one of the times—I use it to discover me."

"What a morbid little exercise." She watched him mockingly: "Profitless, too, I'd think. If I were a drinker, I should use it to undiscover me. As Tom did. . No, it wasn't only that, for Tom. Not only the blotting out." She paused before she quoted " 'It's hope,—it's company' and—I forget the other thing he said it was."

"No, you don't," said Carus "Nor do I. He said it was the next thing to God."

"Did I tell you?"

"Yes."

"Well, I shouldn't have. Just a stupid, pathetic blasphemy. I don't know why you should trouble to remember it."

"No trouble. Like I said, remembering comes easy."

"How your voice varies. . You go from pedantic upper-class, almost to cockney, and then to false American."

"I know, I know." He didn't feel insulted. " 'Habit of mine. Irna laughs at it too."

"Irna?" A cool, questioning look.

"My wife. My second wife; one of Daniel's four parents."

She was narrowing her eyes; abrim with curiosity and determined, he guessed, to ask no questions that might betray it. He went into a private silence of his own; thinking about Irna. She was the one, he knew at this lucid minute, who would mind the most. She would be stricken. Her planning for the boy had seemed to her always so loving and so right. She had put so much energy into the task of Daniel. All the devoted little detail that he had sometimes sneered at in his mind;—(the new wallpaper for Daniel's room; what a fuss.) The best that she could do, always. Poor Irna. The First Act that never came to a Second Act; her insistence on having every one of these expertly typed, so that the hoped-for enthusiasts would find them easy reading. This had irritated him. Now he saw her differently; as a victim. Lonely and striving after fun, after love. After Daniel.

Whose victim? "Oh all right" said Pippin to Carus, "You've failed them all, dear boy. And we know where that began, don't we? Swallow it down."

He said aloud "Failure. Now *there's* a thing."

"I shouldn't have thought you knew much about it," said Geraldine. She spoke lightly. She rose lightly. "'Get you some food. . Before you burst into tears."

"I'm not by way of being a crying drunk. And I don't want anything to eat, thank you."

"You will—" she said, in her cool, maddening way. She went out.

He remembered this feeling. The sense of slackened ropes; the strain going out of the room with her, the luxury in being alone.

Now the room rushed upon him differently. There were ghosts here, too; the ghost of a tortured young man, for example; (over there on that sofa, where that piece of needle-work lay abandoned and that cushion showed the imprint of that head.) The ghost of his torturer lay in the young man's arms.

Foolish, Carus told himself, to think back to there.

At twenty-one anybody could behave like an idiot. Pippin Black certainly had. For all his adventurous knowledge of sex, he had been fooled by Geraldine posing as the vestal-virgin-widow. This had gone on over weeks He had taken his own controlled agonies philosophically; she was an innocent, he said; Tom must have been an utter failure as a husband; so she tortured Pippin without knowing what she did. (Poor little Geraldine who knew nothing of her own body's capacity for delight. He was arrogantly certain

that he could teach her at any time. And still he refrained.)
He didn't doubt that he could make her join him in the
sexual act before they got to their marriage-bed. But he
saw himself as the dominator, who would not let the de-
mands of his flesh break his will.

And he gave nobody his true reason for refusing to take
the Sacrament before the Nuptial Mass. He had said it
to himself, on the day that he was received. "Ten days from
now, the flesh itself will become a Sacrament. And I'll be
safe. Until then, I'm in danger of committing mortal sin."
Not trusting the state of Grace, knowing only his absolute
awe of the first Communion and the fear of sinning after
it: a tortuous scruple that he had withheld from Francis.

Pompous, pathetic little stallion, Carus thought. And
Geraldine of course had been the dominator all the time.
In that, as in everything. He had found it out on a rainy
evening two days before the wedding. It was a precarious
minute; somehow the guests had all disappeared, leaving
them alone together. Suddenly, on that sofa, she had pulled
him down close; in a little while she had made him entirely
aware of what was happening to her. Afterwards she had
pushed him away. Lying still, relaxed, half-laughing, she
had said "My sin; not yours, remember." She had blown
him a kiss. "I'm sorry, Pippin darling; I've been so good
up till now."

Still there, in memory; his angry, baffled body and his
furious shout: "Good? What the devil do you think *I've*
been?"

"I'm sorry."

"If you know what I was going through—*and* you did. .
damn it, why the act—why all that alleged innocence—cold-
ness—not knowing?"

She had said "Safer so. ."

"*Safer*. . Oh, honestly, Geraldine,—there's a very rude word for you; all right, don't be scared, I'm not going to use it."

"I'm sorry, I'm sorry, I'm sorry. ."

Raging at her: "What the hell was the splendid, icy disregard all about? Eh? I swear I believe you insisted on my staying under this roof—over everyone's dead body, including Francis—just to see how difficult you could make it for both of us. Didn't you? Didn't you?"

"Oh no, no. Please no. Please don't be so angry." On and on:—"Please. It's all my fault—forgive me. I'll go to Confession now, this minute."

"And that" said Pippin "will be a big help to me, won't it?"

She had gone away, weeping. He couldn't remember just where she had found him later, to hold his hands gently in hers, and quiet him with words. Where? He thought in the garden. . hadn't they been planting a new tree or something? He had forgotten all but the words, that last phrase, meant for his comfort: "It will be so wonderful, two nights from tonight. When sleeping together will be a thing that we can do for God."

Why had that shocked him so much? His own truth had put the same fact to him; but it used different words. Framed in these, the fact didn't look like his truth or God's. It looked as if it were Geraldine's own invention; a convenient and somehow indecent falsehood.

And he had, most damnably, been given time to brood on it. With more guests arriving, guests all over the house, with Geraldine gracefully, deliberately avoiding him, his thoughts had gnawed it to the bone. Until the hours shrank down and he had seen nothing but the freedom he was losing, wanted nothing but the old life again,—the other beds where he had slept, the other fun. All of it; that was what he had wanted; to be free; to be quit of the spell of God and Geraldine.

Among the many torn-up letters of that last night in the spare room, was the letter saying that he didn't want to sleep with her 'because it was a thing to be done for God.' "What I believe in" he had written "is the truthful lust of loving."

At this point, the middle-aged Carus shivered and felt old. Then he couldn't help glancing at the thought of Geraldine living in chastity for thirty years. He could, he found, believe it of her.

When the telephone rang, faint and tinkly, he wondered how he could hear it. Its place, as he recalled, was away behind the baize door. He could see the old-fashioned thing on its wall-bracket quite clearly in memory.

When it made the same noise again, he went out into the hall. "Oh, *quite* new" said Carus, sighting the table in the alcove under the stairs; the different telephone. He picked it up. He heard a dim voice speaking through a riot of crackle and buzz. "Hullo," he said "Hullo." He could just catch the sound of the voice behind the barrage. It said "Carus." It couldn't have said "Carus." "Hullo; hullo." Now the line cleared for an instant; the voice came through, a distinct, gentle, academic voice asking "Is that you, Carus?" He knew it; he said "Francis. . Father Francis—Father!" and the noises closed in before the line went dead.

It was a long time before he could bring himself to put back the useless telephone. And even then he went on waiting for it to ring again.

CHAPTER FIVE

He wasn't, Geraldine said to herself, the person whom she had loved. He wasn't Pippin, though she kept using the lost, foolish name. She was cooking this meal for a stranger, because he was hungry and must be fed; like a tramp or a tinker come to the back door. No, not Pippin. (Luke's tiresome theory of dead selves, of multiple characters in one life, seemed to be useful here.) Simply a new acquaintance who carried about with him some bequests from an ancestor she had known. Disquieting mementoes; why should he have kept, all these years, that sad, blasphemous phrase of Tom's?

"When did I tell him? Why?" As she broke the eggs into the bowl, she worried at the question. It was important because it looked like betrayal. In no other speech that she could recall had she broken her vowed and lasting silence.

Automatically, she drew the window-curtain aside and looked out across the cobbled yard, to the carriage-house. It must be the reflection of this light, here in the kitchen, that touched that darkened window, making a glow there. She didn't like it; she let the curtain fall.

The carriage-house. "The only happy room." (That, from Pippin, she still remembered.) Antonia, escaping to the dusty shell of it, would never know what comment this little trick of hers made. The place where they escaped, thought Geraldine. From the beginning.

She looked at the day quite often in her mind; she looked at it now.

Godfrey's playroom halfway begun. The planks for the new flooring; the sawdust, the carpenter's bench; the window lacking a frame. Tom standing by the window in the light of a summer afternoon; his gun at his shoulder. Herself thinking "He's better today"; he had been laughing, though the eyes didn't really laugh.

"Watch" said Tom; and fired across the yard, high up at the Manor wall. He was a beautiful shot. He had hit every nasty little rose along the line of fake-Tudor ornament, right in the middle. This shot, accurate as the rest, studded the last rose. (At the inquest, much had been made of the bullets in the roses.) One more loud laugh, and then, she knew, the whole black tent of his misery coming upon him; as though she saw the folds of it falling round his head. (*Mr. Courtney had been suffering from deep depression for many months. The tragic troubles of his country had preyed on his mind to an intense degree.*) Her own voice, light and striving:—"Bravo. Tom. . Bullseye. . Isn't that about enough shooting-practice for today?" The gun lying on the carpenter's bench. Her swift, give-away movement to pick it up, and Tom moving as fast, between her and the bench. He was a very big man; she couldn't hope to get it now. "Run along, Geraldine. You're keeping Master Godfrey waiting and he won't like that." "Why don't you come too?" Silence and the black tent enclosing him. When she said "I trust you—" she had meant it, hadn't she?

(*Mrs. Courtney, giving evidence, said that on return from her walk in the demesne with her little boy, she went into the carriage-house to see how the work was progressing, and found her husband lying under the window... It was* quite obvious to her that he had been about to clean the gun. A ramrod, some rags and an uncorked bottle of methylated spirit were on the carpenter's bench.) Quick work, to get them from the gunroom. Unseen? If old Kevin Hickey really saw her crossing the yard, then he had perjured himself. She was sure that he had. . Hurriedly lining up the stuff on the bench; with the envelope still crackling inside her blouse. Tom had written on the back of the envelope "This is it, Geraldine." Easily burned, once she was alone. She had done well. *Mr. Kevin Hickey, who heard the shot, said that he thought nothing of it until Mrs. Courtney called him, about an hour later. It was obvious to him as soon as he entered the carriage-house—* And against her, against Kevin, unanswerable:—the position of the wound, the angle of the gun, Tom's capable record with firearms. The open verdict. And the Requiem Mass; most fair and right. She was as certain then as now that Tom had been in truth her victim, not his own. (Scarcely worth confessing, her two acts of deception; and a curious scruple to have confessed them to a priest other than Francis. "Very young of me.") Oh, Francis had known; Luke had known. Everybody knew and nobody spoke. She liked to think that she had forced her silence on them. The only word Luke ever uttered came when she saw to it that the playroom was finished. He had said "You have no heart at all." Why? What else would one do?

"And now, Carus Black, your supper appears to be ready" said Geraldine. She carried the tray back to the drawing-room. She found him sitting upright, unrelaxed and watchful. His gratitude for her bringing him a plate of bacon and scrambled eggs, with toast and cheese and fruit, amused her; but, of course, she told him, he knew nothing of her daily round. He remembered a Manor full of servants and silver dishes.

"Did the telephone ring again?" she asked him—"I thought I heard it."

"I answered. There was nobody." He began to eat rapidly. "Very good of you," he said "to feed your enemy."

"My enemy?"

"Surely?" He cleared the plates so fast that she had to force herself not to say "Don't bolt it, Pippin."

"My enemy. . ." she repeated. "Well, yes. You were that for a long time."

"Am I still?"

"No. Of course not."

"Can't see why not," said Carus. "It was unforgivable. The action of a shit."

"I don't care for that language."

"Sorry. Would you rather I said 'Cad'? Action of a cad. ." He drawled it. "More of the period, perhaps. No, a little *vieux jeu*, even then. . What did we say then?"

"When?"

"In 1929."

"Twenty-nine? Who's talking about twenty-nine?"

"You were," said Carus. She laughed at the bewildered face: "Oh no, I wasn't. I don't expect you to believe me, but I wasn't. I suppose when *you* think of the—the cad's action, you think about leaving me at the altar."

That he could still look embarrassed was funny. She went on laughing. "Poor Pippin. . *quelle folie*. . but of course you would think so. As it happens, that's one of the few moments in my life that I cherish. With no regrets at all."

(Not embarrassed now; almost outraged) She said " 'Tell you why. One single, gratuitous torment. One thing of which I can say 'I neither deserved it, nor made it happen.' I can count that against you; not against myself. Score to me."

"Most certainly, score to you," said Carus.

"Only that one moment, mind; that way of doing it. The actual 'No, Father' and walking away down the aisle. You needn't have left it till then. I'd have let you go, I wouldn't have fought. Even so, I couldn't help thinking it was brave of you. Right on the instant, I thought so. And I forgave it you, for that. Eat the peach; I picked it today."

"You forgave it me—then?"

"Well,—very soon after. Why are you looking at me, like that—like a prosecuting counsel?"

He was looking as if it were his turn to score a point. "Your enemy—for a long time—" he reminded her. He peeled the peach.

"Oh, yes. . . for quite another reason—doesn't matter. It's forgiven too, now." Extraordinary, how little desire was left to argue a point that she had argued with him alone in her head so often. Forgiveness, she thought; what does one do in the act of forgiveness, but let the years, the distance, the perspective, take care of it all? Is forgiveness only forgetting? Is that why, when this man, "my old enemy" in my accustomed thoughts, finally appears on the scene, I have nothing to say to him? He diminishes every moment.

Carus got up to put the tray on a side-table. "Off now?" she asked, "It's late. . I don't sleep much, myself, but you must be exhausted."

"May I have a drink first?"

"But of course." She put all the regrets of a neglectful hostess into her voice. This ploy gave her some pleasure; she knew he was waiting for a protest. He filled his glass;

he returned. His eyes, she noticed, were still large and luminous, contradicting the tiredness and the lines in the face that was grown older; so much older. "Have you," he asked abruptly—"Ever loved anybody again?"

"Meaning have I had lovers? No. Chastity isn't as difficult as we all make out. . Ask any intelligent priest."

"I don't, in my walk of life, meet intelligent priests."

When she said, thinking aloud, "I love Antonia, I suppose, more than anybody," she was surprised that he should jump in so quickly with "Tell me about Antonia."

"A very charming, rather naughty girl. Full of problems; all of which," said Geraldine, "will resolve themselves when she takes her vows."

"Good God!" said Carus, "How exactly like you to take the trouble to adopt a child and then hand her over to Mother Church."

She had no answer ready. Though he couldn't know the truth, he had stepped remarkably near to it. (But I wouldn't dream of telling you, Carus. You would argue and batter at me. It isn't in your creed to understand the temptation to love too much, the temptation to give such love to a child that the child becomes more important than God. *Thou shalt not make to thyself any graven image.* . The commandment that everybody shrugs off contentedly, saying 'Well, you don't see *me* carving little wooden idols'. Not realizing, the fools, that anything one loves too much becomes a graven image. Put in God's place. Like the drink, with Tom. But there are, of course, innocent idolaters. The passionate lovers of music and all the other arts would blink if one pointed out the strength of their worship and the slant of it.)

"Well, come on; let's hear some more," Carus was saying.

There was a driving overtone, a special curiosity, wasn't there?—in his voice.

"Why are you interested in Antonia, Pippin?"

"Why shouldn't I be? What are you holding back?"

She said "Nothing." But she was recalling the minute when she had faced the truth about Antonia, seeing the danger for the child as well as for herself. Ten years ago; the seven-year-old out on the terrace, saying goodbye to her; hugging tightly but not as tightly as she herself was hugging. Her own tears falling on the child's hair; and those big staring eyes, the dark terror in the face. "You're going away *forever?* That's it. . Not just for two weeks—*forever—*" and Antonia had started bawling. The hours taken to pacify, to explain. "But if it *isn't* forever, why did you cry?" "Because I'm silly and because I love you."

(Yes, that was the moment. Not to be shared. That was the moment of decision to give Antonia to God.) "I'm keeping nothing back," she said to Carus, "nothing that you'd know about. If it came to religious views, we'd be talking different languages. Wouldn't we? No need to look so insulted. I don't mean you're stupid. It's perfectly natural that you shouldn't understand. After thirty years of freedom."

"Freedom, eh?" The growl in the voice didn't worry her. She got up; went past him to the mantelpiece and turned out the wall-lights there. "I really do think it's time—"

"Stop."

She turned back. He was alight again, furious, for no reason that she could imagine, and she was in no fighting mood; she was tired.

"You listen to me—" said Carus. He was all eyes. "Freedom. . that's what you said."

"Well, yes."

"That's what I have. Freedom."

"Don't you?"

"Oh sure. It's mine for the asking. Except I don't have to ask—I give orders. I'm the chairman of B.C.M., don't forget. I own the bloody world." He wasn't looking at her any more; his eyes were turned to the great tapestry of the stag-hunt: "The bloody world—" said Carus "My world; the whole damned, idiotic place I can trample all over it. All over anybody. Yes, Mr. Black, No, Mr. Black, This Way, Mr. Black. 'Kept your table for you, Mr. Black. That's what I've got. Cash, power,—every useless, beastly, material advantage. Lucky fellow, eh? Would you say lucky fellow?"

"How can I? I know nothing about you."

"True enough. Truest word you ever spoke, to coin a phrase." He took a step towards her. His voice was soft. "You don't know, so let me tell you I've been figuring out, in the last hour or so,—to whom I owe it all. My dissipated body. My financial wizard's brain, with rather more than a touch of atheroma, by now The messes I've made. One divorce and another marriage staggering along because neither of us can be bothered to break it. A son to whom I'm useless. My daily round. The time I spend talking affable balls to people with the souls of apes. The waste of my blood, guts and ingenuity in getting ahead of another big boy, who might, if I wasn't bigger, get ahead of me." He wagged a finger at her now; it was Pippin's gesture in argument. "All of it, now all of it. . My Goddamned success. If that's anybody's fault but my own, there's only one person responsible. And the person, Mrs. Courtney, would be you."

She heard him draw a little, whistling breath. As if, perhaps, he had surprised himself. She made no reply. She put out one more light and walked away from him toward the windows. The room felt hot and smoky. She began to draw back the curtains. The sky was clear; the night sky at last, with the stars pricking through, and a white full moon over the trees. She found herself gazing at the prunus. Tall, dark and shining, the upward shape spread its branches. She wanted to cry to him "Look! Remember?" and she knew that she would not.

ii

She was silent for so long that Carus, watching her, began to forget his own words. Lucidity, strength, had gone out of him. He felt blurred and lost inside the walls of his head. There was that still figure at the window; and the moonlight, and a tired consciousness of the challenge that he had thrown down. He was waiting for her to pick it up. (Sometimes, at the end of an after-dinner speech, with all the red faces grinning and the clapping hands, he wondered what the devil he had been talking about.)

Geraldine had not moved. She said, still looking out into the garden: "I know what you mean. I know what I did to you. Poor Pippin, I'm sorry. I spoiled the fun; I soured the cup. Didn't I?"

The quiet voice was like a song in his head, a melancholy song that he didn't want to hear. She was saying "'Every time I looked at God, Geraldine got in the way. . .' You wrote that to Francis, and it was true. I hurled God at you in all the wrong words. What you don't know is that it's still going on. For other people. I didn't only do it for you.

223

That's how it was for Tom before you, and for Godfrey after you, and now for—" She stopped.

"And now for Antonia?"

Silence. "Wasn't that what you were going to say, Geraldine?"

She didn't answer. She said "I remember a priest telling me once that I should try to be more flexible. I asked him what right *he* had to be flexible at all. . I still don't know. It's so absolutely clear to me,—what I took on when I came into the Church; the whole of it, not just the bits that suited Geraldine Courtney. I can't see it any other way; and I've never lost sight of it. You might say I've done my best; not a good best, but the only one that's true for me. To everybody else, it just looks like an arbitrary prison. . . That's what I live with. I don't put the blame anywhere. Nobody made me like this. I always was like this. And I've always been sorry; too late. Always said so; too late. When we fought,—you with your elephant's memory—who was always the one to say 'Sorry'?"

"You." He became aware that she was scoring again.

"Yes. However atrociously I'd behaved. . . Even when," she gave a small, sad laugh—"No, though,—I can't imagine you remember *that*."

"I rather think I was remembering it tonight."

"The thing here. . in this room?"

"Yes."

"And afterwards," said Geraldine, "all I could do was choose the wrong words."

He tried to say no, but she was cutting across the feeble protest with "Oh yes, yes. I did. And I saw you begin to run, there and then. That was the moment when God and

Geraldine turned into one—into a prison—wasn't it? Wasn't it, Pippin? But you were wrong too, you know."

She turned her back to the window, clutching the long curtains, holding them close behind her; she was almost hidden from him, a shape against the curtains, with a triangle of moonlight above her head, the apex of the triangle pointing downwards.

"Wrong—" she repeated. "And *that*, if you care, is the reason why you stayed an enemy." She let go of the curtains.

"You see, I *was* trying to be different. I thought you'd help me. I wanted to be like you. . loving and lively and untroubled in my faith, as happy in it as you were. I wanted to laugh with you. I was beginning to learn. And I did pray for all the graces that would come with the Nuptial Mass to do the miracles for us. To make me laugh,—make me young in heart, make me 'serve God right merrily' like you. Those were my prayers, the night before."

There had been days, Carus remembered, when he had tried to excuse himself by saying that the Nuptial Mass was all she cared about. She had talked of it so much.

"The night before. ." And he, in the spare room, trying to write the letter. He was tired enough for this to hurt him. He said "Oh, hell. . what it adds up to, darling, is that you might well have made a good job of my life; and I —possibly—of yours. Possibly. . that's all we know. 'Fact remains, we cannoned off each other and went ahead and lived exactly as we meant to live. Eh?"

He waited for her to contradict him. She said "Oh, yes. It's likely that I'd have failed. More than likely. And you'd have gone—like everyone else."

"Everyone? Godfrey. . Where's Godfrey?"

"You must go now. We've talked too much."

"I asked you where Godfrey was."

She said gently "Why do you want to know?"

"It seems so bloody for you not to have anyone."

"I see no reason why possessiveness should be rewarded."

That roused him. "Oh, for God's sake stop being statuesque and saintly. I remember him so well."

"Yes, you remember a little boy with fair hair and blue eyes and Tom's treacly Irish charm. I don't know that you'd feel the same about him now."

"But where—"

"Oh my dear importunate Pippin, I don't *know* where. In London, last time I heard. If you're after the details, you can guess them. We fought. He married a girl I didn't want him to marry; she left him, as I knew she would. Then he followed in Tom's footsteps with the drink, and got the sort of jobs drunkards get. . And went on loathing me." She sounded quite detached about it. "He's always in my prayers; I've given up trying to wipe him out of my mind, because you can't do that with your own child. I've also the idea that I could handle him more kindly, more intelligently, nowadays. But that could easily be an illusion. All I know is I'd try. . if he came back."

She came up to him, putting a hand under his elbow. "You really *must* go now, please."

He stood there stupidly, saying "I'm sorry."

"Don't be. We learn. We grow old. *And all shall be well.*"

The echo sounded. He repeated "*And all shall be well; and all manner of things shall be well.*"; but he didn't believe it. He tried to think of something of his own to say; something entirely for her. It wouldn't come. Every cliché of would-be consolation came instead.

"What are you searching after now?" she asked him.

"I suppose,—the right words."

She laughed. "Don't bother. 'Words are the only things that can really hurt.' Quotation. Who said?"

"No idea."

"You did. Score to me." She put out the light and the last he saw of the room was the moon shining on the tapestry.

"Drive very carefully. You're half-asleep. Goodbye, Pippin. We shan't be meeting in the morning."

iii

She waited, standing at the door while he walked slowly down the steps. Her words appeared to catch up with him on the lowest step; he turned round. "Not—in the morning? Mean that?"

"Oh yes. You see. ." She stopped. Across an age she remembered Daniel. The boy seemed far, small and harmless. It astonished her that the one who had been the whole reason for the furiously-sought battlefield should have lost all importance. Was it funny? Or shocking? She didn't know. It cost her no effort to say "I hope Daniel will be all right." And now Carus looked as though he too had forgotten Daniel. She watched him blunder past the prunus tree on the way to his car.

iv

"With love and delight."

"With ease and affection."

227

"And with perseverance unto the end."

"There you are, you see," said Antonia. She took the last peppermint lump. "Nothing so very difficult, is there? You can remember."

"If you teach me. But last night you didn't have to teach me."

He watched her strenuously while she crumpled up the sticky bag and, for want of a wastepaper basket, dropped it through the bars of the empty parrot-cage. " 'Teach you anything," she said " 'Start on the catechism now if I wasn't so hungry."

"Oh my poor darling."

"I'm not your poor darling. I feed on love."

"And peppermint-lumps," said Daniel. She came back to the horsehair sofa, back into his arms. He kissed her.

"One could, I suppose, taste of worse things than peppermint" she said, drawing away. He looked down into her eyes; he felt responsible and puzzled. "You don't like it, do you? Not really?"

"Well, it's new," said Antonia, "that's all. It feels like being suffocated. Do you kiss a lot of people? I suppose you do."

"Only three. Well, four if you count one who began it."

"Yucks. I hate them all anyway. You didn't sleep with any of them?"

"No."

"Have you ever?"

"Not yet," said Daniel.

"I can't *tell* you what a relief that is to my mind."

Though he laughed, he thought about it. Then he decided that it was a little dangerous to go on thinking. He held her hand.

"That's the nicest," said Antonia. She sat up, leaning forward, gazing at the moonlit window. She had taken off her wet shoes and stockings; she was wrapped in the red, moth-eaten rug. With the silky hair hanging loose, the scarlet billowing tent that the rug made, and the bare feet, she reminded him of something. "Gypsies" he said aloud.

" 'Off with the raggle-taggle gypsies, o'?"

"I like it. We will be, too. We'll run away."

"What about things like money. . And marriage-lines?" she asked.

He said "Oh, wait for the morning. We'll fix it. I can get a job; and the Monsignor can marry us." This gave him pause and at once she must have seen why; she pulled him close, hugging him tightly. "Now you're *not* going into another despair, d'you hear? I won't have it. You're baptized already by desire. That's how it works. I've told you."

"But how" he said "did it happen? Why did I believe it? Any of it? Was it just because Carus had been here?"

"I don't know. I think it's rather magic and splendid, myself. Like the Mysteries."

He was still worried inside. "Suppose I'm mad?"

"Pooh—" said Antonia, "Worms to that."

"Well, suppose it happens again?"

"Oh darling Daniel, suppose what happens again?"

"Losing my memory."

"Goodness, it won't matter. I'll be there to remind you."

Saturday Morning May 30th

"Oh, my God, I believe in You, I hope in You, I love You, I adore You. I offer You all my thoughts, words, actions and sufferings throughout this coming day. May they all be to Your greater honour and glory, and to my eternal salvation. Amen."

Geraldine crossed herself and rose to her feet. Always the same prayer, in the quiet, bare mood of morning. The mood (*Deo gratias*) was no different today. This was her peaceful hour, six-thirty and nobody awake. She was, as usual, well ahead of old Susanna. The pudding-faced Bridget, who came up from the village on her bicycle, was always late. Since the daily Mass on Saturdays was said at seven-thirty, she had just time to do her own room and the bathroom first. She was a quick worker. And the simple tasks, cleaning, dusting, sweeping, had this mercy upon them; that here at least one could be doing no harm, neither to one's own soul nor to anyone else's.

Avoiding the vacuum flask of tea set ready by Susanna, Geraldine put on her white overall. The new rulings on the Eucharistic Fast made the tea permissible. She still preferred to fast from midnight. Tying her head in a white cloth like a nurse's cap, she had no temptation to look in the glass. She was glancing ahead at the chores of Saturday; as regular as the church calendar; they never varied.

Last night's legacy, she realized, was the sense of freedom; freedom from dread. Carus had come at last, and gone.

All was as it had been before he came. And the boy, she said to herself, the boy was another ghost, exorcized, departed, leaving a lightness in the air. The morning mood found the invasions, the explosives of yesterday very strange indeed. She felt as though she had met them with a personality weaker than her own. Today she swung back into herself. (Same old striving self; strong as a lion; with the house to care for and the prayers to say.)

"*Ave Maria, gratia plena, Dominus tecum. Benedicta tu in mulieribus.*"

The brooms and brushes, the cleaning-things for the upper floor, lived in a cupboard at the top of the back stairs, facing the door of Godfrey's room. On her way, Geraldine drew back the curtains from the landing window. She looked out at the morning. Misty and still, the river cut its swathe through the pastureland. Mist touched the trees, but there was a clean-swept sky behind; not a cloud left. She heard the song of the birds.

"*Sancta Maria, Mater Dei, ora pro nobis peccatoribus, nunc et in hora mortis nostrae.*"

What was better, after all, than this, the peace that belonged to the hour? Before people, talk and the tyranny of crossed human wires put a stop to it? Nothing was better, she said to herself, nothing in the world.

Geraldine opened the door of the broom-cupboard. Then she stopped, to listen. That was surely the sound of voices down below; coming from the kitchen. No, it couldn't be. She leaned over the stair-rail. A long moment of silence almost convinced her that she was mistaken. Then a sudden, rocketing laugh went up. There was no mistaking that laugh. But she was still saying "It couldn't be," as she hurried down the back stairs. Impossible. No, and no, and no.

One second after she had plucked open the door, the 'No' turned a somersault; the no became 'Yes', a slumping, resigned yes that made this seem inevitable, as though she had expected nothing else. Here they were; Antonia and the boy.

In a kitchen that she had left orderly at midnight, there reigned the shambles that Antonia, under a cooking-frenzy, could provoke. Every space in sight was strewn; with pans and potholders, with knives and forks, with dish-towels and half-open packets. The coffee-machine burbled; the fat sizzled; the air was full of breakfast smells. Daniel Black, with a sausage halfway to his mouth, sat on the table. Antonia, dressed for some reason in a red rug, with a cord tied round her middle, and the clean white oven-glove slung across one shoulder like a bandolier, was at the stove. She turned the gas-taps low; she set a new relay of rashers and sausages around a golden hillock of fried potato. Putting the dish on the table, she looked up at Geraldine with a cowlike expression.

Daniel slid off the table. Nobody said a word. Neither, Geraldine thought as she stared from one to another, showed a sign of alarm. They seemed, both of them, to be happily aloof amid the shambles. They were two munching, contented animals who eyed her and had no need of her.

Silence, her accustomed weapon, was now quite involuntary. She found nothing to say. For one thing, this couldn't be happening. For another, it was.

Daniel spoke first. He said "Have a splendid sausage?" talking with his mouth full. Antonia, impeded also, said "She can't; she'll be fasting."

"Fasting?"

"Before Mass."

"Jolly *good*," said Daniel, ambiguously, perhaps. He grabbed another sausage. She thought that she might not be here at all, that they could be discussing her in her absence. At this point, however, the boy remembered his manners; he pulled a wooden chair away from the table, inviting her to sit down. He said "We were so hungry. I hope you don't mind."

Antonia said "Alas for girls with big frames who miss their suppers." She ate a spoonful of potato. "I was so empty I got nightmares. I dreamed I was just going to carve the Mother Superior. She was on a little dish and she had been cooked in her robes, like those chickens in pastry jackets."

This made Daniel giggle. He went on giggling. Antonia caught the giggle. They became convulsed, shaking and snorting, saying "Oh *do* stop" and "*You* stop." Antonia began to choke.

"I do see that everything that's happening is quite hilariously funny," Geraldine said, "But at the same time—"

"Choking isn't funny. It hurts."

Away in the hall, she heard the telephone begin to ring. With one more disgusted look at the invaders, she went to answer it.

She listened for a long time to the tiny voice of Mother Paula, speaking from Castleisland. (Why, she wondered, must nuns talk so quietly, even on the telephone?) Reverend Mother wanted to be certain that Antonia was safely home. She was? Ah well. Thanks to Our Bléssed Lady, to whom Mother Paula had made a special petition. The Monsignor had been reassuring, but the fact of the telephone going out of order had made everybody a little anxious. She did not want Mrs. Courtney to think that she had been neglectful. Antonia's note was quite explicit and the Monsignor knew that Mrs. Courtney would understand—here the voice shrank down to a wordless piping, and came back to tell her that they were all praying for Antonia. Mother Paula hoped also that the dear foolish child hadn't got very wet.

"Are you there, Mrs. Courtney?"

It would be true, Geraldine thought, to say that I do not know where I am.

As she went slowly back to the kitchen she caught herself thinking that she couldn't see why Antonia deserved all those prayers. Was nobody saying one for her? She opened the kitchen door.

This time the invaders sprang politely to their feet. Daniel said "I'm sorry if we were rude."

"So am I," said Antonia.

"Yes,—well. ." She looked wearily at the chaos:—"That was Mother Paula."

"It would be," said Antonia.

"How did you get back here?"

"I thumbed a ride. First from a woman and then from a lorry."

"I've told her not to do it again," said Daniel, "it's quite silly and dangerous."

"Who gave you permission to come out of Retreat?"

"Nobody. I didn't think it would be fair to ask. I just left notes saying I was sorry."

"But not to me."

"I beg your pardon?" said Antonia.

"You didn't think of saying you were sorry to me."

"Oh I did. . Honestly. . I never stopped thinking of it, all the way home. But then I got deflected."

"My fault" said Daniel.

"You were in bed at the Nellon,—the last I heard of you." (And confused; and unhappy; and to be let alone, Carus said.)

Daniel said "Me? No, I wasn't. I was in the carriage-house."

It would have to be the carriage-house, wouldn't it? Dazed, Geraldine heard her own voice asking, "Is that where you were—all night? Both of you?"

"Yes. But we didn't commit anything," said Antonia.

The absurdly-framed protest was, she thought, wholly credible. She saw them not as adolescents, but as plaguing, moonstruck children. Yet, when Daniel said "I give you my word that's true," she looked at him in further perplexity. Why was he different today? No longer moonstruck. No less annoying; indeed, more annoying. More palpable and solid; more grown-up. Much too grown-up to be wearing those clothes. Suddenly she hated the corduroy shorts and the neutral-coloured sweater; they made her want to scream.

"Haven't you *anything* else to wear?" It came out as a near-scream.

"What? Oh. . no," said Daniel. "I do look rather scruffy, I suppose. Sorry about that."

"You *must* have some clothes somewhere."

"Oh, yes, I have. In London. And in Sussex. Lots of clothes—" He smiled at her reassuringly. "These were just for hiking."

Antonia said "Shorts are quite splendid, I think, as long as one has nice legs and Daniel has very nice legs, the right shape and not hairy at all."

"Oh shut up" said Daniel placidly.

"You're quite right." Antonia stabbed the butt-end of

a sausage into the mustard which she had made, with mysterious purpose, in a soup-plate. She addressed herself to Geraldine: "It's time we talked things over in an adult manner, don't you think?"

"What. . ? No, I don't. I don't think you're capable of it."

"Oh, well—it was only a suggestion," said Antonia. She smiled; she had become all at once a good-tempered, implacable stranger. Looking at her, Geraldine thought "It's no good any more—any of it." A thought to be contradicted at once. ("All I mean is that I must have a little time to think; to come to a decision.") She couldn't imagine why she said "I'd like a word with Daniel. Alone. As soon as you've both finished your breakfast."

"I've finished," he said, putting down his coffee-cup; this was annoying of him; she wasn't ready.

"So've I," said Antonia.

"Then you might begin on the washing-up."

"But of *course*, Geraldine." The voice was wounded.

"And then get out of that extraordinary thing you're wearing."

"It's a rug. Quite smelly, really. Look, may I ask one thing? Before you start on Daniel?" The last phrase hurt; perhaps it was deserved.

"What is it, Antonia?"

"Are you going to send me back?"

"To the convent? I hardly think you would be likely to make a good Retreat in the circumstances, do you?"

She felt faintly pleased with this answer; less pleased when Antonia yelled "Goody!" and hurled the frying-pan into the sink with a shattering noise.

"Come with me, please," Geraldine said to Daniel. She

opened the door of the room that she called "my office." It was a grim, functional little room, with walls painted olive-green; its furniture consisted of a desk, a filing-cabinet and two chairs. Eminently a room for rebukes, with herself behind the desk and the guilty party standing. Daniel Black seemed immune; he said "That's nice," looking at an old print of the Friary; she had forgotten it hung there.

"All I ask is for you to go. Now," she said without preliminary.

He waited, his head a little to one side, glowing and grinning; he looked cocky, like Pippin.

"Did you hear what I said?"

He nodded.

"Your father, you'll find, will agree."

He raised his eyebrows.

She said "Antonia's seventeen."

"It is very young, isn't it? But in some ways," Daniel said, "I think she's more grown-up than I am."

"I'm not interested in you, Daniel."

"No, of course you aren't. I don't see why you should be. But there's nothing terrible about me. I won't do her any harm, I promise. I really do love her."

"But you must go, don't you see?"

"Why?"

It was the more maddening because his voice was so gentle and serious.

"Perhaps you'll admit you've done nothing but plague the life out of me—out of all of us—since Thursday."

"Excuse me," said Daniel, "But I'm not a bit the same as I was on Thursday. What's more, I don't believe you are, either."

"I haven't the slightest idea what you mean by that impertinent remark."

"You just seem different. . I suppose everyone does, when one gets to know them a little better," he said genially.

"Will you please be quiet!" She put her hand over her eyes. She felt light-headed, impotent. She thought "Carus should be with me. . Or Francis. Or somebody. I oughtn't to be left to handle this alone. ." But it was ridiculous. She could handle anything alone. Why did a couple of children make all look so difficult? Because they were so young, so strong, so silly? She glanced at her watch.

"I'm sorry, Daniel. This is the end of it. Your father's promised to take you away. You might at least—" she couldn't think of the right phrase; she said "go quietly."

"But I'm not a criminal, Mrs. Courtney."

"No," she said, rising wearily, "I don't know what you are and I can't say I really care at the minute. Provided that you leave us all alone. And that's my last word. You know your way out. Goodbye."

From the kitchen there came the unholy noise of Antonia's washing-up. Susanna, with the carpet-sweeper, was abroad in the hall. The drawing-room door stood wide open, giving a glimpse of Bridget on a stool, flapping at a picture-frame with a feather duster. Bridget always hummed loudly while she worked; that she was humming the Kyrie Eleison made it no better.

With a return of speed and purpose, Geraldine seized Daniel's arm, thrust him out through the front door and ran upstairs to her room. It should by now, have been swept and dusted; the bed should have been made. While she peeled off her white overall, picked up her Missal and mantilla, she was thinking "At least I'll be in time for Mass." Nothing odd about that, surely? She always was.

Coming out under the portico, she heard the car's engine running. Daniel had brought it up to the steps for her. He stood beside it, hands in pockets, gazing about him. She thought wildly that she would never be rid of him now, that he would be here always, here in the garden, wearing his awful clothes and looking quietly contented, as if he knew . . . what? Well, perhaps a number of things that she didn't know; only she had no time to linger upon this thought; nor did she want to.

As he opened the car door for her she said "Could I drop you, perhaps, at the Nellon?"

"I'll go down later, if you don't mind. It's a bit early for Carus,—after yesterday." He smiled at her.

"Well, you needn't wake him." She added hopelessly, "It's on my way to the church, Daniel."

"Pray for me," said the boy.

ii

The sound that awoke Carus was a steady roaring. The noise of the aircraft's engine had been going on for hours; surely they must be coming in to Shannon soon. . "*Not past Lundy yet? How long she hangs in the wind,*" somebody said. The roaring grew louder. There was a bump, and he opened his eyes.

He saw a countrified hotel bedroom, and the scatter of his luggage; a bathroom door standing open; he saw slashes of sunlight framing chintz curtains. The colleen from the airline counter was here; she had changed her uniform for a cap and apron; she turned into a housemaid. She had switched off the roaring vacuum-cleaner and now she was apologising. For what? Carus began to remember where he was. He moved his head, testing for hangover. There appeared to be none. Only a peaceful heaviness that made him feel he never wanted to move again.

Blinking at the girl through the chequer-pattern of bright sun and shadow, he said "What's the time?"

"It's a few minutes after twelve, sir."

"Honestly?"

This made her laugh. "It's the truth," she said, nodding at him, " I heard the chimes from the church. But it doesn't matter at all, I can come back later."

"No,—wait," said Carus, rubbing his eyes hard; he must, he thought, have taken care of the Drynomil with an extra Nembutal. "Do you *suppose*," he asked, managing to make this sound very difficult—"you could get me some coffee? *Black* coffee?" He understood her to say that it would give her pleasure.

He lay back on his pillow, remembering; he remembered it all. But it pleased him little enough. He got out of bed.

The bathroom was too bright, with the sun ablaze through transparent plastic curtains. The taps filled the bath too quickly, too noisily. He became conscious of an enfeebling sense of guilt. Unusual to him. Perhaps for falling off the wagon? Perhaps for waking up so late? "Don't kid yourself," he said, turning off the taps. There was only one source of guilt. Daniel.

"And where the hell do we go from here? That's what I'd like to know. . That's what I *will* know, once I've had some coffee. Pend," said Carus aloud, as if he were giving orders to his secretary.

2 4 3

While he splashed and wallowed, he restored every moment with Geraldine. The flat morning mood rejected all.
"If I were capable of blushing, which I'm not. . ." Carus
thought, and stopped there. (He would blush most deeply
for the Poor-Little-Rich-Boy speech, the Boo-Hoo-I'm-A-
Businessman speech.) She, in his recollection, had behaved
well. Damn. . Was this the sort of morning-after when one
sent flowers, and tried to persuade oneself all day that one's
hostess had noticed nothing wrong? It seemed somehow
different, though he didn't know how.

Carus shaved the silver prickles off his chin. He took a
long time over everything. He was pedantic about his
bathroom routine and he liked to quote Samuel Butler's
saying that no man had ever been known to commit suicide
after a complete evacuation. (Irna said it was untrue and
Jennifer said it wasn't Samuel Butler.)

When he came back into the bedroom, the maid had
brought the coffee; she had also brought an orange, a boiled
egg and some toast. She had drawn back the curtains. This
was a first-floor room; through the window he could see
the plump thatch on the yellow cottages (surely not yellow
paint, in his time?) the curve of high grey wall and the
demesne gate (that door was new) with the stone urns
on top.

All very sunlit, and very improbable, still. He blinked
upon Drumnair. He found his dressing-gown, folded in his
suitcase; he had, he recalled, been too bushed to get it out
last night. On the other hand, some resolution had been at
work, for him to take all the Irish road-maps from the dash-
board compartment of the car and stack them on his bed-
side-table. He blinked upon those, too; then upon his own

reflection, the tallowish face above the bright silk dressing-gown.

He drank all the coffee; he ate half the egg and half a piece of toast. Feeling guilty about the orange, he lit a cigarette.

The morning mood began to pick up with the last thoughts of the night. He took the maps off the table. "Get the boy out of here,—and quickly" the night thoughts had said; very sensible of them. Idly he traced the road running south, the road that led to Bantry Bay. Glengariff, now; that was a good idea. Boating and fishing; he looked for hotels in the green A.A. book and found two that seemed promising; no crowd, so early in the summer; simply a question of seeing which hotel they liked the better when they got there.

Out of here. . and quickly.

"You see," he said to Geraldine in his mind, "You're dead. I don't mean as the person I used to know; I don't think you're so different, really (I'm the one who has changed) but as a person living in the world; this world. You're a kind of pathetic ghost haunting a little patch of ground that's precious to you. You're not good for young people. Drumnair isn't for young people. Dan came into it by chance, by a swing-door that must swing him out again. I'll see to that, don't worry."

And Antonia? He wished that the face were not so vivid. He would have preferred to forget her this morning. "Shouldn't have left them alone together," he thought, "—'Given them that You-Have-My-Blessing-Kiddies treatment. Partly my own guilt, partly the drink and the drug; and partly a gesture against Geraldine,—that's what."

He saw that none of it made sense. Sense? It made utter nonsense. A couple of tots; nineteen years old and seventeen. Good God, they were only thirty-six between them.

"And what does Daniel do with his life now, I ask myself? B.C.M.'s out; Oxford's out." (He couldn't help being pleased about Oxford. . . But how, incidentally was he going to break all this to the others? . . *Pend.*) "Daniel doesn't know what he wants; he hasn't a clue; he merely knows what he doesn't want."

But he went on seeing Antonia's face.

Well, he would like to give the beautiful ragamuffin a break; a brief holiday from Drumnair. "Any reason why she shouldn't drive with us to Glengariff? Just for a few days. I can sell it to Geraldine. . 'Really very sweet last night, very gentle; and we certainly ended up as friends. . She knows she's lost out on Antonia; she said so—well, as good as said so. Probably she'll be quite glad to get the child out of the house for a little while. We'll just slip away, the three of us."

The more he looked at it, the more he liked it. He saw Kodacolor pictures of himself and the two kids; in the car; in a boat. And the idea made sense, giving him the chance of getting to know Daniel as he had never known him. Getting to know the girl; feeding the two of them every expensive treat by the way. It was right.

In the rapid glow of the project, he saw Geraldine agreeing thankfully and a splendid time had by all. Decisions could come later. He was here for a holiday, was he not? The grim ghosts, the strange question-marks, the dark heaviness of guilt, all faded while he smoked his third cigarette and looked out of the window.

"Come in," he said to the gentle knock on his door Daniel walked in He looked clear-eyed, hearty, untroubled and a little dark around the lips and chin for want of a shave.

"Good morning" said Dan. "I saw them send up your breakfast so I waited; I hope you've finished. The Monsignor," he added, "doesn't talk with his breakfast either."

"You may cut the ecclesiastical news. How are you?"

"Fine, thanks."

"Did you spend the night with Antonia?"

"Rather a Victorian question," said Daniel, "isn't it?"

Carus laughed. He said "Score to you. I was only thinking you couldn't either of you have been very comfortable."

"It was all right," said the boy. "Could I possibly borrow your razor? I got a bath here, but I do need a shave."

"Go ahead; you'll find all the stuff in the leather roll, in the bathroom. Leave the door open; I want to talk to you."

"I want to talk to you, too." His expression was solidly thoughtful; his atmosphere, by contrast, jaunty. He had a letter in his hand; sheets of small hotel writing-paper. "Been trying to write to Jennifer," he explained.

"Saying what?"

Daniel put the folded sheets down on the corner of the dressing-table. "The letter isn't very good, I'm afraid." He went into the bathroom. "Carus—"

"Uh-huh?"

"You did mean it—last night when I was all sobbing and silly—about not *having* to do B.C.M. or Oxford?"

"Of course I meant it."

"Well that's one of the things I'm trying to tell Jennifer."

"I do see it wouldn't come easy. But I'll help you."

"Thanks awfully."

"Want me to look at the letter?"

"Not yet—" Dan called sharply. He added, "if you don't

mind." Carus watched him shaving and asked "What goes on at the Manor?"

"Oh. . pretty well everything." He sounded quite gay about it. He came back, rubbing his face with a towel. "Have to get out some clothes," said Carus, "Shan't I? Are you still in the dog-house with Geraldine?"

"The dog-house for the carriage-house? Rather good" said Daniel with a giggle. "Well, I was at first. But now I don't quite know. . . She's odd today,—not nearly so sunny."

"Better so. You need to watch out when she's sunny."

"In fact I think she's rather sad."

"Doesn't do any harm to watch out when she's sad."

The boy frowned; he said "Could I have a cigarette?" and then puffed at it in an amateurish way. "At least," he said, "she isn't sending Antonia back to the convent."

"Department of No Retreat?" said Carus. "Good enough. That helps my notion. Here's what I think we'll do. ."

"Look. . could I tell you some things first?" There was a shadow on him now. Carus said "Sure."

"Well, we were up awfully early. I've been up there for hours. Among other things, I went to see Luke." He stopped, fumbling with the cigarette and finally stubbing it out. "Luke was in bed, wearing a sort of silk cape. He was much perkier than I expected. Yesterday he just wanted to die."

"Nonsense. He was saying that thirty years ago. All these Courtneys go on saying and doing the same things."

"Well, but the Book. ." Daniel pleaded, "I do see. But this morning he's got a different angle, somehow. He's sending for a chap from Dublin to look at the bits; and he's giving himself marks for being the only person to know it would be found. .." Here Carus saw the large, light eyes under the black brows, gazing at him with awed respect: —"Did you put it in the box? Honestly? It isn't just one of his stories?"

"No; it's perfectly true."

"I believe it's what I'd have done—if I'd had the wits to think of it. I'd have been so sorry for the poor thing; and for Luke. Just like I was yesterday when we smashed the box. I'm still sorry. . . Because I spoilt all your plan."

"Good God, you couldn't help kicking the stones off. 'Surprised it didn't happen before. None of that matters, Dan, d'you see? All old stuff."

The boy said "How old were you when you buried it?"

"Twenty-one, as I recall. . why? What's that got to do with anything?"

Daniel paced, with his hands thrust deep into the pockets of the wrinkled shorts. "Well, you see, Luke told me a lot of the things that happened when you were twenty-one. It's so hard to stop him once he gets started. I thought you might be annoyed, though."

Carus laughed. "Told you all about me and Geraldine, eh? Right up to the altar? Hell, why not, you're getting a big boy now. Not to worry, Dan, I don't mind your knowing." He rose from his chair. "Well, I must put some clothes on." Daniel continued to look troubled and compassionate. Carus threw a pair of trousers at him. "'May be too big around the middle, but you can hitch them with your belt. Those shorts have just about had it. . Here's a shirt. . Underpants; socks—anything else I can show you today, sir? Oh, try this jacket, it's new, I got it at Saks. Too fancy for me, really."

He dressed more quickly than Daniel. He began to re-pack his suitcases. "Got a surprise for you, I think," he said—"But first I must put a call through to La Belle Dame Sans Merci."

"To who?"

"Geraldine. That is, if she's in residence, and not taking a picnic lunch with the Ladies' Sodality. *That's* more like it," he added, seeing the boy turn from the looking-glass. ". . Fits you, the jacket. . Lucky we're much of a size. What's wrong?"

"Could you—" Daniel said "Not telephone till I've told you something?"

"I thought you'd finished telling me."

"This is something quite serious."

"What have you done—strangled her?"

Daniel grinned. "No. . it isn't about *her*, really. Could we go for a walk?"

"A walk? . . Make it a little one, chum. Can't you tell me here?"

"Comes easier, walking," said Daniel. He was rolling up his dirty clothes in a bundle. "What'll I do with these?"

Carus said irritably "I knew you were going to ask me that. Better give them to the poor. Or stick them in my bag—the Mark Cross job with the strap. We'll get them cleaned, somewhere. Hurry up; I want to pay the bill and cash a traveller's cheque."

Waiting at the reception-desk, he looked about him. "Turned into a roadhouse, this place. . I liked it better when it was kind of dark and fusty. What was the name of the couple who ran it? . . You wouldn't know."

"No," said Daniel, "Sorry."

"Have to give you some dough," Carus said when the girl came back with the change. "Where's your wallet?"

"Gone; like everything—" said Dan gaily.

"It might be worth our while trying Limerick police-station. Your stuff may have been handed in."

"Maybe." The insouciant attitude, Carus thought, must owe itself to the thing on his mind, whatever the thing was. Now, as they came out, Daniel was looking at the car; the new B.C.M., mottled and mud-splashed from yesterday, but still asserting itself in the line.

"Ours—" said Carus.

"Beauty, isn't she?" The voice was wistful.

"Sure you don't want to drive around?"

"I'd rather we walked."

Carus said "Not far, see?" But he liked the feel of the air, and the look of the village-street. "What are all the flags about, I wonder?"

"Corpus Christi. Thursday, it was."

"Corpus Christi. . One I used to like. ." He glanced at the boy's profile. Suddenly he guessed what was coming. "Did Luke tell you that bit of my past history too?"

"Yes. Sort of. What happened, really?"

"Oh, I was received. Then I threw it all away—walked out."

"Didn't you ever want to go back?"

"Well, obviously not. Or I'd be there now, wouldn't I? Is that what's on your mind? If it is, I've only got two comments. One—don't worry about *me*. Two,—if you're serious about it yourself—"

—"I am" said Daniel, "dead serious. Not just because Antonia's a Catholic. I was on to it before."

"All right. Father Francis—the Monsignor, beg his pardon—is your boy. He lives in London; go and talk to him. Quite a distinguished chap nowadays. ." (Yes, he thought; nowadays Monsignor Francis Merrion was a flat name seen on a book-jacket from time to time. But the voice on the telephone last night, the voice calling to him across distances, belonged to somebody quite different; to a friend whom he had failed a long time ago.) "But I shouldn't, if I were you, include that particular piece in your letter to Jenny," he said to Daniel and felt an ungentlemanly desire to laugh. "We'd better break it to her in instalments " They reached the churchyard wall where the sycamore leaned over and Carus promptly sat down on the wall. "Going for a walk," he observed, "is another habit I've lost." He patted the space on the wall beside him, but Daniel remained standing; with lowered head and folded arms.

"Look—your religion's your business, old boy," said Carus, "Just as my lack of it happens to be mine. Check?"

"Check."

"So there's really nothing you need tell me—or anybody, is there?"

Daniel was silent. Carus watched him. Not a bad-looking fellow at all, he thought; the clothes suit him. Not so much like myself when young as we all tell ourselves, though. Less glossy, somehow. Getting religion doesn't really surprise me. . 'more likely to stick to it than I was, I shouldn't wonder. Aloud he said "Well,—I give you my pagan blessing. And now I want you to hear my plan,—then we'll get going."

"Carus. I can't come with you. Anywhere." It wasn't said defiantly; the voice was sorrowful.

"Eh? What's the notion?" He heard his own voice rasp

as it rasped when he sat behind his office-desk; the tycoon's note of challenge.

"I'm staying here."

"*Here?*"

"Yes. I've got a job."

"Well strike me pink" said Carus flatly.

"I hope you don't mind," said Daniel.

He couldn't mind yet; he was winded. He said "What sort of job?"

"Over there. At the Manor. I mean, on the estate—" Daniel's cheeks were flushed and he began to gabble:— "Don't want you to think I got it by sucking up to Luke. He doesn't know. But it was Luke who put it into my head. So I went to see Hickey, that's the man who hires people. 'Came of Luke saying they were short-handed,—that the young ones always moved out. Apparently they do." He came to a stop; he took the cigarette that Carus offered him.

"So I've moved in," said Daniel.

There seemed nothing to say but "Well, well." Carus said "Well, well."

"It was a snip. All over in about ten minutes. I could hardly understand a word Hickey said,—suppose I'll get used to the way they talk. But apparently I'm a Godsend. Nobody stays there long."

"Not unnaturally. If Luke pays as badly as he did in my time— What are they giving you?"

"Two pounds, ten. And part of a cottage."

"Princely" said Carus. Then he thought it was the wrong thing to have said:—"What's the work?"

Daniel rubbed the back of his head with one hand, pushing the hair up on end. "Odd-job man. On the farm and in the demesne. Cutting down trees—driving a tractor—I said I could drive a tractor; shouldn't be difficult. 'Got to help the gardener. . couldn't understand a word he said, either. Hickey was pleased I wanted to clean the tools."

"I bet he was. Cards?" said Carus "Insurance? Labour permit? Have to think of those things."

"Doesn't take long, Hickey said; and we don't have to wait. Luke's got some way around it, for beginners."

"He would have."

"Do you mind, Carus?"

"How much difference would it make if I did?"

Daniel coasted that one. He said "I can't leave Antonia, d'you see? Last night we thought we'd run away. But that sort doesn't look so easy in the morning. So it's got to be this."

"Fair enough." But he didn't really feel that it was fair enough. He didn't feel anything.

"I told her," said Daniel, "through the back-door. Geraldine has put her on a kind of housework-morning; with reference to—St. Martha, is it?"

"It easily might be."

"She says she'll come to the cottage and cook for me," said Daniel. "*Sounds* awful, but she likes it. In fact she's very pleased. She's got a splendid cook-for-all campaign, if Geraldine will play."

"If—" said Carus.

"Well, one doesn't *know*, with her, does one? She was quite quiet just now. I was back from Hickey,—on my way to the Nellon. I was looking at the prunus tree, that magnificent big one, right outside the house; she was standing at the drawing-room window. She didn't smile or anything, but she waved. I'm not scared of Geraldine."

"Well, bully for you," said Carus.

"You do mind. ."

"I don't know. . . It'll be tough sledding. When do you start?"

"Well. . now," said Daniel.

For a moment Carus caught himself thinking "Serf to Luke. . Fine thing." He got off the wall. "Okay. I'll buy it. Nothing else I can do, is there? And talking of buying" he took out his wallet. "No, please," said the boy.

"T'ain't much. I only cashed a hundred bucks. Thirty pounds odd. You take it—and shut up."

"What'll you do?"

"Cash another. And I shan't be sending you any more. Till you ask for it. Oh, don't thank me, for God's sake. . There's an inside pocket to that jacket, chum. . Right. Now I'm making one stipulation." He glanced at an old woman feathering her way up the path to the church. "Just one, Daniel."

"Yes?"

"Don't stay too long. If La Belle Dame Sans Merci gives in about Antonia—and I presume that's the object of the exercise—then you quit. The two of you. Get the hell out. Promise?"

(Now he looks like me, searching for the snag.)

"Dan, this place is a tomb. Quite beautiful as a tomb, I grant you. I'm always unfair to Luke, I think. . The village—well, you've only to look at it. 'Only pretty village South of Donegal, they used to say. 'Wouldn't look as it does if Luke hadn't poured his money into it. . . cared for it. That's the Courtney credo. Luke really only cares about Drumnair. Geraldine only cares about this church. The difference between those two,—you'll find out,—is just their talk. Luke clings to his act, pretends to hate it all,—howls his sorrows to the roof. Inside, the poor old bugger's just as dedicated as Geraldine. No reason why you should join the general dedication. . you or Antonia, see what I mean?"

"I don't, exactly. I like it here."

"You may not go on liking it."

The boy was silent. A cart with a bull in it went clopping up the street.

"So—I've no right to make a stipulation?" Carus asked.

"It isn't that. It's just that I don't know yet. I'm, as you might say, buying it too. ."

"You sure are. And if you think you can sell it to Jennifer, save your time. You won't succeed there. Just put down the bare facts and post the letter—I'll have a bash at explaining tonight."

The boy said "Tonight. ." He sounded stricken.

"Well, you don't think I'm going to arse around Ireland by myself, do you? I'm not on in this scene. Cheer up. There's one thing you can do for me. Write to Irna, eh?"

"Oh, I have," said Daniel "It was much easier than doing Jennifer. Only I haven't posted it, because I know they ought both to get their letters at the same time."

Carus began to laugh; then he said "*Hell*," thinking about that. Then he said "You give Irna's letter to me. I'll see she keeps quiet. What, if I'm not intruding, did you tell her?"

"Just that we'd met; and that I'm staying here" Daniel said. The bare brevity made the statement sound bigger, Carus thought, than was intended. (But have we met, Daniel? Have I met you, and you me? I don't believe I'll know that for a while). He put the letter in his wallet.

"Well . this would seem to be it."

"What was your plan, Carus?"

2 5 6

"Doesn't matter now."

"I'm sorry."

"No need to be sorry. Let me know how you make out." Seeing Dan look as vulnerable as he had looked at certain moments last night, he said "Ah, don't go all gloomy. . Don't feel you've slapped good kind Daddy in the face. I'm not. And you haven't." He jerked his thumb over his shoulder, towards the church. "How's about going in and having a bit of a pray? You'd like it, wouldn't you?"

"Wouldn't you?" said Daniel.

Carus shook his head. "'Bit late in the day, I'm afraid. All yours."

He took the boy by the shoulders, looking into his eyes. "Do it well," he said. He freed himself from the grateful hands and tramped away up the street.

iii

Yesterday, when he knelt in this church, the early morning shadows had hidden much of its beauty. He remembered some other Irish churches. This was a lucky one. He forgot to dip his hand in the holy-water stoup; he forgot to genuflect, facing the altar. He stood staring around him like a tourist.

The Monsignor's words came back to him as he looked at the two blazing windows. He saw St. Michael's scarlet cloak, and the blue of the Virgin's robe. His eyes found the Stations, with the haloes in gold; the altar-cloth with its sparkling edge. And the black crucifix, with the ivory Christ, high up above the tabernacle. He looked at the tabernacle itself, the small secret tent of white cloth. The candlesticks were polished silver, like the vases holding the white flowers. (The Monsignor again. . "You'd expect her to arrange the flowers, but not to scrub the floor.") Geraldine's church. . It dazzled him. It was, this morning, a little intimidating. He needed Antonia here.

Still dazzled, unsure, he went down on his knees in the back pew. He aimed a thunderous "Thank You" at God, and added "Please help me." He didn't know what to say about Carus; he compromised with "Make everything all right for him." Then he got up. As he reached the door, he remembered to genuflect, and so bumped into someone who was genuflecting too. A large man, who grinned at him and said "Good morning" when they were outside the door. Daniel saw tousled fair hair, bright blue eyes and an enormous smile.

"Nice church, isn't it?" He looked as if he were making a joke. He wore an open-necked blue shirt, with the sleeves rolled up and rather dirty grey flannels. "Cigarette for you?" It was a packet of Afton, with only three left in the packet. Daniel said "No, thanks very much. I just put one out."

"In church? Rather bold of you, wasn't it?"

"I didn't mean that. I meant—"

—"You meant I was running short." He took a new pack from each trouser-pocket. "And more in the car, if you're worried. 'Sooner smoke than eat. Sure? All right. You're English, I hear. On holiday?"

What was it about him that made this impact, this disturbance in the mind? Not, the boy decided, an unpleasant one. He didn't dislike the man. But there came from him a gay demand, like a dog, wagging its tail. One felt that he wanted company and would soon suggest a glass of beer.

"I'm not on holiday, exactly," said Daniel.

"Nor am I." The smile grew wider. "Back to school, more. Which way d'you go?"

"I'm going up to the Manor."

"You are, are you? Well, what a thing to be doing on a fine day. That makes two of us. Some," he added, "would say we ought to have our heads examined, they would indeed. Hop in."

It was the dirtiest of small cars, fragile-looking and outdated. "And be quick about it, young man; I'm in a hurry. I don't happen to believe in hurry, but when it's something that scares you, you have to do it damn' quick. Or so I find."

"Yes," said Daniel, "'Comes easier."

"The longest way round, however, is the shortest way home." Daniel didn't see what he meant by this until he had spun the wheel of his shocking car and turned it down the street, toward the South gate of the demesne; then he began to sing. He sang "Merrily, merrily, do we live now!" and presently added "Or do we?" to himself. There was a smell to him; old sweat, old drink, stale tobacco. He went back to his song again. At the gate, Daniel climbed out and opened up for him.

"Thanks. Here we go, then. What's *your* business at the Manor?"

Daniel hesitated. All at once he knew that "Merrily, merrily" was right. Looking at the sunlit trees, at the pasture, the green kingdom, he felt that he had made it his. He was here by sound appointment. He said "I've got a job to do."

This brought a gurgle of laughter. "We *are* in the same boat, then; so we are. Better introduce ourselves, hadn't we?"

"My name's Daniel Black."

"Pleased to meet you. Mine's Courtney. Godfrey Courtney."

iv

Carus kept his foot hard down until the last of the demesne wall went out of sight. Then he slowed up. No hurry. He didn't care if he missed a plane from Shannon He couldn't see Shannon except in terms of yesterday, and yesterday was years ago.

Today was today.

"All yours," he repeated in his mind to the image of Daniel, to the boy standing alone outside the church. "All yours. What'll you do with it? . . 'Hell of an assignment you've given yourself, haven't you?"

He watched the roadside; a reedy pond, with yellow iris lighting up the reeds, and a grey heron, motionless on its stilts. Over to the west, he saw the low mountains and a cragged ruin, desolately tranquil. The boy was pulling at his heart. He wouldn't, he thought, half mind turning, driving back,—to keep an eye to it all.

No. Not allowed

"At least, whatever you make of it, my lad, it'll be all your own work, not ours. And nobody could chart a more disastrous map for you than we've done so far, eh?

"And if it works out—what next? What will you do with your life, I wonder? You and your girl." He couldn't imagine. He saw them escaping; going on to odd jobs and adventures, forgetting him, forgetting that he could help them Not wanting anything or anybody,—only themselves. Perhaps they had escaped already: where they were. ("I like it here.")

"Whatever happens, I was right—I'm not on in this scene."

He speeded up. He might as well drive across to Dublin, hand back the car to the B.C.M. boys, and fly from there. Yes, he would do that. He liked a long drive; and he could always stay the night in Dublin, if there wasn't a plane. He swerved to avoid three geese who came rushing from a farmyard gate to yell at him.

No hurry. And no cause to look ahead. But he saw the speedometer-needle climbing, and already he was looking ahead. To London. To himself invading his own office five days too soon. "Which return, I can guess, will be greeted all around with a deep feeling of no-enthusiasm." He began to review the arrival of a certain clutch of Americans with whom he had talked while in the Middle West. No reason to delegate the handling of their proposition now. He could, he thought, have fun with it,—fun that must include some strenuous entertaining. "I'll call Irna when I get to Dublin. or before."

His thoughts stayed on Irna for a little while. Vaguely, he made a resolution about her; the resolution had no shape nor plan; probably he wouldn't keep it. But he ought to try. "She's going to miss Daniel so much. . Yet I know I can sell it to her, all this, more easily than to the others. She'll be awfully unhappy, but she's pliable enough to understand. And, damn it," he said, "We've all earned our unhappiness, haven't we? I'll say we have. Handsomely. 'Make a point of saying just that to Jennifer. We earned it, high, wide and fancy. ."

He thought about it. "How unhappy am I,—right this minute? 'Wish I knew. When I was younger, I always knew. *And* resented it."

> *You promised I should always be*
> *the partner of Persephone.*

Oh, there were no promises. Only beginnings; only chances. Only doors that you could open—or slam shut. And then they stayed shut.

Gently he turned his thoughts to the past; back down the road there, the past that had been so quiet for so long. Unforgotten always, but pale and still as the tapestry where the hunter launched his spear forever and the lean dogs pranced, curling, and the stag bounded ahead.

The hidden place:

> *that only waits the password to admit*
> *the ancient secret to the young lord of it.*

True enough. It was uncovered now, alive; troublous and blazing; but not for him. He had deserted it long ago. And he had known for years that once you took the wrong road out of Drumnair, you just kept travelling; you couldn't get there again. Daniel could, though.

The road went on.

Milton Keynes UK
Ingram Content Group UK Ltd.
UKHW022226211223
434819UK00004B/117